CHAPTER ONE
The Beetle Plague

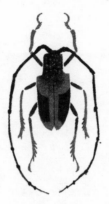

'I've got the Sunday papers,' Bertolt said, pushing Uncle Max's door open with his shoulder and shuffling into the living room backwards. Newton, the copper-coloured firefly that was Bertolt's closest friend, hovered above the boy's cloud of white hair, his abdomen glowing gently.

Darkus and Virginia looked up. They were sitting cross-legged either side of an aqua-blue paddling pool filled with oak mulch and a mound of mugs. Darkus was wearing the Weevil Knieval T-shirt he'd bought in LA and Virginia was dressed in faded denim, old jeans and a

Ceratophyus martinezi

hand-me-down jacket covered in badges.

'We're feeding the beetles,' Darkus said, placing a pot of strawberry jelly amongst the teacups. This was where the surviving beetles from Beetle Mountain lived now, and this room in Uncle Max's flat housed what was left of Base Camp, their den. It was where they met to plan their mission to stop Lucretia Cutter's tyrannical attempt to take over the world.

Baxter, the glossy black rhinoceros beetle that understood Darkus better than anyone, was supervising the handing out of jelly from Darkus's shoulder, waggling his spiky forelegs to show where it should be put.

Virginia was holding a brass plant mister over the paddling pool and furiously pumping a fine spray of water over the oak mulch, to prevent it from drying out. Marvin, the cherry-red frog-legged leaf beetle who wouldn't be parted from her, was hanging from one of Virginia's many braids by his bulging back legs, munching on a blob of banana jelly.

Dusting the soil from his hands, Darkus got to his feet and came over to the coffee table where Bertolt was neatly laying out the newspapers. Virginia put the mister on the floor and joined them.

'There are more stories about crops being attacked, look, here's one about the Colorado potato beetle destroying harvests in Russia. People are beginning to believe what Lucretia Cutter said at the Film Awards and they're panicking.' Bertolt pushed his glasses up his nose and looked nervously at Darkus. 'There are reports of spoilt wheat crops in Germany now too, and three outbreaks of disease caused by a build-up of animal manure. The government is finally saying these are controlled and targeted attacks.'

Darkus moved forward to look at the papers, but Bertolt stood between him and the table.

'And, um, Darkus, there's something else . . .'

Virginia lifted a tabloid, reading out the headline. 'BEETLE PLAGUE! FOOD RATIONED!' She flicked over a page, her brown eyes scanning the words. 'What?! I don't believe it! The papers think Lucretia Cutter's threat is real, but they don't believe *she's* capable of creating the Frankenstein beetles because she makes dresses for a living!'

Darkus shrugged. 'Perhaps they don't want to believe she's found a way to control insects.'

'It's not that,' Virginia snorted. 'It's because she's a *woman*.'

'Virginia . . .' Bertolt tried to catch her eye.

'People always think the best scientists are men.' Virginia slapped the paper with the back of her hand in outrage. 'Listen to this. ". . . *the troubled coleopterist Dr Bartholomew Cuttle, Director of Science at the Natural History Museum and one-time fiancé of Lucretia Cutter, is heading up a team of geneticists and entomologists, men who've all mysteriously vanished in the last five years. This elite force is behind the mad fashionista's beetle army, using Lucretia Cutter's theatrical image to front their attack on the world."'*

'*WHAT?*' Darkus grabbed the newspaper from Virginia's hands. 'But that's a lie!' He scanned the article. 'Why are they're saying that about Dad?'

'Because he's a man,' Virginia said, triumphantly.

Bertolt sighed and shook his head.

'They are blaming him for the beetles! All of them!' Darkus said, reading the article at speed. 'This is wrong. We have to tell them. Dad's trying to stop her.'

'Darkus,' Bertolt said softly, 'it's because he was Lucretia Cutter's guest at the Film Awards.' He picked up a different paper. 'Look, the *Daily Messenger* says as much: "*Dr Bartholomew Cuttle, seen on Lucretia Cutter's arm at the Film Awards, is thought to be the mastermind behind the plague of deadly beetles.*"'

'That's totally unfair!' Darkus felt his face getting hot. 'It's all lies! My dad would never hurt anyone.'

'It's disgusting,' Virginia nodded, 'and they're attributing Lucretia Cutter's genius to a team of men.'

'Genius?' Darkus shouted. 'She is *not* a genius.'

'Of course she's a genius!' Virginia replied. 'She's bred a huge army of beetles that is destroying human food supplies and taking control of the planet. That's incredible. No human has ever ruled the whole earth, and she's going for it, big time.' She shook her head and looked at Darkus. 'Don't worry, they're going to have to acknowledge it's *her* genius eventually.'

'She's not a genius!' Darkus shouted, jabbing a finger at Virginia. 'She's a monster! She wants to starve people, and blame it on my dad and look what she's done to Novak, and Spencer!'

'Hey! Calm down.' Virginia frowned. 'I didn't say I *agreed* with what she's doing.'

'Well, it certainly sounded like it,' Darkus said, scowling at Virginia.

Virginia thrust out her chin, about to protest.

'Um, guys?' Bertolt cleared his throat. 'Let's not fall out again.' He gave them a pleading smile. 'We are all on the same side, remember?'

Virginia huffed out a sigh. 'I'm sorry.' She looked at Darkus. 'I should have said *evil* genius.' She lifted her shoulders. 'I'm just trying to point out that everyone is underestimating Lucretia Cutter.' She pushed the papers around the table. 'Blaming your dad is a false trail. It won't help them find her or stop her.'

'I'm not underestimating her,' Darkus replied. Eleven days had passed since they'd returned from the Film Awards, but to Darkus it felt like years. The image of his father limping away, following Lucretia Cutter up into the rafters of the Hollywood Theater was the last thing he thought about before he went to sleep at night and the first thing in his head when he woke up in the morning.

There was a loud *crack* and they all jumped.

'What was that?' Bertolt asked, looking faintly terrified.

Virginia pointed over his shoulder. There was a thin

crack in the glass of the front-room window.

Darkus cautiously knelt on the sofa, leaning over the back, to look down into the street. Standing on the other side of the road, outside the tattoo parlour, stood Robby, the red-haired bully from school, surrounded by a gang of boys they called the clones. He opened the window.

'Hey, Beetle Boy!' Robby shouted. 'Tell your dad, if he doesn't call off his killer bugs, his son's going to get swatted.'

'Yeah!' Each clone made a fist and punched it into their other hand.

'They're not my dad's beetles,' Darkus shouted back. 'He's got nothing to do with it.'

'Oh, yeah?' Robby jeered. 'That's not what the papers say. They say your dad's a murderer.' He drew a finger across his neck. 'They'll probably bring back the death penalty just for him.'

'The papers are lying,' Darkus shouted. 'None of it is true.'

'Yeah? Well, you would say that, wouldn't you?' Robby sneered, a flash of metal from his railway-track braces. 'But, I've seen you and your gross beetles. We all have.' The clones' heads bobbled about on the end of their necks. 'And we told the police about how weird you lot are, talking to bugs. What the papers say is true. I know it, and I ain't going to stand for it.' Quick as a flash, Robby drew back his hand and flung a stone that had been hidden in his fist.

Darkus felt the flint strike his cheek a stinging blow. He covered it with his hand as he pulled his head back from the window.

'Oh! You're bleeding.' Bertolt gently pulled Darkus's hand away so he could see the cut.

'WE'RE GONNA GET YOU BEETLE BOY, AND YOUR DAD!' came a shout from outside.

'Ignore them,' Virginia said, shutting the window as a barrage of stones hit the glass. She quickly closed the curtains.

'How can I ignore them?' Darkus brushed Bertolt's fussing hands away. 'They're saying what everyone thinks. People believe what they read in the papers. Everyone thinks that Dad is guilty.'

There was an uncomfortable silence as Virginia and Bertolt looked at one another. The growing wail of sirens made Bertolt run to the window. He peeped through the curtains. 'It's the police!' He gasped. 'There are two cars pulling up outside the health food shop. They're getting out. What shall we do?'

'We can't let them in here.' Darkus looked about him in panic. 'They mustn't see the beetles. They'll think it's evidence that Dad is guilty.'

'They can't come in unless they have a search warrant,' Virginia said. 'I've seen it on TV. Tell them your uncle is out and you're not allowed to open the door to strangers.'

'OK,' Darkus nodded, 'but I'm not going to lie about Dad. People need to know that he's trying to stop

Lucretia Cutter. He's one of the good guys.'

'No, Darkus, you can't say anything,' Bertolt said. 'Your dad needs Lucretia Cutter to believe he's on her side, otherwise . . .'

The buzzer sounded.

Darkus looked into the hall, half expecting to see the door being smashed open. 'It's not fair,' he whispered.

'I know.' Virginia nodded, her dark eyes sincere. 'But we know the truth.' She patted him gently on the back.

'I'm going to find Dad,' Darkus clenched his fists, 'stop Lucretia Cutter, and force the newspapers to print an apology on the whole front page.' On his shoulder, Baxter flicked his elytra open and closed, vibrating his soft wings in a thrum of agreement.

'We'll be right beside you,' Bertolt said.

'Every step of the way,' Virginia nodded.

CHAPTER TWO
Damselflight

The hessian bag covering Bartholomew Cuttle's face was making him sweat. A bead of perspiration ran down his cheek like a giddy tear. Despite the stifling heat, he was glad of the cover the cloth provided: it prevented Lucretia Cutter and her goons from seeing that he was alert and trying to pick up clues about where he was being taken.

When the sun shone Barty could make out the silhouettes of the other people in the helicopter, but the world had gone grey an hour ago. Right now, the rain was hammering down on the metal roof like an infinite shower of small stones. It wasn't safe to be flying in this kind of downpour. Torrential rain meant reduced visibility.

We must be nearing the Biome, he thought, leaning forward.

Barty had a clear picture in his head of where everyone was seated. Gerard the French butler was in the cockpit next to Ling Ling, the deadly chauffeur flying the chopper. The goons were sat in a row opposite him, their backs to Gerard and Ling Ling. Craven was first, Dankish slumped beside him and then Mawling's chunky silhouette. Spiky chitinous legs occasionally snagging the fabric of his trousers made it impossible to forget that Lucretia was sitting right next to him. On the other side of the self-proclaimed Beetle Queen there was only silence.

Novak's sitting there, he thought. *The poor girl must be terrified.* He wondered, not for the first time, how she'd become friends with his son. Darkus had asked him to look after her, and he intended to keep his promise.

Lucretia had been furious when the Film Awards had descended into chaos. She had struggled to believe Barty when he'd limped on to the rooftop of the Hollywood Theater saying he'd abandoned his son to be with her, that her vision for the world was the same as his – but her ego was voracious. She had wanted to believe him. She pointed out that she could kill him in a heartbeat, and then instructed Gerard to bind his hands and cover his head with a hood.

They'd been flying for nearly four hours when they made their first stop. Craven climbed on board, fresh from releasing the genetically modified wheat weevils into the grain belt of America. Gerard had removed the hood, offering Barty water while the helicopter took on fuel. He glimpsed a sign saying ALBUQUERQUE before the hood was replaced and they were back in the air again.

The chopper needed to refuel every four hours. Barty silently plotted their route in his head as they travelled through the night. The sinking and then rising sun told him they were flying south. On the third stop, he was yanked out of the helicopter cabin by Craven, marched into a building, and shoved into a room. Pulling off the hood, Barty found himself in a sparsely furnished bedroom.

Gerard woke him with coffee, fruit and sweet bread, and the news that they'd be leaving soon. Barty guessed they were near Mexico City, and as he was guided out to the helicopter with the hood back on his head, he heard men speaking Spanish.

'Happy Christmas, Darling,' Lucretia Cutter said as he climbed aboard the chopper. Barty's heart clenched at the thought of Darkus alone on Christmas Day, but he kept his face blank.

There were three more fuel stops before he was

deposited in a room to sleep again. This time they stayed on the ground for two days, waiting for a storm to pass. When they climbed back into the helicopter, he asked Lucretia Cutter why she wasn't flying by aeroplane. She replied that it was prudent to avoid airports when one had declared war on the leaders of the world. The most powerful and dangerous people alive were scouring the planet, looking for her.

And now it seemed they were on the last stretch of their journey. As the helicopter sank Barty closed his eyes. Waiting in the darkness was his dark-eyed son, clutching his beloved rhinoceros beetle to his chest. Barty sent a silent prayer of love to his brave boy, and turned his covered head towards Lucretia Cutter.

'Lucy, I want to thank you.' He sensed Lucretia Cutter's head pivot to face him. Her greatest weakness seemed to be the affection she had for him, a hangover from their university days. He'd decided to make what he could out of that, to gain her trust and information. He needed to find a way to bring down her empire and thwart her plans. 'For allowing me to be a part of your glorious vision for the future.'

'Ah, Bartholomew,' she replied, 'you will soon discover that I am making all your wildest dreams come true, and "thank you" is too small a word.'

CHAPTER THREE

Titanus giganteus

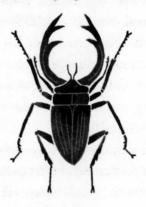

'What kind of beetle do you think she is?' Darkus said, his nose deep in the pages of *The Beetle Collector's Handbook*.

'Who?' Bertolt asked from his watch-post at the window. The police cars had left when Darkus refused to open the door, but they'd said they'd be returning. 'Lucretia Cutter?'

'Yeah, if she's taking the DNA from beetles and adding it to her own, well, you know there are so many different species of beetle, she must have chosen a specific beetle, but which one?'

'That *is* a good question!' Virginia leapt up from the sofa, going to the noticeboard of clues hanging on the wall and examined the picture of Lucretia Cutter hovering above the stage in the Hollywood Theater.

'If we knew what kind of beetle she was we might be able to work out her weaknesses,' Darkus said.

Bertolt stepped over to the bookcase that lined the dividing wall between Uncle Max's flat and what was left of the Emporium next door. The children had replaced all Uncle Max's volumes on archaeology with every insect book they could get their hands on, from their homes, school and the library.

'I think she's a titan beetle,' Darkus said, turning his book around so they could see the picture. 'Her size, her mandibles and those eyes.' He tapped his finger against the page and shivered, remembering the shiny black spheres glaring down at him. 'She looks like the *Titanus giganteus*.'

'The biggest beetle in the world!' Virginia gasped, looking from Darkus's book to the picture on the wall and back again. 'I'll bet you're right.'

'Should we learn more about the anatomy of beetles?' Bertolt asked, staring at Darkus's book.

'Anatomy?' Virginia frowned.

'Yes, how their insides are laid out,' Bertolt replied. 'So we can figure out how Lucretia Cutter . . . works.' He wiggled his fingers over his own torso. 'It may help us to discover her Achilles heel.'

'Yes.' Darkus nodded, flicking through the pages of his book. 'We may be able to find a way to defeat her.'

'Like with a vampire!' Virginia said. 'You have to drive a stake through their heart.' She pretended to stake Darkus and he laughed.

'*Defeat* her?' Bertolt looked horrified.

'We may have to.' Darkus nodded. 'She'd kill us without thinking.'

'Do beetles have hearts?' Virginia wondered.

'I think so.' Darkus turned to the index at the back of his book. 'Although, I know they don't have lungs, because they breathe through spiracles.' He found a page reference and flicked to a diagram. 'It says here that they have a muscle that pushes their insect blood around their bodies.' He looked at Virginia. 'That must be their heart, right?'

'Beetles bleed?' Virginia asked.

Darkus nodded. 'It's called haemolymph and is usually a yellowy-green.'

'Green!' Bertolt's eyebrows lifted as he looked up at Newton.

'Yeah, or yellowish. It does the same thing our blood does, it has antibodies to protect the beetle from illness and help heal wounds and stuff.'

'But Lucretia Cutter's not a vampire,' Bertolt said. 'We don't have to *vanquish* her, we just have to get the police to arrest her.'

Darkus fixed his friend with a pointed look. 'But what

if we *do* have to ... you know?'

'What?' Bertolt frowned.

'*Kill her?*' Virginia's eyes grew wide.

'Oh, no!' Bertolt's hands flew to his cheeks.

'Lucretia Cutter's going to starve millions of people.' Darkus shook his head. 'They'll all die if we don't stop her.'

'She hasn't done it yet,' Virginia said. 'Maybe she'll change her mind.'

'And what if she tries to kill Novak, or Spencer, or Dad?' Darkus looked down at the picture of the *Titanus giganteus*. The enormity of what they were trying to do weighed heavily on him. 'I would have died at the Film Awards if the beetles hadn't saved me.' A vision of Lucretia Cutter's giant jaws, glistening black mouth, her rows of needle-sharp mandibles, filled his head. He shuddered at the memory of her breath – the stench of rotting fruit – and the sensation of falling. 'She would have killed Baxter too, if Dad hadn't saved him.' He looked at his friends. 'We have to prepare for the worst.'

'If we kill her, Darkus,' Virginia said quietly, 'won't that make us murderers?' She looked at Bertolt.

'I thought your dad taught you to preserve life,' Bertolt whispered.

'His life wasn't in danger then,' Darkus said. 'He's out there now, risking everything to stop Lucretia Cutter.'

'He isn't trying to kill her, though,' Bertolt replied.

'Darkus,' Virginia stared at him, her brown eyes wide, 'I don't think I can kill Lucretia Cutter. I mean I love adventures, and I know I used to eat meat, before I understood about sustainable farming and everything, but killing on purpose? I'm not sure I can do it. Even if Lucretia Cutter *is* an evil scumbag.' She bit her lip. 'I wouldn't be able to you know . . . pull the trigger.'

'I could, if I had to.' Darkus gritted his teeth. 'If she was going to hurt Dad.'

'Don't take this the wrong way,' Virginia said, shaking her head, 'but I don't think you're the type of person who can kill either.'

'He's depending on me.' Darkus heard his voice wobble, and he swallowed.

Bertolt put his hand on Darkus's. 'We're going to get your dad back.'

Virginia nodded. 'And we'll find a way to stop Lucretia Cutter's beetle armies, but she needs to be arrested, and confess. That's the only way to clear your dad's name.'

Darkus covered his face. 'Urgh!' he growled. 'Do you know what the craziest thing about all of this is?'

'Um, everything?' Virginia threw her hands up. 'I mean, a crazy beetle woman trying to take over the planet? I understand why no one wants to believe it's happening.'

'No. The craziest thing is that if Lucretia Cutter can do all of this with her beetles,' he pointed to the pictures of decimated crops in the newspaper articles pinned to the wall, 'just imagine the good things those beetles could do if they were led by someone who didn't want to conquer the world – if they were led by someone who wanted to heal it.'

Darkus heard the sound of keys jangling, a door opening then footsteps on the stairs. Uncle Max, dressed in his uniform of safari shorts, shirt and hat, blundered into the room, followed by the short, stout, bespectacled Motticilla Braithwaite. She was carrying an armful of rolled-up maps.

'I'm back,' Uncle Max hailed the children, 'and I've brought Motty and Iris. Iris is putting the kettle on.'

'Make a space on the table,' Motty commanded, her three chins rippling. 'I've got a map of South America for you to look at.'

'The police were here,' Darkus said as he, Virginia and Bertolt knelt down around the table. 'I didn't let them in, but they want to talk to us.'

'Do they now? Well, they'll just have to wait.'

'They said they'd come back.'

Uncle Max pointed at the beetles' paddling pool. 'Got any good flyers we can ask to be lookouts?'

Darkus nodded, 'The ladybirds are the fastest.' He held up his hand, and six red-and-black spotted beetles landed on his palm. He went to the window and cracked it open. 'Split into two groups, one at each end of the road,' he whispered. 'If you spot a police car, the blue and white vehicles with the flashing lights on the top, get back here as quickly as you can.' When studying the flight patterns of beetles, he'd realized why Lucretia

Cutter had used yellow ladybirds as her spies. They reached astonishing heights at great speed and could cover long distances. Thankfully since she'd left the country, they'd hardly spotted any of her deadly yellow *Coccinellidae*.

Uncle Max unfurled the map of South America as Darkus sat back down. 'If the police return, we need to be out of here before they knock on the door. Do you all have your bags packed?' The three children nodded. 'Good. Right, let's get down to business.' He smoothed out the edges of the map and the five of them leant over it. 'The co-ordinates your father passed to you at the Film Awards, on that scrap of paper,' Uncle Max placed his finger on the map, 'are here.'

Darkus's eyes greedily scanned for information. 'In Ecuador?'

'North-west.' Uncle Max nodded. Motty handed him another map, which he unrolled and placed on top of the first. 'This is a more detailed map of the region.' He ran one finger along the top of the map and one down the left-hand side then brought his fingers together. 'And, if we can trust the co-ordinates the French butler gave your father, *this* is where Lucretia Cutter has built her Biome.'

Baxter fluttered down from Darkus's shoulder and marched to the spot Uncle Max was pointing to.

'Sumaco Napo-Galeras National Park,' Bertolt read. Newton fizzed and flickered excitedly.

'That's where Dad is.' Darkus stared at the series of wiggling contour lines that suggested the Biome was halfway up a mountain.

'I've checked with all my contacts in the airports between LA and Quito, and it doesn't look like Lucretia Cutter has travelled by plane, which makes sense if she doesn't want anyone to know where she's going,' Motty said. 'And no one has seen her since she disappeared into the sky after the Film Awards.'

'She's vanished?' Virginia asked.

Motty nodded. 'If she did the whole journey in her Sikorsky S-92' – she paused at the blank looks on the children's faces – 'that's her helicopter – well, a Sikorsky S-92 will only do a thousand kilometres before it needs to refuel. It would have taken her a good few days to get from LA to here.' She pointed to the map. 'Four or five days at least, and that's if they only stopped for as long as it takes to refuel, but they'd not be able to travel through bad weather, and they'd need comfort breaks, a pilot has to sleep and eat.' She tipped her head to one side, and after a second tipped it back the other way. 'I'd estimate a journey like that, when you're trying to avoid being seen, so flying mostly at night, might take ten or eleven days.'

'But that means,' Darkus counted off the days on his hands. A bolt of positivity shot through him. 'Dad's only just got there.'

Motty nodded.

The door of the living room swung open and Iris Crips, dressed in a flowery blouse and navy pinafore, with her springy grey hair tied back, came in carrying a tray of tea, orange juice and biscuits. 'Oh! You've started without me,' she chided, setting down the tray.

Virginia launched herself at the biscuits.

'I do beg your pardon, Iris,' Uncle Max apologized.

'Mrs Crips, we know where you son is,' Darkus said. 'Spencer's in Ecuador.'

'He's is in the Sumaco Napo-Galeras National Park.' Bertolt pointed.

'That's a long way away.' Mrs Crips stared at the map, blinking.

'Not if you've got an aeroplane,' Motty said softly.

'And we have!' Virginia bounced up on to her knees, spraying biscuit crumbs everywhere.

'First, we've got to go to ICE to speak to the entomologists.' Darkus reminded them. 'Dad said, "Go to the entomologists, they'll help you."' He looked at Uncle Max.

'Yes, and we will need their help. I have no doubt of that.' Uncle Max nodded. 'There are reports of fresh beetle invasions every day, and there's worse to come, you can be sure of it. Lucretia Cutter is just getting started.'

'ICE?' Mrs Crips's forehead furrowed.

'The International Congress of Entomology,' Bertolt explained.

'It's the day after tomorrow,' Darkus said.

'We fly to Prague in the morning for the congress, and then head straight from there to Ecuador,' Uncle Max said. 'I had thought we'd stay here tonight, but if the British Constabulary has decided we should help them with their enquiries, I'd rather not be here when they come knocking.' He waggled his eyebrows. 'It would really rather put a spanner in the works if I were to be arrested.'

'Why would they arrest you?' Darkus asked, shocked.

'Well, it wasn't only Barty who was in LA at the Film Awards, now, was it? I was there,' he looked at Darkus, then Virginia and Bertolt, 'and you, and you and you.'

'You mean they might arrest all of us?' Bertolt squeaked.

'It's possible.' Uncle Max nodded.

'Right, get your bags.' Iris Crips stood up and pulled her car keys out of her pinafore pocket. 'Tell the beetles to get in their case. You're all coming to stay at mine.'

Everyone sprang into action. Motty rolled up the maps and Darkus went to the open suitcase beside the paddling pool.

'Everyone in,' he said, pointing at the warren of paper cups wedged into oak mulch inside the case. 'Quick as you can.'

Baxter flittered down, landing on the inflated wall of the pool, twitching his antennae as the Base Camp beetles filed past him.

Uncle Max jammed his pith helmet on his head. 'Now remember, we mustn't let anyone know the location of the Biome, not even friends. We can't even let on that we know where it is. Half the world is looking for Barty and Lucretia Cutter right now. We need to make sure we get to them before anyone else does.'

'But, why don't you tell the authorities where she is?' Mrs Crips asked. 'Let them deal with her.'

'Because, Iris, there's a good chance they'll rain bombs down on the place, and blow it to kingdom come,' he replied. 'We don't want to risk the lives of Spencer or Bartholomew, now do we?'

'Or Novak,' Bertolt added.

'Oh!' Iris Crips shook her head vehemently. 'No, we don't want that!'

'There's no need to look so alarmed, Darkus.' Uncle Max smiled at him. 'I'm pretty certain Lucretia Cutter is expecting retaliation. All her eyes will be on the skies and her Biome will be protected.'

'Do you think so?' Darkus asked, the knot of fear in his stomach tightening.

'Yes, I do, and the threat gives us an advantage.'

'It does?' Bertolt looked as frightened as Darkus felt.

'Yes, we'll be on the ground, looking like a harmless little family taking a holiday.'

'Weird-looking family,' Virginia muttered.

'Exactly.' Uncle Max nodded. 'And that's why no one will suspect we're on a mission to save the world.'

CHAPTER FOUR

Henrik Lenka

'**W**e are landing, Madame,' Gerard shouted over the rhythmic throb of the helicopter blades and the machine-gun rattle of the torrential rain.

'Good, tell Lenka to come out and meet us,' Lucretia replied. 'Craven, Dankish, you will go straight to the security dome and make preparations for any form of attack on the Biome. Send out the beetle borgs.'

'Yes, ma'am,' Craven barked.

'Lenka? *Henrik Lenka?* You said he didn't work with you any longer.' Barty did his best to sound annoyed. 'Are you trying to make me jealous?'

'He doesn't work *with* me. Not in the lab. He has a limited imagination and a tawdry lust for money,' Lucretia replied. 'I threw him off the research team when I discovered he was talking to a journalist called Emma Lamb. He was going to sell her my secrets.'

'He hasn't changed, then,' Barty said wryly, and Lucretia snorted.

'I should have killed him, but he begged for his life, and for old times' sake, I let him keep it. I couldn't let him leave and tell the world what I'm doing, so he's the facilities manager at the Biome now.' There was a note of amusement in her voice. 'He looks after the sanitation.' She laughed. 'I make him clean the toilets.'

Barty felt his stomach lift as the helicopter touched down. The hessian bag was snatched from his head. Blinking and squinting, his eyes adjusted to the sudden light of day.

'We're here.' Lucretia Cutter's fathomless compound eyes bore down on him. She'd disposed of the sunglasses at the Film Awards. 'Would you like to come and say hello to your old friend?'

'I have never called Henrik Lenka a friend,' Bartholomew replied. He lifted his bound hands. 'Perhaps you could untie me first. I would rather he didn't get to enjoy my incarceration.'

Lucretia reached out and severed the ropes with one slash of her claw. 'There's no need to tether you here.' She fixed him with an ink-black smile. 'If you run away, the jungle will kill you more painfully that I ever could.'

Craven, Dankish and Mawling jumped out of the helicopter into the torrential rain. Gerard got out, opened an umbrella and came round to the door beside Novak, reaching up to help her down.

Lucretia Cutter wheeled around to face him. 'No!'

Gerard froze.

'You will stay away from the girl. You are sentimental, Gerard, I have seen it in your eyes when you look at her. You are not to go near her any more.'

Gerard took two steps back and bowed his head.

Barty looked at Novak. Her face was blank, expressionless.

Lucretia turned to her bodyguard and chauffeur, who lightly leapt down from the pilot's seat. 'Ling Ling, take the girl to the cells.'

Novak stood up, getting down from the helicopter and walking past the French butler without giving him a glance. He held out the umbrella as she passed and she took it.

The door opened beside Barty. Mawling grabbed his arm, yanking him down to the ground.

'Thanks for the assistance,' Barty glared up at the muscle-bound wrestler in his black vest and unbuttoned camo shirt, 'but I'm quite capable of walking.' He was going to say more, but the view silenced him. At the end of the helipad clearing, nestled amongst the luminous greens of rainforest foliage, rose a giant dome constructed from glass and steel hexagons. It reached up into the canopy of trees, the size of a stadium. Barty spotted one, then more, satellite domes arranged at a distance from the main building. He stood staring in wonder as a river of rain fell out of the sky and soaked him to his skin.

Mawling grunted and gave him a shove. Barty stumbled forward, Lucretia fell into step beside him. 'What do you think?' she gurgled. 'Isn't it the perfect place for a laboratory?'

'It's incredible,' he whispered.

She stalked towards the dome, eagerly, and Barty hurried after her. 'It's invisible from above,' she declared. 'And what you can see,' she waved her hand at the dome, 'is just the tip of the iceberg. Two-thirds of the facility is below ground.'

'Two-thirds?' Bartholomew looked about him, incredulous. There was no obvious entrance to the Biome. Plants and impossibly tall kapok trees, centuries old, grew thick between the central dome and the six smaller outer domes.

When Lucretia Cutter reached the edge of the landing pad, a rectangular hole the size of a van opened up in the ground. An invisible grass-covered door sank down and slid out of sight to reveal a sloping tunnel. Lights flickered on as Lucretia Cutter lurched down the incline.

Barty followed her out of the torrential rain and on to

a floor of white stone. Inside the tunnel the walls were a glossy white polycarbonate, with a ceiling of tessellating lights. Ahead of them a giant hexagonal door lifted. Standing in the doorway was a tall man with spiky silver-blond hair, a humourless face and ice-blue eyes. He looked at Bartholomew Cuttle with undisguised hatred.

'Henrik Lenka,' Barty said, without extending his hand. 'It's been a long time.'

Chapter Five
Arcadia

Lucretia Cutter strode past Henrik Lenka, who turned
his back on Barty and scurried along beside her.
'Lucy, I'm so glad you're home. I—'

She silenced him with a wave of her hand. 'Prepare
the Hercules suite in the residence dome for Bartholomew.
Make sure he's comfortable. Get him whatever he asks
for – and, Henrik – be nice to our guest.'

Barty followed them, a pace or two behind.

'The Hercules suite?' Henrik snarled.

'That's what I said. Run along.'

'But I need to hear – what happened at the Film

Awards? Did you do it?'

'The wheat weevils have been released. The world has been notified. The Biome is on high alert and the beetle borgs have been sent up into the canopy of the cloud forest to watch the skies.'

'Then I should be helping you, not fluffing up pillows for *him*.' He jerked his thumb over his shoulder at Barty.

Lucretia Cutter grabbed Henrik Lenka by the collar with a chitinous claw, lifting him off the ground. 'I wouldn't allow you to be a part of the defence of this Biome if my life depended on it.'

'Please! It was a mistake. What can I do to prove to you—'

She dropped him and he stumbled backwards, falling to the floor. Pivoting on a claw, Lucretia lurched through another rising hexagonal door. Barty's eyes lifted with it, and he found himself gazing into a green paradise of vegetation, flowers, beetles, birds and beasts.

'Why did you bring him here?' Henrik Lenka barked. 'He's not one of us. He'll betray you.'

'Like you did?' Lucretia spat, glaring at him over her shoulder. He turned his face away from her scalding hatred. She waved a human hand at him. 'Bartholomew is bound to be hungry after his long journey. Go to the kitchens and order him some food. Have it sent to his suite.'

Henrik glared from Lucretia to Barty as he scrambled to his feet, and then stormed away.

'Ling Ling, I want an update on the Biome's status. We need to be ready for whatever comes our way.'

Barty jumped as Ling Ling stepped forward beside him. He hadn't realized she was there. She bowed and was gone.

'So,' Lucretia purred, 'what do you think of my Arcadia dome?'

'I, I, I don't know what to say,' Barty stammered. 'It's like nothing I've ever seen.'

'Come this way.' Lucretia slid a human arm through his and led him into the cavernous dome. 'Once you've seen Arcadia, you'll think Noah's ark was nothing more than a row boat.'

A river coursed through the vast space, bubbling up on one side of the structure and tumbling out of the other. On the near bank, he saw three huge river turtles, and across the water a family of giant otters.

'Careful of the fire ants.' Lucretia pointed, and Barty saw that his right foot was barely a centimetre from a bustling trail of *Solenopsis*, eviscerating everything in their path. 'And don't go for a swim, unless you fancy being nipped by predacious diving beetles or piranha.'

'You made all of this?' Barty said, his voice a breathless croak. 'It's unbelievable.' With a tiny shake of his head, he turned his gaze upwards, to the steel and glass roof of transparent hexagons a hundred metres above him. The rainstorm had passed, grey mist was giving way to blue sky. 'How long has this been here? How did you

build this place? How did you plant it? How did you even get the land?' The questions were tumbling out of his mouth, leaving no space for answers. 'I mean, we're in the Amazon! How did you even get permission?'

'The Ecuadorian government got into a bit of debt,' Lucretia replied. 'They were considering selling a chunk of rainforest to the highest bidding petroleum company, for oil drilling. I stepped in, matched the highest bid, requested a smaller piece of land for my research, only a million hectares. I guaranteed no oil drilling and protection of the indigenous tribes who live here. They inherit the land upon my death.'

'Don't pretend you care about indigenous tribes.' Barty couldn't hide his surprise.

'On the contrary.' Lucretia looked away. 'They are part of the ecosystem of the rainforest. I'm more than happy to protect them.'

Barty was struck dumb by what he was hearing and seeing. He pulled his shoulders back, standing up straight. His head no longer felt heavy. The tiredness and aches from the long helicopter journey were gone. 'So, where's this famous laboratory you've been talking about?'

'Here, in the Arcadia dome,' Lucretia replied, looking amused. 'And below us,' she stamped a beetle claw on the dirt path, 'is my insect farm.'

'Insect farm? I'd like to see that. Are they all transgenic? I have to admit to being curious about the beetle borgs? What are they?'

'One thing at a time, Bartholomew.' Lucretia stepped off the path and swept aside a waterfall of hanging creepers to reveal the metallic doors of a lift. 'You're like a child in a sweet shop.'

'It's odd. I feel lighter, stronger . . .' Bartholomew followed her into the lift, '. . . younger!'

'It's the oxygenized atmosphere in Arcadia. It's set at thirty per cent.'

'That's nine per cent more than the earth's atmosphere.' Bartholomew gazed at Lucretia Cutter's face, part human, part beetle. Compound eyes perched atop a human nose, descending into giant jaws, stunted mandibles and flailing palps, all sitting within a human skull. She wasn't wearing her sunglasses and wig any more, there was no need to hide what she was. He gasped. 'You're bringing back giant insects!'

'Ha! Hardly a brilliant deduction, seeing as the answer is staring you right in the face.' She made a theatrical gesture to her own body as the lift doors opened. 'Really, Bartholomew, do keep up.'

Barty had to pick up his pace to match her long strides, and he marvelled at how much easier it was to jog in an oxygenated atmosphere. He felt great. 'You like your hexagons.'

'They are as close to magic as science gets,' Lucretia replied. 'Nature loves hexagons; just ask the bees. Or look into my eyes.' She turned so he could see. 'They're constructed of hexagonal cells.'

Barty moved closer to Lucretia. 'They are beautiful,' he said, his gaze unwavering as he studied her face.

She froze, her neck retreating, pulling back from his stare. As the door rose behind her, Barty wondered if underneath all that chitin and bile she still harboured feelings for him. She'd done a good job of persuading him she had no feelings of any sort, but he thought he sensed a flicker.

She spun away, stepping into the laboratory. 'There's someone I want you to meet.'

The laboratory was an open-plan hexagonal platform with only two solid walls. A silver balustrade, at waist height, separated the lab from the jungle of Arcadia. A young man, too skinny for his lab coat, stood at a sloped desk covered in dials and switches in front of a wall of toughened glass. A rectangular door of reinforced steel at the end of the desk was the only way into the room beyond the glass. Inside, Barty saw a cylindrical chamber that stretched from floor to ceiling. *That must be the pupation chamber!* He stared at the giant egg-like capsule suspended within the cylinder of fluid, his eyes following the spaghetti of wires and tubes making a nest at its base, and he wondered how it worked.

'This is Spencer.' Lucretia's face was reflected in the polished white surface of the lab benches. 'He's the Biome lab assistant.'

'Madame Cutter!' Spencer bowed his head, blinking furiously through rectangular glasses. 'You're back!'

'Spencer, this is Dr Bartholomew Cuttle. He has come to work with us. I want you to show him around and explain how we do things here. You will be assisting him.'

'Yes, Madame,' Spencer looked stunned as Barty shook his hand. 'Pardon me, sir, but are you *the* Dr Bartholomew Cuttle?'

'Yes, I believe I am,' Barty replied, noticing a large dung beetle poking its head out of the breast pocket of Spencer's lab coat.

'It's an honour to meet you, sir.' Spencer smiled and cherubic cheeks sprouted like crab-apples beneath his spectacles. Barty thought how young he was – only a handful of years older than Darkus.

'You must call me Barty.' He put his hand on Spencer's shoulder.

'Enough,' Lucretia declared. 'There's work to do.'

Bartholomew winked at Spencer, then bounded after her.

'The Biome is built on a hexagonal footprint,' she said as she walked. 'The Arcadia dome is designed to accommodate the river. We generate electricity from the current, and charge our power generators with it.'

'You power the whole place using the river?'

'We are on the edge of a waterfall. The current is strong, but no, we use solar power too.'

'Impressive,' Barty replied.

'On each side of the Arcadia dome is a smaller dome connected by an underground corridor.' She threw her hand up to indicate the one they were travelling through. 'The ones you need to know about are the residence dome, the infirmary, and the supplies dome, which has a recreational space.'

'Oh, do you have a ping-pong table?' Barty smiled winningly at Lucretia. 'I love ping-pong,' He heard a stifled gasp from Spencer, but Lucretia ignored his impudence. 'No ping-pong? That's a shame. What's in the other domes?'

'One houses the security centre, power generators, facility controls and server room, one houses the prison cells and the refrigerators, and the last dome is mine.'

As they turned the corner, Barty heard the rumble of cascading water then stopped dead as he saw the wall ahead was sheet glass. He was hit by the panoramic view of the rainforest. *The Biome is high up*, he thought, *at least halfway up a mountain*. The cloud forest was shrouded in mist, beautiful and wild, its secrets and mysteries a powerful magnet. He came right up to the glass and looked down at the thunderous waterfall tumbling hundreds of feet down the sheer cliff face at his feet.

Spencer came to his side. 'You never get used to it.'

Ling Ling appeared along the corridor. Lucretia made it clear with a hand gesture that they were to stay where they were and went to talk to her.

'Spencer,' Barty hissed in an urgent whisper. 'Listen to me, I . . .'

Spencer gave a tiny shake of his head, his eyes rolling up to the ceiling. Barty looked up and saw a small black semi-circle protruding from the ceiling. A camera.

'I err . . . just wanted to say, that, um, I am looking forward to working with you, and that . . .' Barty tipped his head forward, as if nodding, and as soon as his mouth wasn't visible to the cameras he spoke softly but clearly, *'I'm here to stop her and to bring you home.'* He straightened up. 'I may get a bit lost in this white labyrinth, so I'm going to need your help.'

Spencer's eyes darted over Barty's face, searching for evidence of truth.

'I'm excited to learn more about the work you've been doing here.' Barty clapped his hands together. 'Lucretia has promised me a place by her side at the cutting edge of scientific research. I find her work fascinating. Her transgenic developments are extraordinary. She has become a power to be reckoned with.'

Spencer nodded. 'She is very powerful. It would take an army to defeat her now.'

'Yes.' Barty nodded emphatically for the camera, but said in a low voice. 'Although, Goliath was felled by the boy David.'

'That's just a story, Dr Cuttle.' Spencer's expression made him look older than his years. 'This is real – very, very real.'

'Spencer, stories only last if they tell a universal truth.' Barty saw the reflection of Lucretia returning, in the glass, and changed his tone. 'I'm sure there's plenty you can teach me once we are in the lab, I'll need to be brought up to speed.'

'Bartholomew, there's something I want you to witness,' Lucretia said, sounding very pleased with herself. 'Spencer can show you to your room afterwards.' They followed her through a dizzying series of turns and tunnels, ending up in a room with white leather sofas and a large flat-screen television on the wall.

'You'll like this,' Lucretia said as the TV flickered on. 'I've given Australia a second Christmas.' She pointed a black claw.

Worldwide Network News was showing images of Sydney harbour. They cut from footage of the city to the beach, and everywhere you looked, crawling and flapping about clumsily, were thousands upon thousands of chunky metallic brownish green scarabs. Branches of trees were so heavy with coleoptera that they were bending down to touch the water.

'Did you know the poor Christmas beetle was in decline, due to habitat destruction? I was so saddened by this news that I thought I'd send the Australian Prime Minister a gift of several billion of them.' She threw her head back and chittered.

The news cut to an image of Kirribilli House, the second official residence of the Australian Prime Minister. It was barely visible under the blanket of beetles.

'What do you hope to achieve with this cheap trick?'

Barty asked, unable to hide his disgust.

'Did you know that Australia has the second biggest sugar cane harvest in the world, after Brazil?' Lucretia drew herself up on to her hind legs. 'Together with the Christmas beetles, I sent their Prime Minister a proposition. I've offered to decimate the Brazilian sugar cane industry with my bugs, in exchange for their sworn allegiance. The Christmas beetles are there to demonstrate that I am capable of delivering my end of the bargain. You see, Australia will be the first country to bow down to my rule – shortly followed by America – who, after losing their wheat harvest, know that I can wipe out their soybean harvest too with a single command.'

'You're dreaming.' Barty shook his head. 'The American President will never bow down to your rule.'

'Am I?'

There was a knock on the door and Dankish padded in.

Lucretia looked surprised to see the thug. 'What do you want?'

'Uh, we went back to the helicopter, to get the luggage.' He paused, clearly nervous about delivering his news. His eyes were glued to the floor.

'And?'

'The latch on the luggage compartment of the helicopter is broken, and all the luggage is gone. It's empty. It must have fallen out on the flight.'

'You *idiot*!' Lucretia hissed, lurching threateningly towards him.

'Madame.' Ling Ling appeared from nowhere. 'The President of the United States is on the phone for you.'

'HA!' Lucretia Cutter instantly forgot Dankish and the lost luggage. She swung round to face Barty, victorious, her ghastly mouth a grinning pit of molasses. 'See? They will all bow down to me eventually or their people will starve.'

CHAPTER SIX
Helicopter Hideaway

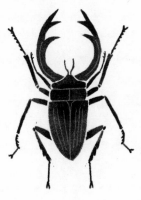

'*H*umpty?' Pickering hissed, prodding his cousin's blubbery bottom with his bony forefinger. 'Wake up! Wake up! Do you hear me? Oh, for goodness' sake!' It irritated him that Humphrey slept so soundly, and snored so raucously. Pickering had climbed into the helicopter luggage compartment first, because he'd wanted any wild animals that found them to kill and eat Humphrey first, but now he was trapped inside by Humphrey's mountain of a body, and he desperately needed a wee. 'Humphrey Gamble, will you wake up, you giant oaf!' He raised his hand and slapped his sleeping cousin on the rump.

Humphrey snorted and rolled towards Pickering, like a gargantuan fleshy boulder, crushing him against the wall of the helicopter. Pickering thrashed about. 'You're SQUASHING ME!' he squawked.

'Huh?' Humphrey sat up and farted.

'Oh, my . . .' Pickering made a retching sound. 'YOUR INSIDES STINK!'

Humphrey looked, bleary-eyed, at Pickering. 'Oh, no, we're still in the blasted jungle, aren't we?'

'*Arghhh, huuhhh, ug, argh!*' Pickering spluttered.

'Shhhhhh, they'll hear you. It's just a bum burp.' Humphrey rubbed his eyes with his sausage-like fingers. 'What time is it?'

'How should I know what time it is? Neither of us has a watch!' Pickering snapped. 'All I know is that it's getting light outside and we need to get out of here before we get caught – or choke to death.'

'*I'll* choke you, if you're not careful.' Humphrey held his hands up threateningly, and Pickering immediately calmed down. 'Anyway, I can't help it,' Humphrey grumbled. 'It must have been those purple berries we ate yesterday. They've made me gassy.'

He rolled towards the luggage compartment door, pushing it open with his feet, and slid out, waggling his legs until they found the ground. Once he was standing he held his hand out for Pickering, who accepted it and leant on Humphrey to scramble down.

The air outside was still. Fog drifted around them like a terror of waltzing ghosts. The leaves at the edge of the clearing glittered menacingly with moisture, and Pickering was overcome with dread. He longed for the dirty air of London and his old life, before he'd discovered the beetles. Then he remembered the day Lucretia Cutter had paid him a visit, the money she'd promised him, and his heart throbbed. They were here to make sure she kept her promise and get what was rightfully theirs, half a millon pounds.

Pickering followed Humphrey into the forest, all his senses alert. The sun was rising, and they didn't want to get caught beside the helicopter by Lucretia Cutter's men.

When they'd first made their escape from the helicopter luggage compartment, directly after landing, they'd stumbled into the forest fringes and hidden. There was the big commotion about the missing luggage. Dankish, Mawling and Craven had come to blows about who would tell Lucretia Cutter that her luggage was gone.

'If we admit to being in the helicopter,' Pickering worried, 'they'll know it was us that threw out the luggage.'

'I don't see what all the fuss is about,' Humphrey replied. 'It was just a bunch of dresses.'

They'd decided that they'd keep a low profile, biding their time until they could talk to Lucretia Cutter in person and explain that they had only thrown her luggage out of the helicopter because they'd wanted to spend some time with her. Pickering was certain that if they could get Lucretia alone, and explain everything they'd been through to see her, she'd be flattered. He had read in his romance novels about how ladies like it when a man risks life and limb for love. Then they could talk reasonably about the matter of the money she owed them.

Humphrey wasn't so sure, and since they'd landed he'd become increasingly grumpy. Ten nights trapped in the luggage compartment of the helicopter had left him half crazed and very hungry. He'd thought they were going to land in Hawaii or Florida, in a holiday home by the beach, so when they'd finally jumped out of the chopper, he was horrified to see that they were in a jungle, with no fast-food restaurants for hundreds of miles. Humphrey's limited conversation had reduced to grunts, snorts and death threats. Pickering was certain that if they didn't find food soon, Humphrey would eat him.

They had no idea where they were, or which country they were in, and they couldn't set off into the rainforest without risking getting lost or killed, so they were stuck until they could find a way to talk to Lucretia Cutter.

The first night in the forest had been torture. They'd tripped over a half-man, half-skeleton, dressed in a white lab coat, rotting on the forest floor, and decided that going up to the Biome and knocking on the door might not be a very good idea. Then after trekking around the entire building they realized there *wasn't* a door. Exhausted and irritable, they found a big tree with a hollow in its roots. Humphrey thought it would make a comfy place to sleep. He grabbed an armful of leaf mulch from the hole to make it comfy, and was startled by a huge reddish brown tarantula that lived there. It lifted its front two legs, hissing, before it leapt at him bearing its fangs. Humphrey fell backwards screaming, Pickering threw a stick at the spider, and the pair ran into the forest.

Pickering suggested they should sleep up a tree, but Humphrey had problems climbing. Eventually, they agreed that one of them would lie on a fallen tree trunk and sleep while the other kept watch. Humphrey slept first. Pickering sat up, terrified by the haunting night cries of howler monkeys. When it was his turn to sleep, Pickering had just nodded off when he was shaken awake by a wide-eyed Humphrey, who pointed silently at a large jaguar watching them from the edge of the clearing. Humphrey roared as loudly as he could and ran at the large cat, which bounded away. The petrified cousins sprinted back to the helicopter, leaping into the luggage compartment, closing the door on the rainforest and sleeping fitfully until dawn.

After their night of terror, they had decided to make the luggage compartment their bedroom. They spent their days in the fringes of the forest, foraging for food and waiting for Lucretia Cutter to come outside for a stroll. They waited and waited, seeing Craven, Dankish and Mawling, as well as Ling Ling, and even once the French butler, but Lucretia Cutter never came outside.

As if this wasn't enough to terrify him to death, Pickering couldn't shake the feeling that they were being watched. Perhaps it was all the living things that stared at them from every branch and hole in the forest, but he swore he could feel human eyes watching them, and so he jumped and spun round with every crack and rustle of the forest.

At night he cuddled his baby blanket to his face, his Muckminder, and imagined it was Lucretia Cutter's cheek. His heart went pitter-patter at the thought of her name. He must be brave and keep his and Humphrey's spirits up. He was certain that battling the jungle would be the way to win his lady's heart, and he would be rewarded with true love and a trunkload of cash.

CHAPTER SEVEN
Fighters and Flyers

'**I**'m nervous,' Bertolt whispered.

'It's going to be fine,' Darkus said under his breath. 'Once we've had our boarding passes scanned and looked at the camera thing, we'll be sifted into one of those queues.' He pointed with his forehead. 'They're looking for bombs and weapons, not beetles.'

'I know, but my heart is racing, and I feel sick.'

Bertolt did look a bit green. 'Once we're on the other side, you'll feel better,' Darkus said.

Bertolt nodded.

Uncle Max and Virginia came striding out of the

airport newsagent's, followed a by a chattering Calista Bloom – Bertolt's mum – and a politely nodding Barbara Wallace – Virginia's mum.

'What's the matter?' Darkus asked, seeing his uncle's furrowed brow and dark expression.

Virginia shoved the *Daily Messenger* in front of him and Bertolt. 'The world governments are threatening to bomb Lucretia Cutter! Well, actually, it says your dad *and* Lucretia Cutter, but . . .'

'What!' Darkus leapt up.

Bertolt took the newspaper from Virginia. 'Hang on a minute. It says here that international powers are *discussing* the possibility of a targeted strike. It doesn't say that they are actually going to do it.' He pushed his glasses up his nose and looked at Darkus. 'It could be a bluff, to try and scare her.'

'It could be.' Uncle Max nodded. 'We have to hope they don't know where she is.'

'Lucretia Cutter's not stupid,' Virginia said. 'She will have expected this and prepared for it. I'm sure your dad's safe, Darkus.'

'What are you children talking about, that makes your faces so serious?' Barbara Wallace asked, as she and Calista Bloom approached.

'Nothing,' Bertolt said, smiling sweetly as he folded up the newspaper and tucked it under his arm.

'Are you all ready to go, Bertikins?' Calista Bloom giggled apologetically as Bertolt blushed. 'Oh! Sorry, yes,

I forgot. I mustn't call you that any more. Silly me.'

'Yes, Mum, I'm ready.' Bertolt stood up and let his mum hug him. 'Be gentle,' he hissed. 'Remember? The fireflies!'

'Of course, dear, how could I forget? I was up half the night helping you stitch the new lining into your blazer.'

'Shhhh!' Bertolt glared at his mother.

'Oh, Berti . . . I mean, Bertolt.' She pinched his chin affectionately. 'No one is listening!'

Darkus grinned. Bertolt hated breaking rules, but they'd thought long and hard about how to bring the beetles to Prague, on to Ecuador and into the Amazon, and the best idea they'd had was to divide the Base Camp beetles between them. Bertolt had twenty-seven fireflies hidden in tiny pockets stitched into the lining of his blazer, although Newton remained in his favourite place, nestled deep in Bertolt's thick white frizzy hair. Darkus had the fighters and the flyers, the titans, bombardiers, Hercules, Atlas, tiger and dung beetles, hidden in pouches on his canvas belt and in his trouser pockets. All three children were wearing khaki combat trousers, with pockets down each leg, in preparation for their trek into the jungle. Baxter and the biggest beetles were hiding in the compartments around his belt. The smaller beetles – the bombardiers, the tiger beetles and the dung beetles – were divided up amongst his trouser leg pockets, which were lined with oak mulch and damp moss.

In her trouser pockets, Virginia carried the frog-legged leaf beetles, the ladybirds, the giraffe-necked weevils and the jewel beetles. Marvin had disguised himself as a hair bobble, wrapping himself tightly around the end of one of her braids.

They each had a rucksack, containing the survival packs Barbara Wallace had given them for Christmas together with a portable pooter, pyjamas, underwear, washbag, cagoule and T-shirts. They had to travel light: only one giant suitcase was being checked in, and that contained all the equipment they needed to look after the beetles, plus their penknives, sleeping bags and camping gear.

'Right, it's time to go through to departures,' Uncle Max said, looking at Darkus. 'Are you ready?'

Darkus nodded.

'Follow me,' Uncle Max said, and Virginia and Bertolt kissed their mothers goodbye.

'Good luck,' Barbara Wallace said to her daughter. 'I'm very proud of you, Virginia.'

Darkus saw tears welling up in her eyes, and turned to Uncle Max, not wanting to intrude.

'Just hang back until I've set all the alarms off,' Uncle Max said, as they scanned their boarding passes and stared at the cameras taking their picture. He strode ahead, lifting his hat to the lady who indicated which queue they were to join.

Darkus, Bertolt and Virginia each stepped up to the

conveyor belt and put their coats and backpacks into a plastic tray. Uncle Max rolled his tray along towards the X-ray machine, walked up to the body scanner and stepped in. There was a wailing noise, and a flashing light went off. A man on the other side asked him to step backwards, but instead Uncle Max stepped towards him.

'I say! What does that noise mean?' he exclaimed loudly.

'Please, sir!' the security officer barked. 'Step back through the machine.'

'Do you think it was my watch?' Uncle Max rolled up his sleeve to reveal a large chunky metal watch.

'Please, sir! Step back!'

Darkus ran his thumbs along his belt, releasing the poppers. 'Are you ready Baxter?' he whispered, to the glistening eyes staring up at him from the open compartment.

Uncle Max stepped back in the wrong direction. The security man lost his patience and blew a whistle. The security woman who was standing on the children's side of the body scanner moved to help her colleague. Darkus quickly lifted out the rhinoceros beetle, throwing him up into the air. Baxter cracked open his elytra and his amber wings shot out, propelling him up.

'Go! Go! Go! Go!' Darkus whispered as all the other beetles took off, following Baxter up into the high ceiling of the airport.

'Aarghhhh!' A woman screamed and pointed. *'BATS!'*

Bertolt stepped towards the female security officer. 'Is it my turn to go through the machine now?' he asked.

'No, kid, this man has to return and go through again.'

'Whose bag is this?' asked a security officer from behind the X-ray machine.

'Oh! That's mine!' Uncle Max exclaimed, walking towards him.

'GET BACK HERE, SIR!' the original security guard shouted. 'Will you kindly remove your watch and your shoes, and pass back through the body scanner.'

'Goodness!' Uncle Max said. 'Well, now I'm all confused. Where should I go first?'

The woman took Uncle Max's arm and pulled him back through the machine, which was set off again by his watch. Everyone in the queue was staring at Uncle Max as he performed the part of a confused bumbling Englishman perfectly.

'Excuse me. Is it my turn yet? Bertolt asked again.

'Go, kid, go through.' The female security officer waved him through without even looking at him. Bertolt skipped through the machine, which didn't make a sound. The security staff were all watching Uncle Max as he very apologetically took off his hiking boots and unclipped his watch while delivering a monologue about 'technology these days'.

Darkus walked through the body scanner next, followed by Virginia. They grinned at each other as they picked up their backpacks and slung them over their shoulders. Bertolt was waiting for them underneath the metal beam that all the big beetles were now perched on.

The three children turned their backs on the security checkpoint and opened their rucksacks wide. Darkus looked up and made a high chirruping sound by sucking his back teeth. Immediately, all twenty-one beetles dived down, opening their wings to steer their flight, landing in the bags. The children did up their bags, and looked round to see how Uncle Max was doing.

Uncle Max was stripped down to his boxer shorts and vest, proclaiming loudly that he had metal pins in his leg from a biking accident years ago, and that he couldn't very well take his leg off to go back through the blasted machine. Darkus gave him the thumbs-up, and as soon as Uncle Max saw the sign, he stopped acting up.

'Oh, you know what it could be?' He lifted his safari hat off his head and handed it to the security officer. 'It's a pith helmet. It has brass rivets.' He hopped through the machine without setting it off. 'Ta-da!' he cried triumphantly.

The security officer shook his head as he placed the hat in a tray on the conveyor belt and waved Uncle Max through. Uncle Max picked up his shoes and clothes from the trays and put them back on. 'Now, old chap, what's the issue with my hand luggage?' he asked the officer emptying out his rucksack.

The man held up three bottles of water.

'What were they doing in there?' Uncle Max exclaimed.

'Dearie me! I'm losing my faculties. A thousand apologies.' He nodded as the officer held them over a bin. 'Of course you can get rid of them. They're only water. Are we all done? Marvellous stuff.' He waved at all the security staff. 'Thank you. You're all doing a wonderful job.'

The children walked ahead of Uncle Max until they were out in the main departure lounge. 'That was brilliant!' Virginia chuckled.

'Why, thank you, Virginia.' Uncle Max beamed as he fastened the laces of his boots. 'Are all the beetles accounted for?'

'Yes,' Darkus nodded, 'but the big ones are still in our backpacks. We need to get them back into their pouches before someone gets crushed or loses a leg.'

Uncle Max pointed to the door of a disabled toilet. 'Why don't you three pop in there and sort out the beetles? I'll keep my eyes peeled.'

Darkus nodded, and Virginia and Bertolt followed him into the room and shut the door. Five minutes later they all shuffled out. 'Ready,' Darkus said.

'Great. Now, we are at gate X, because it's a privately chartered flight.' Uncle Max put his safari hat back on. 'Follow me.'

Motty was waiting for them on the tarmac, dressed in her battered brown leather jacket and khaki cargo pants. She saluted the children as she saw them striding out of the airport doorway.

'Are we ready to fly?' she asked.

Baxter clambered out of the neck of Darkus's over-sized green jumper and waved his legs.

'Yes.' Darkus smiled at the rhinoceros beetle. 'We are.'

As they filed on to Bernadette, Motticilla's trusty black Beechcraft 90 aircraft, Darkus felt a surge of excitement. Finally, he was on his way to strike a blow against Lucretia Cutter.

CHAPTER EIGHT

ICE

'I don't understand.' Darkus stood on the stage, in the wings of the Panorama Hall, the lecture theatre where the International Congress of Entomology was taking place. 'Where is everybody?'

'What do you mean?' Professor Appleyard asked, poking his head around the gold curtain and peering out. His grey eyebrows lifted, turning the wrinkles on his forehead into deep furrows.

'All the entomologists.' Darkus pointed at the scattering of empty yellow seats in the auditorium. 'Why haven't they come? Don't they know how important this is?'

'Darkus, they *have* come,' Professor Appleyard, replied, looking out into the hall. 'Everyone's here.'

'But there are only a few hundred people.'

'Well, obviously, not every single entomologist on the planet comes to this congress, but there is a representative here from every major university, zoo and museum in the world.'

Darkus felt this news like a body blow. He was shocked. 'But insects are so important – to the planet, to the world's ecosystems, to humans. I thought there would be more scientists.'

'I'm afraid entomology is an often overlooked science. Very few universities teach it any more, other than as a part of zoology or biology.' Professor Appleyard shrugged. 'The entomology community is small, but it is passionate. Historically it's always depended on the passion of enthusiastic amateurs, just like you.'

'But, Professor,' Darkus grabbed his sleeve, 'I thought there'd be thousands of entomologists here.'

'What did you think? That you'd be leading an army of people with butterfly nets and pooters into the Amazon?' Professor Appleyard chuckled – then, looking down at Darkus, he stopped laughing. 'Oh, I see, you did.' He frowned. 'I'm sorry.'

Darkus's heart sank as he looked around the room. 'This is not enough people,' he said, thinking of all the beetle infestations being reported on an hourly basis. He felt sick. He'd been worried that what they were trying to do was difficult, but right now it felt impossible. He peered at the scientists – there were women in bug T-shirts knitting, some friendly-looking bald men, a couple of young men with very long hair, and an old man with the longest grey beard Darkus had ever seen. He took in thick glasses, tweed jackets, asymmetrical haircuts and butterfly scarves. Men and women, young and old, who all seemed nice, polite – and as about as useful in a fight as a lace glove. This was not the eager army of gung-ho entomologists he'd hoped to lead to the Amazon to battle Lucretia Cutter's beetle army.

'She's already won, Baxter.'

The beetle on his shoulder reared up and shook his head.

'Baxter's right. There's only one of her,' Virginia stepped up beside Darkus. 'We don't need an army of scientists to defeat Lucretia Cutter, but we may need an army of entomologists to combat the destruction caused by her beetles.'

'Have faith,' Bertolt said. 'They'll all want to help, you'll see.'

'It's show time,' Professor Appleyard whispered. He walked to the lecture podium in the centre of the stage and tapped the microphone to make sure it was on as the polite applause died down.

'Hello, can you hear me out there?' There was a low polite murmur. 'I'm here, as many of you will know, to talk about the multiple Coleoptera infestations that have been recorded over the last few weeks, since Lucretia Cutter's declaration at the Film Awards in Los Angeles. The destruction these insects are wreaking is bordering on catastrophic for human food supplies and agricultural economies. Today we, the entomologists of the world, must decide what we will do about it.'

'Don't you mean, if these wild claims are to be believed!' a gruff voice called out from the auditorium. 'Since when did the world of science blindly believe the preposterous statements of a fashion designer?' He laughed.

'I heard that she's just a front, that this is Dr Cuttle's work.'

Darkus peeped round the curtain, trying to see who had made the comment, but all he saw was a sea of faces, nodding.

'I quite agree. First we must establish the truth of these claims, and prove the unique nature of these beetles Lucretia Cutter claims to have sent out into the world to attack our harvests.' Professor Appleyard removed his spectacles, polishing them with a corner of his shirt and replacing them on his face. 'But, to those of you who doubt Lucretia Cutter's capabilities, I must ask you to see through the veneer of the Lucretia Cutter brand and cast your minds back to a truly brilliant scientist you will have known by the name of Dr Lucy Johnstone. She was a central part of the work we attempted on the Fabre Project, and I am certain many of you will remember her and have read her scientific papers.' There was a murmur of surprise. 'If you look past the dress and the morphology of the creature calling herself Lucretia Cutter, you will see that she is in fact Dr Lucy Johnstone.'

This statement caused outbreaks of heated chatter, and Professor Appleyard stood still, allowing the conversations to calm down. When he was certain he had everyone's attention again, he continued: 'Those of you who know about Dr Lucy Johnstone's ground-breaking work with Dr Bartholomew Cuttle, will also know that the claims she is making, while admittedly far-fetched, are not impossible. And so I must proceed to the second matter: the question of whether it is possible that she has engineered a genetically modified army of coleopterans to attack and weaken the structure of human society. Well, to answer this question I must invite some friends on to the stage. Please will you welcome Darkus Cuttle – Bartholomew Cuttle's son – Virginia Wallace and Bertolt Roberts.'

Darkus looked at Virginia and Bertolt, and then all three of them walked on to the stage. Once out of the safety of the wings, Darkus felt very small, and the murmuring from the audience grew.

'Are you getting children to carry out your experiments now, Professor?' the gruff voice called out again, and Darkus saw that the man was sitting in the third row. He had a military demeanour, with his hair slicked neatly back, and he was wearing a green coat with shoulder lapels. A ripple of laughter travelled round the room.

'I think you'll find Darwin was but a child when he developed an affinity with Coleoptera,' Professor Appleyard replied. 'It would be ignorant to dismiss wisdom because it comes from a young mind.'

'Let the kids speak,' boomed an American voice. Darkus turned and spotted a big man with a bushy beard and shoulder-length hair, wearing an Entomological Society of America T-shirt. The man gave him a thumbs-up.

Darkus stepped forward. 'I am here, with my friends, to prove that the genetically modified beetles do exist, to clear my father's name, and to ask for your help.'

Bertolt knelt down at the front of the stage and bowed his head. Newton zoomed out of his hair, his abdomen flashing, and twenty-seven fireflies followed his cue, leaping from the tiny hidden pockets in Bertolt's blazer. They rose up around Newton, who was the largest and shone the brightest. Newton became the north star, and the fireflies all found their place and hovered, their lights painting a picture of the night sky's major star constellations.

Professor Appleyard cued the dimming of the theatre lights. The audience of entomologists sighed with awe at the vision, pointing out the Plough and the Great Bear in wonder.

Virginia stepped forward, and without speaking a

word, did a handstand. Marvin dropped off her hair bobble on to the stage. The jewel beetles and giraffe-necked weevils in her trouser pockets flew, dropped and marched down on to the stage beside the shiny red frog-legged leaf beetle. An overhead camera was switched

on, and a picture of the lengthening line of beetles was broadcast on to a screen at the back of the stage. Virginia began a game of mirrors, executing a measured silent dance of postures and poses that the beetles copied, sometimes in pairs, to replicate her moves.

'What *is* this?' the military man called out. 'Party tricks?'

Darkus glared at the heckler. He lifted Baxter from his shoulder, holding him up in the air for a moment, so the entomologists could see the *Chalcosoma caucasus*, then he threw the beetle high up into the air. Baxter lifted his elytra and unfolded his flying wings, vibrating, so that he hovered above Darkus's head, facing the entomologists. Darkus mimicked the sounds of stridulation with saliva on his back teeth and a chorus line of Scarabaeidae flew out of the deep pockets in his trousers and the compartments in his belt. The beetles came together in formation, in front of Darkus, flying in patterns, creating the model of a rotating double helix with Baxter crowning the top.

This was what they'd rehearsed, back at home, but now they were here performing it, Darkus felt foolish. He was angry that there were so few entomologists, angry with his dad for sending him here, angry that at a desperate time like this he was on a stage performing party tricks. The military man had a wry, unconvinced look on his face, as if what he was seeing was no more than a circus act, and Darkus felt a hot rage flare up inside him.

He tilted his head back and made a high-pitched jagged noise, and suddenly the beetles forming the double helix exploded apart and zoomed back together to form a phalanx, rising up and diving towards the audience, with Baxter at their head. The fireflies broke their map of the stars and danced about above the audience's heads, flashing and flickering alarmingly. Virginia's troupe of acrobats scurried to the edge of the stage, their elytra raised and ready.

'That's enough now, Darkus,' Professor Appleyard said sternly. 'Call them back.'

Darkus raised his hand, palm flat, and called out: 'Beetles to me!'

All the airborne beetles zoomed up in a loop, still in formation, and flew back to Darkus's hand, landing and scrambling down his arm and into their personal pockets. The last beetle to land was Baxter, who settled on Darkus's shoulder.

Virginia and Bertolt made sure that their beetles had safely returned, and came to stand beside Darkus.

'That was a little off script,' Bertolt whispered.

'That was awesome!' Virginia hissed.

'So, as you can see,' – Professor Appleyard had to raise his voice to be heard over the alarmed conversations taking place in the auditorium – 'it is no fiction that genetically modified beetles exist – and Lucretia Cutter controls an army of them.'

'But why?' someone called out. 'What does she want?'

'Well, that remains to be seen,' Professor Appleyard replied, 'but it looks as though she's asking all the governments of the world to place her in a position of sovereignty at their head. She wants to rule the world.'

There was a stunned silence.

Professor Appleyard continued: 'And she plans to use human food supplies as a way of achieving that. She is laying siege to the world.'

'But how can we fight this?'

'How do we stop her?'

'How do we know his father isn't the mastermind behind this attack?' The military man was pointing at Darkus. His heart sank as he saw the panic on people's faces. He'd come to Prague looking for answers, for allies, for an army, but as he looked around the room he saw nothing but confused and suspicious grown-ups, who were having trouble believing what they'd just seen. If Lucretia Cutter was going to be stopped and Dad saved, he realized, he and the beetles would have to do it on their own.

He turned and marched off the stage.

'Darkus!' Virginia called after him. 'Where are you going? Come back!'

Darkus kept walking.

CHAPTER NINE

The Thingamabob

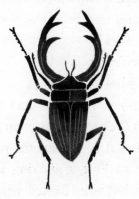

'**Y**ou should have stayed,' Bertolt said, coming into the dressing room and seeing Darkus slumped on the sofa.

'No.' Darkus shook his head. 'We shouldn't have to put on a show to persuade them what we are saying is true.' Baxter was sitting in his cupped palms. He brought the rhinoceros beetle close to his face. 'Don't they have eyes? Can't they see what's happening? Lucretia Cutter will have the whole world in the palm of her hand before they've made up their mind whether or not to do anything about it.' Baxter lifted up his front leg and petted Darkus's nose. 'Oh, I'm all right, Baxter. Don't you worry about me.' He smiled and the rhinoceros beetle opened his mouth, smiling back.

'Darkus,' Virginia said, sitting down on a chair opposite, 'we totally agree, but Dr Yuki Ishikawa came up on to the stage after you stormed off. He was in the audience the whole time.'

'Dr Ishikawa's here? I didn't see him.' Darkus sat up.

They'd met Dr Yuki Ishikawa in Greenland. He'd refused to come with them to the Film Awards, but his wisdom had helped Darkus save Baxter from the cold weather, and given him the idea that helped them win the battle in the Hollywood Theater.

'They treat him like some kind of Jedi,' Bertolt nodded, coming to sit beside Darkus.

'Yeah, he was brilliant.' Virginia's brown eyes shone. 'He's taken samples of Lucretia Cutter's beetles, from the ones we collected in our pooters at the Film Awards and from the genetically modified wheat weevils she released in Texas. He shared some of his observations with the other entomologists.'

'The first thing he discovered is that the beetles she's breeding have short life spans,' Bertolt said.

'The adults die after just one or two days,' Virginia added.

'And they appear to be mostly male,' Bertolt said.

'So he's come up with two ideas to tackle the infestations,' Virginia said. 'The first is to distract the male beetles with the pheromones of female beetles.'

'The entomologists are going to set up pheromone traps, to lure the beetles away from the crops,' Bertolt explained. 'And then they are going to use the Sterile Insect Technique where they only release sterile males so that if any beetles mate there won't be any babies!'

'The entomologists were all a-buzz with ideas of how to tackle the infestations,' Virginia said, 'suggesting natural predators, like you used at the Film Awards, and other ways to protect untouched crops.'

'So, we do nothing,' Darkus snapped. 'Set up pheromone traps and clear up the mess. Sounds like a great plan.'

'I thought you'd be pleased,' Bertolt said, crestfallen.

'Dealing with the infestations isn't going help get Dad back, is it? Or clear his name?' Darkus scowled at Virginia. 'Being here is a waste of time. I thought there'd be loads of brave entomologists, who'd want to come with us to the Amazon and take on Lucretia Cutter. Dad said they'd help us, but half of them think he's guilty.'

Virginia put her hands on her hips. 'Your dad never said they'd fight Lucretia Cutter. He didn't actually say *what* they'd help us with, did he?'

'Darkus, entomology is a science,' Bertolt said softly. 'It's not a sport. It's hardly a surprise that they're not weapon-wielding bodybuilders, is it?'

'Yeah, well, we don't need their help anyway.' Darkus stuck out his chin. 'It's always been us and the beetles against the world.'

'We're on the world's side, idiot,' Virginia tried to tease him into smiling, 'it's Lucretia Cutter who isn't.'

'Ahem.' The three of them looked round to see Uncle Max leaning against the wall, listening to their conversation. 'I do hope you're including me in that "us", Darkus?'

There was a knock at the dressing-room door.

'Hello there.' The giant American man with the bushy beard opened the door and poked his head in. He had rosy cheeks, friendly blue eyes, and beetle tattoos down his arms: a stag on one and an Atlas beetle on the other. 'I'm looking for Darkus Cuttle.' He stepped into the room. 'May I shake you by the hand, sir?'

Darkus stood up, awkwardly, and shook the man's hand.

'I'm Hank, from the Entomological Society of America.' He pointed at his T-shirt. 'We sure are grateful for all that you're doing to help protect our harvests. Dr Ishikawa said he would never have come to ICE if you hadn't flown to Greenland to alert him of Dr Johnstone's experiments.'

Darkus felt his cheeks getting hot. Virginia folded her arms and beamed out an *I told you so* look at him.

'Thank you, Mr, err . . .'

'Burton, but you can call me Hank.' He pointed at an empty chair. 'May I?'

'Please do,' Bertolt said, as they all nodded. 'What can we help you with, Mr Burton – I mean, Hank, sir?'

'Actually, I may have something that will help *you*.' He unzipped his black leather bum-bag. 'I can't work out for the life of me what this thingamabob does.' He handed over a square black screen the size of a matchbox. 'When you turn it on, a white hexagon lights up with six triangles inside, but nothing happens when you press them.'

'Why do you think this will help me?' Darkus turned it on and looked at the device, puzzled.

'Because it was found outside the Hollywood Theater, in a pile of clothes near the stage door.'

'I don't understand.' Darkus looked at Hank.

'It seems that someone threw all of Lucretia Cutter's luggage out of her chopper before it took off. Everything was brought to us, at the ESA, in case it could help us combat the attack on the wheat harvest. Most of it was clothes and useless stuff, but we did find that thingamabob.'

Bertolt sprang forward, taking it out of Darkus's hands, studying it intensely.

'Thank you,' Darkus said.

'No, thank *you.*' Hank dipped his head. 'I wish there was more I could do to help you. Professor Appleyard told me what you children did to prevent Lucretia Cutter's attack. It was mighty courageous.'

Darkus looked at Bertolt. 'Do you know what it is?'

'It looks like a fancy TV remote control.'

'Can we take it with us?' Darkus asked.

'Of course. It's yours. Only wish there was more I could do.' Hank drummed his palms on the arms of the chair. 'I hear you're going giant beetle hunting? I would sure love to come with you guys. I'm handy with a shot-gun.'

'Have you any idea where to find Lucretia Cutter?' He tipped his head. 'Whole world's looking for her, sure know a bunch of folks who'd kill to find out where she's holed up.'

Darkus glanced at Uncle Max. 'I'm sorry.' He shook his head.

'Well, if you need me, for anything at all, you can contact me here.' He held out a piece of paper. 'I have to go back to Washington and advise the White House on the best way to deal with these attacks. Dr Ishikawa's findings will be a great help. If we can lure some of the wheat weevils into honey traps, we may be able to save some of our harvest. Right now, the best we can hope for is damage control. This attack has hurt our economy real bad.'

Darkus took the paper and as Hank Burton got up to leave, a familiar face appeared in the doorway. 'Dr Ishikawa.' He bowed his head. 'It's good to see you.'

Bertolt and Virginia followed his lead as the smiling scientist entered the room.

'It is wonderful to see you again, Darkus Cuttle.' The skin around Dr Yuki Ishikawa's eyes concertinaed as he smiled. 'I wanted to give you my best wishes for your journey, and bring you these.' He took three tiny bamboo cages from a cloth bag. They were similar to the one about his own neck containing a beautiful pink preying mantis. 'They are for your beetles. There are many predators in the Amazon, and we know how dangerous a predator can be, don't we?' He laughed, his eyes twinkling. 'Your actions at the Film Awards were inspired, young man. I could not have done better myself.'

Darkus felt his face getting hot for a second time. 'Thanks. I wouldn't have thought of releasing the birds if you hadn't said that thing about every creature having a predator.'

'Ah, but you *did* think of it, and that made all the difference.' Dr Ishikawa handed him the largest of the three cages. 'For Baxter, to keep him safe in the jungle.'

'Are you coming with us this time?' Darkus asked.

Dr Ishikawa shook his head. 'There is great need for my work here. I can do the most good disarming Lucy Johnstone's foot soldiers, her transgenic beetles. So here I must stay.'

'You *have* to help this time.' Darkus stepped closer to Dr Ishikawa. 'Please. We don't know what we'll find out there. We'll be hopelessly outnumbered.' His voice was strained and he found himself blinking back tears. 'I don't know how to fight her,' he admitted.

Dr Ishikawa gave a little shrug. 'Then, perhaps, you shouldn't.'

Darkus gave an exasperated sigh. Why did Dr Ishikawa always speak in riddles.

'You are the Beetle Boy.' Dr Yuki Ishikawa fixed Darkus with his eyes as dark and calm as underground pools. 'Only you know what that means.' He touched his finger to Darkus's forehead. 'Think.' He paused. 'Be a scientist. Observe. Be curious. Ask questions.' He moved his finger and pointed to Darkus's heart. 'Do what you feel is right.' A broad smile spread across his face, as if he'd solved a complicated puzzle, and he nodded. 'Yes. The Beetle Boy must do what he feels to be right.'

CHAPTER TEN
Novak's Nightmare

Novak sat up, her breath snatched in stunted gasps. She was on the floor of the dimly lit white cell, in her bed, with the covers thrown off. She'd had the dream again. Closing her eyes, she pressed her hand to her heart. She pictured it beating inside her chest, willing it to slow down. It was *her* heart, it belonged to her, and it needn't beat so fearfully or so fast. She was going to protect it with the same passion with which it pumped blood around her body.

Her carefully drawn breaths calmed her racing heartbeat, and Novak thought about the air she was breathing

80

in. Humans needed to breathe air into their lungs, to oxygenate their blood, and while she drew breath, she was still human.

In the dream, her eyes had filled with darkness, becoming black. Her senses had spiked and every hair on her body had risen up, communicating information to her about her surroundings. Novak was frightened of her beetle senses. She tried to block them out and ignore them. She didn't want to be like Mater. She'd rather die.

Looking down at her black chitinous shins and clawed feet, Novak pulled her knees into her chest and wrapped her arms around her legs so that she didn't have to see them. She'd give anything to be a normal girl. To turn back time, to before she'd been put in the pupator. She should have run away, but she never could have imagined what they were going to do to her.

She rested her chin on her knees and looked down at the chunky silver bracelet on her right wrist. She whispered to the turquoise stone in its raised silver setting. 'Heppy, are you awake?' The setting swung open on a hinge, revealing a beautiful rainbow-striped jewel beetle.

'Oh, I'm sorry, Hepburn, did I disturb you?'

The jewel beetle lifted her elytra and stretched out her wings before folding them away and clambering up on to Novak's kneecap.

'I'm frightened, Heppy,' Novak whispered. 'I don't want to go in the pupator again. We have to get out of here.'

The jewel beetle nuzzled her beautiful bobble of a head against Novak's chin.

Novak smiled. 'Ah, thank you, little one.' She lifted a finger and stroked it gently down Hepburn's back. 'I love you too. Right now, you are the only friend I have.'

She thought about Darkus. He'd promised to take her home, just before her mother had grabbed her, wrenching her away from him and from any hope of safety. She knew that Darkus kept his promises – he'd be looking for her, trying to find a way to get to her – but no one could find her here. The Amazon jungle was an enormous place. Novak knew that Darkus wasn't coming to rescue her this time, and he may not even want to. After all, his father had betrayed him, choosing to be with Mater rather than his own son.

Novak clenched her teeth. She hated Bartholomew Cuttle for what he had done to Darkus. Her mother was cruel to her, but at least she'd never pretended to be kind and caring. She'd never pretended to love Novak.

Novak lifted Hepburn off her knee and stretched her legs out in front of her, looking at her clawed feet. Darkus had said he thought they were awesome. He'd asked if she could walk up walls. She hadn't known the answer until she tried, and found she could. Her feet were made of two strong outer claws that tapered off into sharp points, and between the claws was a knife-like blade so sharp it had sliced open Ling Ling's cheek. Novak had never tested what her body was capable of –

she'd spent all her energy hiding the changes caused by the pupation, even from Gerard. She had bound her feet and worn thick tights to cover her black shins. But here, now, in this cell, she was helpless, and the only tools she had that might help her escape a second pupation were those she possessed because of her beetle genes.

She got to her feet, standing up on her claws, holding Hepburn in her cupped hands. 'You have to help me, Heppy,' she whispered. 'I need to find out who I really am.'

Hepburn fluttered her wings, lifting off Novak's hands and hovering in front of her face. She waggled her front legs in a gesture of encouragement, and Novak laughed.

'OK, OK.' Novak rolled her chin down to her chest, closed her eyes and took a deep breath. She parted her thick silver hair at the nape of her neck and teased out first one, then a second black feathered antenna, which rose up, curling out of the top of her head like two feathered fans. She concentrated on her breathing, placing her thoughts in her skin, where each hair was standing to attention. She felt her eyes roll back in her head and fill with darkness.

This wasn't a dream. She was making this happen.

The fine silver hairs on her body shivered. The world outside the triangular walls of her white cell came into her consciousness as a series of sounds, smells and obstacles. She sensed a man with rasping breath and strong body odour sitting on a chair outside the cell.

'Dankish,' Novak whispered. 'I can see him.'

She lifted her head and clenched her fists. She needed to test how her human muscles and chitinous feet worked together. She spun round and ran at the wall, managing to get both claws up before she fell to the floor, hitting her elbows hard.

'Ouch!' She got up and walked back to the opposite wall – as far away as she could get in the small cell – and tried again. This time she ran up the wall diagonally, gouging great scratches into the plaster. Feeling the strength in her feet, she slowed, strolling into the centre of the ceiling and hanging upside down, like a bat. Her claws were incredibly powerful and easily able to take her weight.

Her silver hair hung down and her black flagellate antennae flicked and fanned, sensing the world around her. Her beetle eyes picked up more detail in the dimly lit room than her human eyes could. Everything around her, even the air, was more visceral.

Hepburn flitted up, hovering in front of her face then dancing about. Novak smiled at the beetle's delight.

'Look, Hepburn,' she said. 'We're sisters.'

CHAPTER ELEVEN
Scud

'Oi, Crips,' Novak heard Dankish growl, 'what you got there?'

'Food, for the girl.'

'Hepburn, quick.' Novak pushed against the ceiling, letting go with her clawed feet. Somersaulting in the air, she landed in a kneeling position, one knee up, her arms out. She held out her wrist, with the bracelet compartment open. Hepburn zoomed down and dropped, clumsily, into the hidden chamber. Novak snapped it shut, then flattened her antennae down, back over her head, tucking the furled ends neatly into the nape of her neck. She ran her fingers through her hair, covering the feathered feelers with her silver locks. Tipping her head to her chest, she rolled her beetle eyes back down, seeing with her human eyes once more. Sitting down cross-legged, she grabbed the blanket and covered her knees, doing her best to look meek and scared.

There was a timid knock at the door. It opened to reveal a young man in a white lab coat. He smiled and shuffled in, carrying a tray. The lights turned up as he entered.

'Hello, I'm Spencer,' he said, blinking at her through rectangular glasses. 'I, um, I brought you some food.' He looked down at the tray. It held a plate covered by a silver dome and a glass of water.

'Thank you. You can put it down there.' Novak watched, amused, as Spencer clumsily laid the tray on the floor, knocking the silver dome off the plate of melon and banana slices, apologizing profusely as he replaced it.

'I'm Novak,' she said.

'Oh, yes, I know. I mean . . .' He straightened up. 'Your mother, she—'

'I don't have a mother,' Novak cut him off. 'Would a mother treat a daughter like this?' She gestured to the cell.

'Err, no, I, ah suppose, not . . . I mean, *my* mother wouldn't.'

A small black frog-like face popped up out of Spencer's top pocket, with two shining beady eyes either side of a ridged armour-plated head.

'Oh!' Novak clapped her hands together. 'You have a beetle!'

'Scud!' Spencer chided. 'You're supposed to stay hidden.'

'No, it's OK. I love beetles.' Novak knelt up. 'Hello – Scud, is that his name?'

'Yes, Scud, like the missile. It's funny, because, well, you know,' Spencer chuckled, 'he's a *dung* beetle.' Novak frowned, not understanding the joke, and Spencer blushed. 'Oh, I see you have a little friend too!' He nodded at Novak's bracelet.

She looked down. The bracelet was open and Hepburn was excitedly clambering out. Once her abdomen was free of the case, she flipped up her elytra and flew straight to Spencer, landing on his nose and clambering in circles, stopping to kiss him every few seconds.

'Hepburn!' Novak exclaimed. 'What are you doing?'

'She's a very friendly *Cyphogastra javanica*,' Spencer laughed, gently lifting Hepburn from his nose and peering through his glasses at her. 'No! It can't be.' He became agitated. 'Where did you get this beetle?'

'Why?'

'I know her.' He examined Hepburn from all angles while she appeared to hug his thumb. 'But I haven't seen her for nearly five years.'

Novak got to her feet. 'How do you know she's the same beetle?'

'Are you kidding? I'd never forget her. Look at how beautiful she is!' Spencer chuckled as Hepburn strutted backwards and forwards across his hand like a model on a catwalk. 'And she knows it.'

Novak's pulse quickened. 'Then you must know Darkus Cuttle?'

'Dr Bartholomew Cuttle's son? No.' Spencer shook his head. 'Should I?'

'But Darkus brought Hepburn to me. She came from Beetle Mountain.'

'Beetle Mountain? What's that?'

'Darkus is the guardian of the beetles from Beetle

Mountain. It's this amazing place built out of teacups filled with lots of different species of intelligent beetles. Or at least it was . . .' Novak's voice petered out as she remembered that Mater had burnt it to the ground.

'Lots of different species?'

'Yes, and Darkus has a beetle friend too, a rhinoceros beetle, called Baxter.'

'The beetles *survived*?' Spencer exclaimed.

There was a bang on the door. 'What's going on in there?' Dankish grunted.

'Just a minute,' Spencer called out, and then his voice dropped to an excited whisper. 'This is incredible! When I set the beetles free, I wasn't sure they'd be able to cope out in the world, but I couldn't leave them there.'

'What do you mean, you set them free?' Novak asked.

'The intelligent beetles – Scud here, and Hepburn – they were bred in Lucretia Cutter's laboratory. They carry human DNA. Dr Cuttle's DNA, to be precise.' He pushed his rectangular glasses up his nose. 'Their life in captivity was cruel. They wanted to be free.' He shrugged. 'So, one day, I smuggled them out of the lab, in one of Mum's cake tins, and let them go.'

'You did! Oh, how brave!' Novak clasped her hands to her chest. 'Wasn't Mater angry?'

'Furious.' Spencer nodded. 'When she realized what I'd done, she sent her goons.' He pointed to the cell door. 'They grabbed me and put a funny-smelling cloth over my mouth – I passed out. When I woke up I was trapped here, in the Biome, and made to look after the insect farms downstairs, supplying healthy specimens for her experiments.'

'You're a slave?' Novak gasped.

'The work's not bad. I quite like it, actually.' Spencer smiled weakly. 'But I miss my mum, and I worry about her. She doesn't know where I am.' He sighed. 'At least the beetles got away. I've always wondered what happened to them.' His expression brightened. 'And if Dr Cuttle's son is looking after them, then I know they are in good hands. They must have bred if there's enough of them to fill a mountain. I hope I get to see it one day.'

Novak thought it best not to tell Spencer what had happened to the mountain. 'Thank you for bringing me food,' she said, lifting the silver dome. 'I'm starving.'

'That's OK.' Spencer said, shuffling backwards. Novak noticed he was clenching and unclenching his fists. 'Um. And. It will probably be your last meal for a while.'

'Oh?' Novak looked at him.

'Lucretia Cutter has scheduled your pupation for the day after tomorrow. You must be nil by mouth for at least twenty-four hours before you step into the machine.'

'I see.' Novak looked up at him. 'Don't suppose you have a cake tin you can smuggle me out in?'

Spencer swallowed and shook his head. 'I'm so sorry,' he whispered.

'C'mon, Crips!' Dankish shouted. 'I don't want to get into trouble.'

'Don't be sad for me, Spencer.' Novak reached up and stroked his cheek. 'She bred me for this, but I would rather die than be put in the pupator again.'

Spencer's chin sank to his chest and Novak thought he was about to cry, but instead he whispered:

'If I can help you, I will. I promise.'

CHAPTER TWELVE
The Astronomical Clock

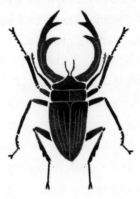

*U*ncle Max marched them swiftly into the Old Town Square, weaving through the market of Christmas-themed stalls. 'You can't come to Prague and not see this!' He waved his arms at the mint-green, honey-comb-yellow and dove-grey buildings. They looked like pictures Darkus had seen on chocolate boxes. 'And that is the oldest working astronomical clock in the world! Isn't it a thing of beauty?'

Darkus looked up at the enormous clockwork time-piece on the wall of the Town Hall. It was constructed of bronze cogs, gold symbols and had moving celestial orbs on the clock hands. A bell sounded, and a skeleton – the figure of death – struck the hour. Each chime reverberated in his chest like a final heartbeat. Twelve apostles presented themselves at the top of the clock, but Darkus turned away. He couldn't watch. Time wasn't on his side: the whole world was looking for his dad and Lucretia Cutter, and when they found them they were going to send bombs.

Uncle Max shepherded them across the Charles Bridge at a fierce pace. 'Construction of this bridge began in 1357 during the reign of King Charles IV.' He pointed at the castle. 'That is the largest and one of the most incredible castles in the world,' he said, hurrying them on to a bus. 'Such a pity we don't have time to see it.'

Darkus had never been to a city that looked more like a place of fairy tales. He stared at the castle as the bus pulled away. *If this was a fairy tale*, he thought, *I should be the hero*. His heart sank: he'd never felt less heroic.

He looked at Baxter sitting proudly on his shoulder and felt like a fraud. None of the entomologists were coming with them to the Amazon. Not one. They all had to go back to their own countries and fight the beetle attacks. Everyone seemed to think that because he'd driven Lucretia Cutter away at the Film Awards, he was more than a match for her, but he knew that wasn't true. She was monstrous, and freeing the birds had been a spontaneous idea. He'd done nothing special. He'd been so confident the entomologists would help him, that they'd be coming with him to the Amazon, he hadn't thought to feel afraid about the oncoming battle. But ever since the congress, fear had been gnawing at his insides.

Václav Havel airport was a short drive out of Prague city centre. Darkus, Virginia and Bertolt followed Uncle Max into terminal three, a small concrete building for privately chartered flights. Gathering them around him, Uncle Max spoke in a low voice. 'Motty's on the other side of security, waiting beside Bernadette. We need to get the beetles past the security checks again, and then we'll be able to head out to the plane.'

The three children nodded. They knew what to do. Uncle Max was loaded up with metal items, to send the detector machines crazy: a watch on each wrist, sock suspenders, a necklace, his belt, metal-tipped shoelaces, and loose change in every pocket imaginable. As the security men gathered around the bumbling apologetic Englishman, the beetles fluttered silently over their heads and the children skipped innocently through the machines.

Out on the tarmac, Bernadette was waiting for them, her staircase reaching out like a helping hand.

'Hi, Motty!' Virginia said, hopping into the co-pilot's seat. 'Need any help for take-off?'

Motty smiled at Virginia. 'I think I've got it covered, but I'll let you know if I need you.'

At last Uncle Max came through the aircraft door,

giving the ground crew the thumbs-up to remove the stairs. 'Ready for take-off, captain,' he called to Motty. He grinned. 'Will all passengers please take their seats and fasten their seatbelts.'

'How long is the flight to Ecuador?' Darkus asked.

'It's not a simple journey,' Uncle Max replied. 'We go to Lisbon first, top up with fuel, then make the journey to Caracas, which is nearly nine hours. We refuel again, and then fly on to Quito in Ecuador. It will take us around twenty hours with all the stops.'

'A whole day and night flying!' Virginia marvelled. 'Brilliant!'

'I hope Mum's OK.' Bertolt blinked. 'She's probably missing me by now.'

'I just hope no one finds the Biome before we get there,' Darkus said.

'Lucretia Cutter's managed to keep its location a secret for this long.' Uncle Max patted Darkus's back. 'It can't be easy to find. Now, go and get the beetles into their case and grab a seat.'

Darkus nodded. The Base Camp beetles had to be in the suitcase for take-off, for safety and comfort. He counted them as they filed into the mulch-filled case, settling and burrowing into their preferred nooks and crannies. Uncle Max's reassurances about the Biome being hard to find hadn't made Darkus feel any better. He hoped Dad was all right, not hurt, or trapped in one of Lucretia Cutter's cells. His head drooped as he wondered how on earth he was he going to get inside her Biome and find him. This wasn't like the last time they'd fought Lucretia Cutter: this was more dangerous. They were going deep into a jungle to fight her. He heard Virginia's words, about him not being the kind of person who could kill, and he told himself that he could, that he would if he had to, but deep inside, he was frightened that Virginia was right.

He thought of the billions of beetles that Lucretia Cutter controlled, and then looked down at the suitcase. There had once been so many beetles. Together, they might have been able to make a difference, but now? He sighed. They were hopelessly outnumbered.

He felt the tickle of Baxter's claws climbing up his neck.

'Hey, Baxter, where are you going?' He tried to look, but the rhinoceros beetle was already climbing round the back of Darkus's ear and scrambling up through his thicket of dark hair. Darkus looked up. He could feel the beetle, but couldn't see him. 'What are you doing?' Baxter shuffled forward and then, wings out, he launched himself off Darkus's head, his hind legs wrapped around two strands of fringe. He lurched forward, jerking Darkus's head up and then clattered down against his nose, swinging from side to side, his four free legs waggling idiotically, his mouth wide open in a huge smile.

'OK, OK,' Darkus laughed. 'I'll try and cheer up, you

crazy beetle.' He lifted Baxter down, and pulled the bamboo cage Dr Ishikawa had given him from his coat pocket. 'You don't need to go in the suitcase.' He kissed Baxter's thorax. 'You can stay with me all the time now we've got this.' Baxter wrapped all six of his legs around Darkus's thumb and hugged it tight.

Darkus eased Baxter into the little bamboo cage and gave him a lump of banana to munch on. Looping the strap over his head, he tucked the cage inside his green jumper. It was comforting having the rhinoceros beetle so close to his heart.

He zipped up the suitcase and strapped it into a seat, before going and sitting down in his own.

Bertolt sat down beside him. 'We're cleared for take-off.' He smiled at Darkus looking over his glasses. 'Better put our seatbelts on.'

Darkus nodded and fastened the belt across his lap. He looked out of the window at Václav Havel airport. He couldn't help feeling the trip to Prague had been a waste of time. He'd thought they'd find an army of entomologists here, raring to fight Lucretia Cutter. Instead, he'd been doubted by a room full of dithering scientists. If they had flown straight to the Amazon they could have already got Dad, Novak and Spencer out of the Biome.

'You're very quiet,' Bertolt said.

'I'm fine.' Darkus closed his eyes, gripping the armrests as the plane sped up, rocketing down the runway and lifting off the ground. In the darkness of his own head he heard the chimes of the skeleton on the astronomical clock. *We're running out of time*, he thought.

He heard Virginia whisper to Bertolt: 'Is he OK?'

'Um, yes. I think he's tired.'

'I'm going to go to the cockpit when the seatbelt light goes off. You coming?'

'No,' Bertolt replied. 'I think I'll stay here and read. You know,' he lowered his voice, 'make sure he's all right.'

CHAPTER THIRTEEN

The Land of Predator and Prey

The heat of Ecuador hit Darkus as soon as the cabin door was opened. He took his jumper off, tying it round his waist, and opened the bamboo cage, so Baxter could clamber on to his shoulder. Uncle Max had said there were only two seasons here, so close to the equator: a summer season and a rainy one. January fell in the middle of the rainy season, and sure enough, despite the heat, fat droplets of rain were flinging themselves at the ground as if it were a long-lost relative.

Darkus, Bertolt and Virginia bundled out of Bernadette, and into the airport, under an enormous rainbow-striped golfing umbrella held aloft by Uncle Max. 'I've hired us a jeep,' he said, as they walked towards a grey Portakabin with a handwritten cardboard sign in the window saying *Alquiler de Coches*. 'We're driving out of town to a hotel called Selva Vida Lodge, which is as far into the rainforest as we can get by car. We'll rest for a night, and tomorrow we will begin our trek into the jungle.' He surveyed the horizon and sighed. 'It's such a shame we don't have more time. Quito is one of my favourite cities. I'd love the chance to show you around.'

'You've been here before?' Virginia asked.

'Oh, yes. I studied the archaeological dig at Tulipe, a fascinating site, built by the Yumbo people somewhere between 800 and 1600 AD.'

Motty hopped into the passenger seat of the jeep as Uncle Max started the engine and Virginia, Darkus and Bertolt scrambled into the back.

'Quito is the capital city of Ecuador and is built on the foundations of an ancient Incan city,' Uncle Max shouted over the din of the engine. 'There are many interesting ruins around here.'

'Wait, there are no seatbelts!' Bertolt cried.

'Oh, well, better hold on tight,' Uncle Max laughed as the jeep bounced down the road away from the airport and the rain hurled itself at the tarpaulin roof. 'Did you know that Quito is the second highest capital city in the world?' he said over his shoulder. 'It's in the foothills of the Andes Mountains. It's also the city second closest to the equator, AND,' he hooted with glee, 'it's right beside an active volcano!'

'Volcano?' Bertolt squeaked.

'It's the perfect place for our greatest adventure,' Virginia said happily.

'It's not the volcanoes you have to worry about,' Motty said, knowingly. 'It's the earthquakes.'

'Earthquakes?' Bertolt wailed.

'Brilliant!' Virginia smiled at Darkus. 'It's good to finally be here, isn't it?'

Darkus nodded, looking out at the glowing greens and bright browns of the Ecuadorian farms. The colours were different here. Uncle Max drove for several hours, pointing out and naming mountains, volcanoes and plants, telling stories about the history of Ecuador. All the while Darkus stared at the tree-covered mountains ahead. His father was in there somewhere, hidden and held captive by Lucretia Cutter.

'I'm coming, Dad,' he whispered, and Baxter – the only one close enough to hear him – tenderly rubbed a tusk against his neck. Sometimes Darkus thought it crazy that a beetle understood him better than anyone else, and sometimes it made perfect sense.

Back in London, Darkus had thought the waiting to leave had been awful, but now he was here, in Ecuador, he felt worse. His thoughts kept crashing into each other like thunderclouds, raining drops of dread on his heart. He told himself the Biome was just a building with a laboratory inside it and possibly an insect farm, containing millions of beetles. Lucretia Cutter's beetles. A powerful, angry army of them.

Darkus had been racking his brains ever since the Film Awards, trying to think of ways he could destroy Lucretia Cutter's beetle army, but one thought tripped him up time and time again.

If I kill her beetles, does that make me as bad as her? He stared up at the tree-covered mountains where she was hiding. *What is the difference between me destroying thousands of her beetles and her burning down Beetle Mountain?*

The truth was, he didn't want to kill *any* beetles, not ever, not even Lucretia Cutter's.

He touched his forefinger to the sharp point of Baxter's horn. Baxter and the other beetles from Beetle Mountain were all once Lucretia Cutter's beetles. They came from her laboratories.

Virginia's words berated him. *I don't think you're the type of person who can kill.* He looked at her. The rain had stopped, and she was on her knees, unhooking one side of the tarpaulin roof. She poked her head out, above the top of the jeep, the wind whipping back her braids as Marvin clung on for dear life.

'Look! Chickens!' Virginia whooped, pointing. 'Bananas! Look! Look! A cow!'

I'm not an adventurer, Darkus realized, his heart sinking. *Virginia's an adventurer.* Words his uncle had once said about his father came to him: '*His adventures were in thought. He explored the very fabric of nature, experimented with possibility, and all within the confines of his own head.*'

Maybe I'm like Dad. Darkus looked down at Baxter, whose elderberry eyes gazed back at him, unblinking. *Maybe I'm a scientist.* The rhinoceros beetle opened his mouth, smiling. *Who is standing up for the beetles here?* he thought. *No one. Why is everything always about humans?* He turned his head and looked out of the window at the lush vegetation randomly interrupted by an oil well or a farm. He *was* the Beetle Boy. Maybe it wasn't just Dad, Novak and Spencer that he should be rescuing. Maybe the beetles needed rescuing too. A tiny seed of a plan sprouted in his mind.

Turning off the road on to a dirt track, orange mud sprayed up through the open windows and Virginia squealed with delight. Darkus gritted his teeth to stop from accidentally biting his own tongue as the jeep hopped down the trail.

'UuuuuUuuuuuuUuuuUuuUuUuUuuuu!' Virginia's mouth hung open as she enjoyed the bumpy vibrato. She fell silent when, out the other side of a grove of tall trees, the jeep came to a sudden stop in front of a lake. 'Oh, wow!' Virginia stood up on the car seat, looking about. 'This place is amazing.'

'Are we all OK?' Uncle Max turned round.

'I feel sick,' Bertolt admitted quietly. 'Are we here?'

'Not quite.' Uncle Max pointed. 'The lodge is over the water. We get there by boat.'

Bertolt moaned, but Virginia couldn't get out of the jeep fast enough.

A footpath led to a wooden walkway, suspended above the water on poles. On the far side of the lake, Darkus could see a wooden structure hidden amongst the trees. A rickety old motorboat with a blue canvas covering was already *putt-putt*ing across the water towards them. On the near bank, a cloud of mosquitoes vibrated above the surface of the lake, occasionally penetrated by a brightly coloured, goggle-eyed dragonfly looking for a spot of dinner.

'We get one night in a comfy bed,' Uncle Max said, lifting the suitcase out of the back of the jeep, 'so enjoy it.'

'I'm looking forward to getting back in a hammock,' Darkus said, and Uncle Max laughed.

'This is the BEST place ever,' Virginia said as Darkus came to stand with her at the end of the wooden jetty. 'Even better than LA.'

'Can you smell the forest?' Darkus looked beyond the lake to the lush green expanse of trees and smiled.

Virginia nodded. 'The whole place stinks of humid trees and it's glorious.'

She was right: this was the most wonderful place on earth. He spotted a pair of red-and-green macaws up on a high branch, and, suddenly remembering the Film Awards, lifted the bamboo cage to his shoulder.

'In you get, Baxter. We mustn't forget, this is the land of predator and prey. I don't want you to get eaten.' He nudged Virginia. 'You should put Marvin in his cage too, look.' He pointed at the birds.

Bertolt cautiously shuffled along the walkway to join them. Newton was already inside the tiny cage around his neck. 'You should strap yours to your head, like a hat,' Virginia giggled, 'in case Newton gets homesick for your hair.'

The boat pulled up alongside the jetty, and they piled in. Even Bertolt smiled as they glided serenely across the lake to the lodge.

On the far shore, a zigzag of boardwalks took them to the entrance. Darkus and Virginia ran ahead, excited to see where they were spending the night. The lodge was a large wooden building, with a reception, restaurant and hanging-out area. A cluster of log cabins, each on stumpy stilts with a pointed roof of bamboo canes, were scattered around it.

The manager of the lodge, a cheerful Ecuadorian called Miguel with a toothy smile led them to their cabin.

'Family suite,' he said, pushing open the door.

Virginia bounded in and looked around. 'Awesome!'

Two giant double beds and one single, each with white mosquito nets draping down over them, stood on a floor of polished soft wood. There was a circular table in the centre of the room, on it a glass bowl of delicate orchids and above, on the ceiling, a rotating fan keeping the room cool.

'This is how I imagine paradise.' Bertolt pushed the bathroom door open so they could see the beautifully lit sanctuary of cappuccino-coloured mosaic tiles and white porcelain.

'Motty and Virginia, you take one bed,' Uncle Max pointed. 'Darkus and Bertolt, you can take the other. I'll take the single. No one wants me snoring in their ear.'

'Oh, dear.' Motty was standing beside a wooden desk on the other side of the hut. Fanned out across the top was an assortment of international newspapers. She held up the *Daily Messenger* so they could read the headline:

FASHION EXPLOSION – COUTURE FACTORY BOMBED!

International forces identified the Indian Cutter Couture textile factory as a possible source of the rogue beetles which have been plaguing food harvests around the globe. In a series of strategic strikes, planned with the support of the Indian government, the Cutter Couture textile factory was reduced to rubble last night. There are no reports of casualties, and locals said the factory had been abandoned for some time.

Witnesses later reported that the bombing of the factory lit a fuse that triggered an explosion and the collapse of an abandoned farmhouse three miles up the road.

This second explosion released a mile-wide swarm of coconut rhinoceros beetles and Oriental flower beetles, which descended on the neighbouring farmland. Desperate farmers are now reporting plagues of beetles attacking their coconut palms and mango crops.

'They *are* bombing her!' Bertolt's eyes grew wide. He looked at Darkus.

'Yes.' Virginia walked over to Motty, taking the newspaper. 'But Lucretia Cutter bombed them right back. That swarm of coconut rhinoceros beetles and Oriental flower beetles, and the fact it was empty means she was expecting them to blow up her clothing factory. She *wanted* them to.'

'But it means that if they find it, they *could* blow up the Biome!' Bertolt said, his voice trembling.

'Although . . . if they are bombing her factory in India,' Darkus realized, 'that means they don't know about the Biome yet.'

'I'd bet any money that wherever Lucretia Cutter is is the safest place in the world,' Uncle Max said with a sigh. 'And I'd hope that any government would think twice before dropping bombs in the Amazon rainforest. It would do terrible damage to the ecology of the planet.'

'You would hope they'd think twice,' Motty muttered, 'but humans can be very stupid.'

Darkus's head ached. He needed to clear his head and get some air. Stepping out of the cabin, he noticed –

across the clearing – a viewing tower. A giant ladder had been strapped to an enormous tree trunk and at its top was a circular platform, which enabled the viewer to look in any direction. Darkus was drawn towards it.

'Hey,' Virginia shouted, jogging up beside him. 'Where are you going?'

'I want to climb up there and take a look.' Darkus pointed.

'Oooo, me too.'

'Wait for me,' Bertolt called after them. 'What are you doing?'

'We're going up there,' Virginia called over her shoulder, pointing up.

Bertolt paused, looking at the high tree. He swallowed, but then scurried to join them. 'Remember to check for snakes,' he said. 'My book says to always check for snakes before climbing anything.'

Darkus went first, with Bertolt in the middle and Virginia at the back. When they reached the platform, Darkus leant on the wooden balustrade and Virginia whistled as all three of them stared out over the undulating treetops.

'It's like a sea of broccoli,' she said, and then, after a minute, 'I'm hungry.'

The sun was setting and the sky was smeared with pink and yellow.

'Lucretia Cutter is in there somewhere,' Darkus said, resting his chin on his hands. 'And so is my dad.'

Virginia and Bertolt nodded.

'Do you think . . .' Darkus paused, '. . . do you think Lucretia Cutter's beetles are bad?'

Virginia screwed up her face as she thought about the question.

'I don't suppose *they're* bad,' Bertolt said. 'It's that Lucretia Cutter's making them do bad things.'

'Yeah.' Darkus nodded. 'That's what I think too.'

CHAPTER FOURTEEN
A River Runs Through It

*H*umphrey growled at the howler monkeys up in the trees. They were hurling branches and large seeds at him, taunting him with hooting cries and laughing.

'I hate nature!' he bellowed at Pickering. 'It's scratchy and bitey, and it hurts!'

Pickering nodded vigorously, agreeing with his raging cousin for once. The jungle wasn't the way he'd imagined it to be. It was a hostile, brutal place. He was hungry, itchy, and terrified of being mauled by a caiman or a jaguar. As each day passed he became more and more certain that if they didn't get into Lucretia Cutter's big greenhouse soon, he was going to die in this jungle. 'We need to find a way into that big dome,' he said.

'We could just go and knock on the window till they let us in,' Humphrey replied. 'I'm past caring whether she's angry about the dresses.'

'We *could*!' Pickering was struck dumb by the simplicity of the suggestion.

A rock hit Humphrey on the back of the head. He looked up and roared at the mischievous monkeys, shaking his fist, only to be hit in the face by a coconut, knocking his two front teeth down his throat. He choked, coughing them out on to the jungle floor.

'MY TEEFFFFF!' He fell to his knees, shuffling around in the leaves, searching for his front teeth, but they were gone, lost in the leaf mulch.

'Right! I've had enouthhh!' he lisped tearfully. 'Geth me ouka here, Pickers, or I thwear I'll eat *you*, I'm that hungry.'

'Come on.' Pickering covered his head with his arms to protect himself from more monkey projectiles. As they scrambled back to the helipad, he was relieved to find that the monkey missiles that hit him were soft, but as he got to the clearing, he caught a whiff of the orange-brown monkey dollops that were now splattered on his head, arms and shoulders.

'WHY?' he shrieked. 'WHY DO I ALWAYS GET PELTED WITH POO?'

'At leasssth you have your teeth,' Humphrey grumbled.

'I can't go and knock on the window like this.' Pickering looked at his shoulders smeared with monkey poop. Lucretia Cutter would never want to kiss him now. He turned to his cousin. 'And look at you, you're covered in blood.'

'I don't care,' Humphrey muttered, wiping his chin with the back of his fist.

'There's a river on the other side of the greenhouse dome. Let's take a dip in it before we go knocking on the window.'

'Fine,' Humphrey agreed, stomping off in the direction of the water.

It took them the best part of an hour to reach the river, which was swollen from the rain. The surface of the water was tranquil, but before they dipped a toe in the water, Humphrey and Pickering checked for caimans. When they were certain that there was nothing in the water planning to eat them, they stripped down to their pants, which they'd been wearing for well over two weeks, and waded into the muddy waters. He couldn't see the bottom, but Pickering was relieved to find the river was only waist deep.

'Look, the river flows into the greenhouse!' Pickering pointed upstream, to where the glass dome straddled the waterway. He flapped his hands with excitement. 'It looks like the river runs right through it. Do you think we can get in this way?' He lurched forward, dragging his spindly legs though the water till he reached the middle

of the river, and a strong current pulled his body towards the dome. 'Humphrey, come look.' He stumbled forward and grabbed on to a low hanging branch, his feet lifting off the river bed. 'The river flows down through a tunnel, and there's a grate, but it only goes down as far as the water. We could duck under it and swim in!'

'Really?' Humphrey came up behind Pickering and peered past his cousin into the dark tunnel.

'Let's swim in, sneak about until we find the living quarters and steal some fresh clothes.' He looked at the remnants of the flowery dress that he'd put on that morning of the Film Awards, now hanging forlornly from a tree branch beside his battered straw hat. He'd ripped the skirt from the dress when they'd first marched into the jungle, so now it was more of a sweat-stained tunic. He'd kept the straw hat, because he'd hoped it would keep the mosquitoes at bay, but both his and Humphrey's face and body were covered in large welts where they'd been bitten. He was desperate to get away from the jungle, but if there was any way for Lucretia to see him in a different set of clothes, he'd choose it.

'That's not a bad idea,' Humphrey admitted, smacking his lips, and Pickering could tell that his cousin was thinking about the food they might find if they did get in.

'Come on.' Pickering let go of the branch and waded towards the grate. 'I'll bet there's a big tasty roast dinner in there somewhere.'

There was a loud snap behind them, like a big branch

breaking. He and Humphrey spun round, scanning the jungle on both sides of the river. 'What was that?' Humphrey asked.

'Do you get the feeling that we're being watched?' Pickering whispered.

'It's those flipping monkeys,' Humphrey growled.

'No.' Pickering shook his head. 'I've felt it ever since we first set foot in the jungle. It's like there are human eyes looking at me, following us.'

Humphrey laughed so hard he shoved Pickering, who lost his footing in the river and fell over, coming up spluttering.

'What did you do that for?' he shouted.

'C'mon, Pickers,' Humphrey cackled, 'who is going to be following us through the jungle? Who on earth would want to?'

Pickering knew his cousin was right. He shrugged. 'I just can't shake the feeling we're being watched, that's all.'

'Come on. My tummy's rumbling. Let's go inside.' Humphrey strode up to the grate and bobbed down, his head plunging under the muddy water and rising on the other side of the barrier. 'Piece of cake,' he said.

Pickering swam over to the grate and turned round, sinking into the water backwards. In a blur of movement, he thought he saw the face of a blonde woman up a tree. He bounced back up on the far side of the grate, grabbing the bars, staring at the spot where he thought he'd seen a familiar face, but there was nothing there, just violent green foliage.

'I think I may be losing my marbles,' he muttered, shaking his head.

'That happened years ago, Pickers,' Humphrey snorted. 'Remember your funny bicycle with the trailer? And all that rubbish you picked up from the streets, thinking you could actually sell it?' He gave a great belly laugh and shook his head. 'Bonkers!'

Pickering scowled. 'Well, at least I've got all my teeth.'

Chapter Fifteen

The Predacious Pool

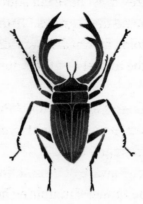

Pickering waded through into the dark tunnel after his cousin. He focused on the pale fleshy back moving forward in front of him.

'There's another one of those grate things here,' Humphrey said. 'We're going to have to go under the water to get past it.'

'Get on with it, then.' Pickering snapped.

Humphrey bobbed down, and there was a long pause before he resurfaced on the other side.

'This grate goes down much deeper,' he spluttered. 'I almost didn't get under.'

'I hardly think that's going to be a problem for me.' Pickering gloated, holding his nose as he ducked under.

There was a gap of about a metre between the river bed and the bottom of the grate. Pickering smiled to himself as he bounced up on the other side, thinking of the panic Humphrey must have felt squeezing under.

'There better be no more grates,' Humphrey growled, uncertain about going forward. It was almost pitch black in this section of the tunnel and the water was up to their stomachs now.

'I'll go first if there's another one.' Pickering replied. 'Come on, we're here now. I thought you were hungry?'

'I am,' Humphrey agreed.

Pickering became aware of a rumbling sound as they moved through the tunnel. Humphrey held up his hand, but the current dragged Pickering forward. The floor dropped away and Pickering screamed. Humphrey grabbed him by his hair as Pickering threw his hands up, grabbing on to his cousin's arm. He was hanging over the edge of a waterfall, and the only thing that was stopping him from being swept away was Humphrey's weight. He clambered along Humphrey's arm, wrapping his legs around his hefty torso. The pair looked down at the drop into darkness.

'How far down do you think it goes?' Pickering wondered. The tunnel walls were metal and the ceiling and sides were smooth.

'Maybe we should find out.' Humphrey said.

'I'm not going down there!' Pickering exclaimed. 'I'll break my neck!'

'You might not,' Humphrey reasoned.

'But I might!'

'Well, I'm not going back to the jungle,' Humphrey said. 'And if this is the way to get a decent meal,' he pointed down into the darkness, 'then that's the way I'm going.'

'Now who's crazy?' Pickering unhooked his legs from Humphrey's waist and looked around in a panic.

'I'll sit on the edge and slide down.' Humphrey looked at Pickering. 'You can sit on my lap if you want.'

Pickering straightened his neck in shock. This was the kindest thing Humphrey had ever said to him. 'Really?'

'I've got enough padding for both of us,' Humphrey grinned, lowering himself down till he was sitting with his legs hanging over the waterfall, his left hand flat against the wall of the tunnel, to stop from being swept over the edge. He slapped his knee. 'C'mon then, Pickers.'

Pickering scrambled on to Humphrey's lap and closed his eyes.

'Are you ready?' Humphrey asked.

Pickering nodded.

'One, two, THREE!'

Pickering felt Humphrey shove him and he screamed as he tumbled – alone – down the waterfall. After a few seconds he realized the waterfall was sloped, like a slide, and then he shot out into a small lagoon in a dimly lit room.

'Are you dead?' Humphrey called down after him.

'You hateful, traitorous, wretched OAF!' screamed Pickering.

There was no reply, but a minute later Humphrey came thundering down the waterfall like a cannonball, belly-flopping into the pool with a thunderous slap. He surfaced a moment later, spluttering and rubbing his tummy.

'You could have killed me!' Pickering shouted at him.

'You're alive, aren't you?' Humphrey shrugged. 'And we're that little bit closer to dinner.' He looked about. 'Where are we?'

'Look. Over there.' Pickering swam towards the outline of a hexagonal door. 'Oh, there's a strong current here.' He swam harder. 'It's dragging me down.' He doggy-paddled frantically, fighting the current and focusing on getting to the door.

'Ouch!' Humphrey squealed. 'Get off!'

'I'm nowhere near you!' Pickering shouted as his hands scooped at the water, pulling him forward.

'Not you. *Ow!*' Humphrey slapped at the surface of the water. 'There's something *alive* in here with us and it's biting me.'

Pickering thrashed about in the water, kicking his legs faster in panic. He had to get to the door. 'What is it?' he cried. 'A shark? A crocodile?'

'No,' Humphrey roared. 'They're little and there's loads of them. Arggghhhhh!' He half-waded, half-swam towards Pickering.

'Stay away from me,' Pickering screamed. 'I don't want to get bitten.' There was a ledge at the foot of the hexagonal door, he was nearly there. He threw his long arms up in front of him, hurling his body forward and grabbing on. The current was weaker here, and he was no longer being dragged backwards. He felt his way up the door.

'There's no handle!' he cried out in despair.

'NNNNNNaaaarghhhhhhhhhhhhhhhhhhhh!!!!!!!!!!!' Humphrey screamed. 'HELP ME! GET ME OUT OF HERE!'

Pickering stared in panic at his cousin, who was thrashing about, half drowning in the water. Any second he expected a shark's head to surge up out of the water and tear Humphrey apart. 'What is it?' The terror was rising so fast in his chest that he wanted to vomit.

'They're inside my pants!' Humphrey shoved a hand into his underwear and pulled out a handful of black shapes. 'They're biting my peanuts!'

'What are they?' Pickering stared at the small black beasties, suddenly less frightened.

'They're blasted BEETLES!' Humphrey flung them across the water and exploded into an incandescent rage. 'Swimming beetles! Did you know beetles could swim?'

Pickering shook his head as Humphrey ranted.

'I *hate* beetles more than any other horrible creature on this planet.' He repeatedly punched the water. 'DIE! DIE! DIE! ARGHGHHHHHHHHHHHHHHHH!'

'Calm down, they're only beetles,' Pickering barked. 'Someone will hear us.' Now that he knew the biting monsters were insects, and not a massive shark, he felt a lot braver. 'Ouch!' Something pinched his elbow. He looked down at the surface of the water and in the dim orange light he could see the surface shimmering with dark brown spoon-sized shapes. He tried to push the water away, but the black shapes dived down, and a second later he felt a thousand tiny bites to his stomach and thighs. He thrashed around, trying to brush the insects away. 'Aaarghhhh! My nipples!' he howled as the beetles started biting on top of their bites. 'WHAT KIND OF BEETLES ARE THESE?' he cried as he slapped his chest, trying to kill the nasty nippers.

'Predacious diving beetles,' said a dopey voice above him.

Pickering looked up. The door was open. Dankish bent down and grabbed Pickering by the arms, lifting him out of the pool and tossing him on to the floor. The beetles retreated back into the water.

Humphrey flailed his way over, unbothered by the current, and Dankish helped him out, laughing as he danced about shaking his bottom and pulling at his pants, trying to get the last insects out.

Dankish took out a small square black screen out of

his pocket. He touched it, and a white hexagon appeared. 'Craven? You'll never guess who I've found in one of the beetle pools? It's those two weird guys from the Emporium . . . Yeah! Them!'

CHAPTER SIXTEEN

The Cloud Forest

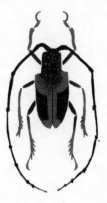

*D*arkus, Virginia and Bertolt rose at dawn and got dressed in their trekking gear. They wore army fatigues, and filled their pockets with Base Camp beetles and a few tiny pots of jelly. Bertolt buttoned up his khaki shirt, tucking it in and straightening his collar. Darkus and Virginia left theirs undone, wearing them like jackets over their black T-shirts. Each of them carried a rucksack containing a small pooter, a bottle of water, their survival kit and their personal stuff: Bertolt had a picture of his mum, Virginia a beanbag teddy bear called Dot that only had one eye, and Darkus had his

Beetle Collector's Handbook.

Darkus knew the Amazon held many dangers, but his main concern was for their beetles. He'd read that beetles were a source of food for birds and other hungry creatures. He didn't want Baxter to get snatched off his shoulder by the quick hands of a hungry monkey. He was grateful for Dr Ishikawa's gift. With Baxter in the bamboo cage around his neck, he could be sure the rhinoceros beetle was safe.

Uncle Max had employed a local guide called Angelo to take them into the forest, but he'd refrained from telling him their final destination. Motty'd heard the staff back at the lodge whispering about a witch who lived deep in the forest, and Uncle Max thought it best not to mention where they were going. With the co-ordinates of the Biome plotted on a map safe inside his rucksack, everyone fell into line behind Uncle Max and Angelo, and with Motty bringing up the rear, they set out to find Lucretia Cutter's lair.

The forest was surprisingly dark. Sunlight struggled to pierce the canopy, never getting as far as the forest floor. The air was thick with moisture from the respiring trees and the group was silent as they walked but for their breathing. The forest above their heads was far from quiet. Birds called and answered, brash chirrups piercing the eerie torch songs of lonely would-be lovers. Hidden toads and frogs croaked in chorus, and monkey hoots and whoops bounced from tree to tree, but despite the cacophony Darkus couldn't see any of the creatures he could hear.

He found that even though the warm air was saturated with oxygen, the breath he was drawing into his lungs didn't seem to quench his body's thirst for it. His breathing came hard as he marched forward into the most diverse place on earth. After an hour of walking, they stopped for a rest and he stared up into the canopy, wondering why he couldn't see any of the animals he could hear. After a few minutes of remaining still his focus shifted.

'Look!' he cried, spotting a sleeping sloth hanging upside down from a tree branch. 'A sloth!'

'Where?' Virginia swung round to look.

'Wish I could sleep like that,' Uncle Max said, chuckling.

And then the rain came. Darkus had never understood the word 'monsoon' – how heavy could rain be? But this was nothing like the rain in England. This was a torrential downpour, so heavy he could barely see a metre in front of him. Their guide signalled that it was dangerous to continue, and directed them to a sheltered spot. They waited the storm out, watching as their path become a brown stream and two large otters swam by.

And then, just as suddenly as it had arrived, the rain stopped and the sun came out. The air was immediately heavy with moisture, and it was impossible to know whether the moisture in the air was condensing on your skin and forming droplets of water, or whether the dense warm air, like an unwanted layer of clothing, was drawing sweat from your body. Darkus's dark hair stuck to his face, and his normally olive cheeks were flushed pink.

They ate as they walked. Uncle Max had obtained sandwiches and fruit from the lodge, and as the day wore on, their exclamations of wonder and pointing dwindled to nothing but grunts as they pulled aside vines, clambered over mossy rocks and tripped over twisting roots.

By mid-afternoon, Uncle Max declared that they'd made good progress and should look for a place to make camp for the night. They stopped to drink water from their bottles, and the guide indicated there was a clearing a bit further along the path.

'Darkus!' Bertolt waved him over. 'Come and look at

this.' He was standing beneath a tree, peering up at the trunk. 'It looks like a jewel beetle of some kind. It's beautiful.'

As Bertolt shuffled through the leaf mulch to get closer to the tree, Darkus saw the head of a snake rise up out of it. 'Bertolt!' he shouted, running towards his friend.

Bertolt screamed, stumbling backwards and falling to the ground as the snake's head darted forward. Angelo leapt at the attacking snake with his stick, pinning its head to the ground by its neck, before picking it up and moving it away from the group.

'Bertolt! Are you OK?' Virginia and Darkus helped their friend up from the forest floor.

'Yeah— ouch! Thank you, Angelo.' Bertolt winced as he tried to stand up. 'The snake didn't get me, but I think I've twisted my ankle.' He put on a brave face as he limped away from the tree. 'I'm fine. I just need a minute.'

Darkus looked at Uncle Max.

'How about I give you a piggyback until we find a spot to set up camp?' Uncle Max suggested to Bertolt.

'No, really, I'm fine,' Bertolt said, looking pale.

'I insist.' Uncle Max took off his rucksack and handed it to Motty. 'Come on, hop up. We need to get set up before it gets dark.'

Bertolt scrambled on to Uncle Max's back with Virginia's help. 'You're as light as a feather, Bertolt!' Uncle Max exclaimed, setting off after Angelo.

'It was a fer de lance!' Virginia whispered to Darkus. 'It could have killed him.'

Darkus nodded. 'But it didn't.' His eyes searched the ground as they walked, his heart knocking against his ribs as the image of the rising pit viper played over and over in his mind.

'I've got a first-aid kit,' Motty said to Bertolt. 'I'll strap your ankle up as soon as we've made camp.'

They finally came to a clearing of high ground surrounded by stout-trunked trees. Angelo pointed up to a long pole, a slender tree trunk that had been felled and suspended across from one tree to another, on the other side of the clearing. It seemed this spot was regularly used as a camp – there was even a charred fire pit.

Uncle Max took out a folded plastic sheet, which he called a basha. He tied a stone into one corner and threw it up over the pole. Removing the stone, he then pulled the plastic sheet out, passing guy ropes through loops at the corners and sides. He and Angelo climbed up surrounding trees, tying the ropes around the trunks, stretching the sheet out across the clearing, making a roof and giving them shelter from the rain.

Darkus and Virginia scrambled under and wriggled out of their backpacks. They pulled out their hammocks, made of orange parachute silk suspended inside a transparent tent of mosquito netting.

'Here, give me yours, I'll hang it for you,' Darkus said to Bertolt who'd crawled over to sit beside him.

'Yes, let Darkus and Virginia do the beds.' Motty said, pulling a washbag out of her backpack and extracting a roll of bandage. 'I need to take a look at that ankle.'

Virginia and Darkus suspended the five hammocks from the central tree, tying the foot of each to a different tree around the clearing so that they formed an orange star under the basha. Then they dug out the old fire pit and built a fire from dry kindling that Uncle Max had brought in a plastic bag in his rucksack, whilst he hunted about looking for dead wood that wasn't too wet.

Bertolt sat with his back against the central tree, his foot on Motty's lap as she gently removed his boot and sock. Darkus saw that his ankle was swollen, and purple with bruises.

'Ooh, that's nasty,' she muttered, unreeling the bandage. 'It looks like a sprain.'

'I'll be fine, though, won't I?' Bertolt asked anxiously. 'I'll be able to walk tomorrow.'

'I'm sure you will,' Motty said, but she sounded unconvinced.

CHAPTER SEVENTEEN
Escarabajo Gigante

Darkus woke with the sun. He clambered out of his sleeping bag, untucked the mosquito-net tent and stepped out into the wet Amazon morning. Everything was dripping water, but at least there was no rain falling from the sky, and the patch of ground beneath their basha seemed mainly dry.

Motty was up, sitting cross-legged on the ground, reviving the embers of last night's fire.

'Morning,' Darkus said, quietly, not wanting to wake the others.

'Morning, Darkus,' she replied with her thin-lipped,

pug-like smile. 'I'm trying to get enough of a fire together to make coffee. I need petrol to put in the old tank.' She patted her chest. 'We've got a long hike ahead of us today, and my legs aren't as young as yours.'

'Do you think Bertolt's going to be able to make it?' Darkus asked.

'He wants to try.' Motty said. 'I offered to take him back to the lodge last night, but he got very upset.' She paused, then nodded. 'I'm sure he'll be able to make it.' She pointed over to a tree. 'Your uncle made him a walking stick last night.'

Darkus saw a long Y-shaped stick, and beside it four smaller ones.

'What are the other ones for?'

'They're for each of us, to check the ground ahead of us for snakes. Angelo says they are everywhere.'

As the smell of coffee flavoured the air, the rest of the camp started to stir. Virginia had to help Bertolt down from his hammock, and even though he said he felt much better, Darkus didn't believe him. Bertolt couldn't put weight on his right foot without his face twisting in pain.

Angelo appeared out of the trees and cheerfully helped them pack away their basha and hammocks.

In under an hour, their bags were packed and they were walking again.

Bertolt used the crutch Uncle Max had made him to good effect, wedging it under his armpit and leaning on it every other step, but it slowed him down and tired him out. Virginia walked beside him, chatting away merrily to keep his spirits up, and Motty walked behind them.

Darkus walked at the front with Angelo and Uncle Max, keen to push forward and find the Biome. As the morning wore on he couldn't help feeling a mounting frustration at their slow progress. He watched Angelo stride easily through the forest, aware of its trips and traps. As the trees become dense and the ground harder to traverse, Angelo unsheathed a giant knife – a machete – and hacked at branches to clear the way for them.

They stopped to eat lunch and give Bertolt a rest, while Angelo went scouting on ahead to clear a path. Darkus wolfed down his sandwiches and got up, wandering after him. He heard Angelo yell, and rushed forward, eyes alert. The sound had come from a dense copse of trees. He gripped his stick, prepared to see a jaguar. Angelo came thundering towards him, leaping over tree roots like an Olympic hurdler. Darkus dived to one side, narrowly avoiding getting barrelled over by the terrified man.

'¡Un monstruo! Monstruo!' the guide shouted.

'What is it? ¿Que es?' Uncle Max jumped up and grabbed Angelo by the upper arms. '¿Que es?'

'¡Un escarabajo gigante!' Angelo pointed back along the path excitedly. '¡Uno de los animales de las brujas! ¡Un escarabajo gigante!' He wrenched himself from Uncle Max's grasp and ran away, back along the path they'd forged that morning.

Darkus knew the word *escarabajo* was Spanish for 'beetle'. He crept forward. *Gigante* was almost the same as 'gigantic' in English. He saw the guide's fallen machete and picked it up.

'Baxter,' he whispered to the rhinoceros beetle in the bamboo cage around his neck, 'can you sense any danger?'

Baxter shook his head, and Darkus moved forward with more confidence. There was a snap behind him. He glanced over his shoulder to find Uncle Max and Virginia right behind him. He passed the big knife to his uncle. They could see how far the guide had got, because branches were hacked away and the path clear. When they reached an untouched curtain of leafy foliage, he looked at Uncle Max, who nodded, holding the machete up high. Darkus carefully pulled it to one side and then cried out, putting his hand up to tell his uncle the knife was not needed. He stumbled forward, falling to his knees in front of a giant Hercules beetle, the size of a baby elephant. The beetle's horn was sheared off and it was on its back. One of its legs was missing and the others were swimming weakly in the air. Its eyes looked dry, and Darkus knew that the beetle was dying.

'Virginia, quick, get my banana,' Darkus cried out, and he heard her feet pound away.

Carefully, Darkus moved to the side of the beetle. It had been in some kind of fight, perhaps with a caiman, although it was most likely to have been a frightened human. Darkus made soothing clicking noises as he approached the beetle side-on and slid his arms around its mottled thorax. 'Help me,' he said to Uncle Max. Together, they slowly lowered the beetle down on to its five legs.

'There we go,' Darkus stroked the beetle's elytra. 'That's better, isn't it?'

The giant beetle's legs slowly clawed at the forest floor, like it was swimming in soil, digging itself down a foot before it ran out of strength.

Virginia was back. Skidding down on to her knees, she held out all their bananas. Darkus peeled them and, breaking off chunks, he reached under the beetle's head, holding them in front of its mandibles. Sensing the fruit with its trembling antennae, the beetle opened its mouth, and Darkus carefully fed the bananas to him.

'Is it going to be OK?' Bertolt asked from the path, Motty beside him.

Darkus shook his head. 'I don't think so.'

'There must be something we can do,' Virginia said, her voice cracking.

Darkus just kept shaking his head. He was trying not to cry.

'The guide said this was one of the "witch's monsters",' Uncle Max mused. 'I'm guessing the witch is Lucretia Cutter.' He looked at Darkus. 'When I asked for a guide at the lodge, they refused to bring us in this direction. They said there was bad magic here. I had to go to the village to find Angelo, and because of Miguel's superstitious attitude, I didn't let on where we were going.'

'We must be getting close, then,' Motty observed.

'He's one of the most beautiful creatures I've ever seen.' Darkus bit his lip. The underside of the sheared stump was soft and velvety. He gently stroked it, making soothing sounds. 'Look at him. He's magnificent,' he whispered. 'Imagine him flying!'

'There's nothing like this in nature,' Virginia said, sitting down on the other side of the beetle and stroking the fluffy hair sprouting out around his thorax. 'He's definitely one of *her* beetles.'

Darkus lifted up Baxter's cage. 'Is there anything we can do for him, Baxter?'

Baxter bowed his head, and Darkus's head drooped. 'No, I didn't think so.'

'We should push on, Darkus,' Uncle Max said softly. 'We've still got a way to go, and now we've no guide.'

'I can't leave him like this.' Darkus got to his feet and looked about. He tugged at a fallen branch, dragging it over and leaning it against the beetle. 'We've got to hide him from predators. Let him die in peace.'

Virginia nodded, jumping up and helping to cover up the giant Hercules beetle. Soon they'd created a dense cover of camouflage. Darkus stepped away, satisfied that they'd done the best they could. He looked at Uncle Max. 'I'm ready to go now.'

They retrieved their backpacks and started walking,

Darkus and Virginia reading the map and Uncle Max up front wielding the machete.

They'd been walking slowly for a couple of hours when Bertolt stumbled and cried out. 'I think we need to think about setting up camp,' Motty said. 'It will take us longer than last night, without the help of Angelo.'

Uncle Max nodded in agreement. 'We'll stop as soon as we come to a good place.'

Darkus slowed down to help Bertolt, putting his arm under his shoulder and letting his friend use him as a crutch.

'Thanks, Darkus.' Bertolt smiled and blinked. 'I didn't want to say anything, but my armpit is red raw from leaning on that stick.'

'You're doing great.' Darkus smiled at his friend. 'You should have said you needed help.'

'I don't want to be any trouble.' Bertolt blinked.

They had walked for about twenty minutes when Virginia halted them with a loud, 'SHHHHHH.' She put her finger to her lips. 'There's something up there,' she whispered, pointing up into the rainforest canopy. 'It's been following us for about ten minutes.'

Darkus looked up, alarmed. 'Don't worry,' Uncle Max shielded his eyes and peered up into the canopy, 'it's probably a monkey.' But he held the machete ready.

Darkus saw a small dark figure, high up in the branches, blonde hair scraped back from a grubby but familiar face. 'It can't be,' he whispered.

'Who are you calling a monkey?' Emma Lamb called down to Uncle Max.

'Emma?' Uncle Max said. 'Is that you?'

Emma Lamb, the reporter who'd helped them in their first battle at the Emporium and who'd sworn to expose Lucretia Cutter, jumped from her tree to a lower branch, then another, finally swinging down to the ground.

'You're alive!!!' Virginia cried. She was so happy to see the reporter that she hugged her.

'Yep, definitely not dead.' Emma Lamb lightly thumped her fist against her ribs. 'Although several stone lighter.'

'Oh, Emma,' Uncle Max was beaming, 'am I glad to see you! I tried to send a message, but when we landed in Quito, and they told me it was uncollected, I feared the worst.'

'I can't go back to civilization right now.' She shook her head. 'Have you seen what's going on? It's crazy. Before the Film Awards, I managed to persuade a guy on the inside to share some of Lucretia Cutter's Biome secrets with me.'

'You've got someone who can help us?' Darkus asked.

'Not any more.' Emma Lamb frowned. 'Lucretia Cutter must have found out he was talking to me. He's gone silent.'

Virginia gulped. 'Silent?'

'Don't feel too bad for him.' Emma Lamb patted her on the shoulder. 'Henrik Lenka knew what he was doing.

He's a nasty piece of work, one of those people who hedges his bets and sucks up to whichever side is winning in a fight. I think he was talking to me in case Lucretia's plan failed, and he needed to wriggle out of a prison sentence. Either way, he knew the risk and I paid him very well for his information.'

'Henrik Lenka?' Darkus looked at Bertolt and Virginia.

'From the Fabre Project!' Bertolt said.

'Did he tell you anything about Lucretia Cutter breeding giant beetles?' Darkus asked. 'We found a beetle the size of a baby elephant back there. It was dying. We couldn't do anything to save it.'

Emma Lamb tipped her head as she thought. 'He did say something about one of their experiments escaping the Biome.' She frowned. 'He called it a "dinobeetle", but I thought he was pulling my leg. He said they'd led it out of the Biome on a chain, to see how it coped with the atmosphere. The thing broke its own horn off trying to get away, and left a leg behind in the chains.'

'They're chaining the beetles?' Darkus asked, shocked.

'Poor dinobeetle,' Bertolt said, and the children fell silent, thinking about the gentle giant they'd left dying under forest leaves.

'Emma, please tell us you have a camp we can rest our weary bones in?' Uncle Max said, changing the subject. 'We are about ready to expire.'

'I've been copying the monkeys and sticking to the treetops. I just sling my hammock wherever I find two suitable branches. It's safer up there.'

Uncle Max's face fell. 'Oh.'

'However, I do know of a clearing a safe distance from the Biome, where you can set up your camp.' She grinned and set off through the trees. 'It's this way, follow me.'

CHAPTER EIGHTEEN

On the Lamb

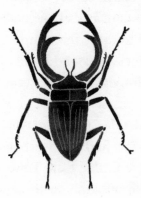

'Peeny-wally for your thoughts,' Virginia said, pointing up to the fireflies fizzing about above Darkus's head.

He looked up and smiled. 'Emma says the Biome is half a day's hike that way.' He pointed to the narrow path in front of him. 'My dad is less than a day away from us.'

Virginia stared along the path. The sun was setting and it was getting dark. 'Tomorrow,' was all she said.

'Virginia,' Darkus lowered his voice, 'I'm worried about Bertolt. We can't take him into the Biome with an injured foot.'

'Darkus, we've been together the whole way.' Virginia frowned at him. 'You can't leave him behind. We're a team.'

'But we don't know what we are going to come face to face with in there,' Darkus replied.

'Precisely.' Virginia lifted an eyebrow. 'Which is why we need him. He's clever in a way that you and I are not.'

Darkus looked towards the campfire, at their motley band of rebels. Uncle Max and Emma Lamb were tying up hammocks, Motty was tending the fire and cooking while Bertolt sat beside her, examining his ankle. He thought about Lucretia Cutter and what they were likely to face in the Biome, and his heart clenched with fear. When he'd rescued his dad from Towering Heights he'd done it alone, with only the beetles and Novak to help him. It had been simpler that way.

'You hungry, Darkus?' Uncle Max called over to him. 'Motty's made some rice and beans.'

'Coming,' Darkus replied, accepting Virginia's hand and standing up. He sat down beside Bertolt and smiled at Motty. 'It smells lovely,' he said politely.

'No, it doesn't,' Motty replied, 'but it will fill your belly.'

Emma picked up a metal bowl and held it out. 'Fill her up, please, Motty. This is the finest meal I've seen in a month.'

Uncle Max sat down beside Emma. 'So, your Dr Lenka, what did he tell you about the Biome? Anything useful?'

She nodded, while she chewed and swallowed. 'The whole place is built on a pattern of hexagons.' She produced a piece of folded paper from a pocket in her trousers – a crude map drawn in biro. 'This central hexagon is the biggest dome, and from what I can tell it's full of plants, like a huge greenhouse. I've been all the way round the domes, spying on them from the outside to get as much information as possible. Lenka told me that each of the satellite domes has a different use. This one contains the rooms for the scientists, this one is for staff.' She pointed at two of the smaller hexagons. 'Lucretia Cutter has one for her personal use that you can't see into, then this one is for food supplies, laundry, that sort of thing . . . and then there's this one.' She paused and looked around the circle of attentive faces. 'This one is the important one.' She pointed to a hexagon beside a square that she'd marked as *door*. 'This one contains the security monitors, generators, server room, climate control and air conditioning. If we can get into this dome, then we can see everything that's happening in the Biome, and possibly control what's going on.'

'What's that one for?' Darkus pointed his spoon at the one hexagon Emma hadn't labelled.

'It's the prison cells,' she replied.

'That's where Dad and Novak will be.'

'Spencer is probably in the scientists' quarters,' Bertolt added.

'This is a river,' she followed a line straight through

the central hexagon, 'and this is a cliff. The river becomes a waterfall here. Lenka told me that below ground, under the central dome, is a huge insect farm.'

'Below ground!' Darkus was feeling more despair by the second. The Biome was huge. It could take a long time to find Dad and Novak, even with the help of the beetles, and then he had to get them out of there.

'Our biggest problem,' Emma said pointing at the square marked *door*, 'is that the only way into this glass labyrinth is through this door in the ground. It's a mechanized trapdoor with an entrance tunnel behind it.' She leant back. 'I've been out to it at night. There's no way to get it open, and there's no other door into the building.'

There was a long silence as they all stared at the scruffy piece of paper.

'I'll bet I can open it,' Bertolt said, sitting up straight.

'What?' Emma frowned. 'I doubt it. I've tried everything.'

'Darkus, pass me your bag!' Bertolt unzipped the front pocket, pulled out the thingamabob and held it up, switching it on. A white hexagon appeared. 'With this.'

Emma's smile stretched from ear to ear. 'You kids never cease to amaze me. Where did you get it? Can I see?'

Bertolt handed it to her and she turned it over, her fingers running over the surface, pushing and pressing it.

'An American entomologist called Hank gave it to us,' Darkus said. 'When Lucretia Cutter's helicopter took off, a load of her luggage was left behind, and this was found in one of her bags.'

'This looks like the devices I've seen her thugs using.' Emma handed it back. 'What you have there, Bertolt, is the key to the Biome's front door.'

Darkus looked at the little black square.

'And if we can't make it work,' Emma spooned the last of her rice and beans into her mouth and swallowed, 'there's always plan B.'

'Plan B?' Virginia asked.

'We get in through the river,' Emma said, running her tongue over her top teeth. 'I saw your old neighbours trying to get into the Biome that way this morning. It seems to have worked, unless they're dead.'

'Humphrey and Pickering?' Uncle Max asked.

She nodded. 'The reedy stick-like man and the giant oaf. The ones who were arrested after the Emporium collapsed.'

'They're here?' Darkus was flabbergasted. 'But how? I mean . . .'

'I think they arrived with Lucretia Cutter. They appeared around the same time her helicopter landed.' Emma shrugged. 'They've been crashing about the forest like a couple of suicidal morons, attracting every hungry predator for miles.'

'Imagine if they got eaten by a jaguar,' Virginia giggled.

'Virginia,' Bertolt chided, 'that's not very nice.'

She rolled her eyes. 'Says the boy who trapped them both in a burning pile of furniture and tried to torch them to death.'

'I didn't! I mean, I wasn't trying to . . .'

Darkus laughed.

'Right, time for bed, I think,' Uncle Max said, getting to his feet. 'Tomorrow we'll hike to the fringes of the forest beside the Biome and plan our attack.'

Chapter Nineteen

Tannhäuser

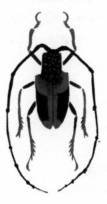

*L*ucretia Cutter had agreed to see him. This was his chance to talk to her about Novak. Barty took a deep breath and stepped through the doorway. The mezzanine floor above the laboratory reminded him of a lobby in an expensive hotel. The long bar against the back wall led to a viewing gallery, looking out into the Arcadia dome. Lucretia was standing with her back to him, looking into her Eden. In the middle of the floor stood a grand piano. Glancing down to the floor below, he could see the lab, the glass wall and the base of the pupator.

'What do you want, Bartholomew?' She didn't need to turn around to know that he was standing behind her.

'I'm not comfortable about forcing Novak through another pupation,' he said. 'It could kill her.'

'Don't think of the girl as a human with a name. Think of her as a genetic experiment. She only got a name because she lived. For a while I called her Handbag.' She laughed.

'I cannot.' Barty shook his head. 'I will not.'

'I do so enjoy your weaknesses,' she laughed softly. 'Do you know, your inability to kill is one of the reasons I don't see you as a threat? Your hopeless belief that good will out makes you impotent and harmless.'

'Novak is a child.'

'Enough. The girl *will* experience the full pupation,' Lucretia snapped. 'I cannot become who I wish to be without another metamorphosis, and I cannot be sure it will work until it is tested. It has to be tested on her because she is my genetic mirror. We are the only two humans to have gone through the pupation and survived. My mission is too important to take the risk with my own life, so she *will* go through a second metamorphosis whether you like it or not.'

'Please, Lucy, have a heart,' Barty begged. 'Whatever you call her, she's your daughter.'

Lucretia snorted. 'Novak's pupation will take place tomorrow. If you don't want to be there, that is your choice.'

There was a long silence.

Barty walked over to the piano. 'Do you still play, Lucy?' He ran his fingers over the ivory keys, playing a random series of notes. 'I remember you were really rather good once.'

'That's gratifying to hear.' She tipped her head back. 'Yes, I still play. Music is the soul's expression, after all.'

'You still believe you have a soul, then?'

'Souls aren't exclusive to humans, Bartholomew,' she replied. 'Elephants, monkeys, beetles, all living creatures have souls. I believe trees have souls, don't you?'

Barty levelled his gaze at her unreadable compound eyes. 'What you are planning to do, what you are already doing, is going to result in the deaths of millions of people. You are committing genocide. I fail to see how you can talk about expressing your soul through music, when you set about committing mass murder with a smile on your lips.'

Lucretia's nostrils flared with anger. She swept over to the piano in a series of lurching steps, and sat down. She placed her two human hands on the keys, nails painted black, fingers weighed down by diamond rings, and began to play.

'Is everything so black and white to you?' she said softly as she played the first notes of a tune that Barty faintly recognized. 'Aren't humans, as a species, committing mass murder on an immeasurable scale? Forty per cent of all of the earth's animals have become extinct in the last fifty years. Aren't our population growth and addiction to wealth killing this planet? We are hastening our own demise, fighting wars over fossil fuels and nuclear weapons.' She played a series of chords, the music building. 'What is there about humanity that you think is worth saving? Doesn't your heart grieve for the last elephants, the last giraffes? Don't you wonder what will be left for your grandchildren? Don't you want to stop it all?'

'But of course . . .'

'You don't see how. Do you? You lack vision. The meek shall inherit the earth, the Bible says, and we think that means meek humans, but why are we so obsessed with our own species? Yes, the meek *shall* inherit the earth; in fact, I plan on giving it to them. I plan on giving it to the beetles.'

Barty felt her words like hammer blows to his chest. 'Do you really think you can take on all the governments of the world?'

'I already have.'

'Lucy . . . they will send nuclear bombs.'

'Ha!' She laughed and played, and played, lifting two beetle legs on to the higher and lower octaves of the piano. 'The big boys with their bad bombs, we must all quake when the bullies shake their fists. Well, *not me*. The Biome is a self-sustaining environment with a hyper-oxygenated atmosphere. The hexagonal design of each panel of military grade glass – used in the windshields of stealth bombers – is impenetrable. But even then, more than half the facility is underground. We are safe here. If they bomb me, I'll destroy more of their crops, like I did in India. If they use nuclear weapons – well, the Amazon rainforest is the lungs of the earth, they may as well be bombing themselves. They'd destroy their soil, their harvests and their water supplies. I have turned the planet into a giant chessboard, and I have them in checkmate.'

'But why?'

'I am going to change the course of the human race, Bartholomew. I'm going to wipe out the human population. I'm going to re-wild the planet. The humans that will be allowed to live will be the ones that put the environment before their own meaningless lives.'

'I can see how you think this might be a solution, but . . .'

'There is no solution to global warming. We have pushed the planet far beyond the point of no return.'

'That is absolutely *not true*, Lucy.' Barty moved round the piano so he could see her face. 'You will be punishing the weakest first. The poorest and the youngest will die from starvation.'

'That can't be helped. I'm not here to save human beings. I'm here to save the planet – I'm the only one who cares enough to do anything about it.'

'You're wrong.' He brought his fist down on the piano lid, but she kept playing, the rhythm of the music becoming more insistent. 'There are millions of people who care.'

'*Where?*' she hissed. 'What I see is people protecting the wealth and power they have by electing politicians who keep the rich rich and make the poor poorer. They do not care about the environment, and choose not to believe in climate change.'

'That is not everybody,' Barty argued.

'Where are the revolutions?' she cried. 'Where are the human beings insisting that the environment be the key issue upon which a government is elected? I can't hear their protests.' The melody folded and doubled, becoming feverish. 'Humanity is weak, and that is why the earth needs *me*. Humanity is a plague. It's not just climate change; it's sheer space. We're running out of places to grow food for the human horde.'

'There are other ways to tackle population growth.'

'None that will have a big impact, fast enough – and anyway, the people in power won't allow it. *This* is the only way, Bartholomew.' She smiled at him, a ghastly leer. 'Just think of how beautiful this planet will look when I'm done with my cull and the giant insects return.'

'Who made you God?' he whispered, shaking his head.

'I did! And the people will worship me and carry out my edict, or die.' She leant forward, taking a deep breath in through what was left of her nose, the music rising, as a waterfall of notes cascaded down the keyboard.

Barty suddenly recognized the tune. It was the over-ture to *Tannhäuser*. Lucy had taken him to the Royal Opera House to see it a long time ago. She'd always loved Wagner. He stepped forward and placed his hand on her shoulder, closing his eyes as she played.

'Are you really not afraid of their bombs?' he asked softly.

'Let them do their worst.' She leant into the keyboard, her body moving with the music. 'The underground superstructure of the Biome can seal off the upper glasshouses. We would be untouched by an explosion and free from the impacts of nuclear fallout. We are equipped to survive for some decades here – although the effect on the rest of the planet would be terrible.' She laughed. 'You know that old adage that the cockroach is the only creature that could survive a nuclear holocaust? Well, it's not true. *The beetle is.*'

'You've thought of everything.'

'Bartholomew,' she looked up at him, 'you opened my eyes to the beauty of this planet. You dragged me to the cliff's edge and made me open my heart and mind to the natural world, and then you abandoned me to stare down and watch humanity extinguish species after species, bulldoze and burn habitat after habitat. How many more miles of the Great Barrier Reef can you stomach losing? How much more plastic must be found in the guts of whales? How many square miles of rainforest traded for oil? *It has to stop*. The human cull is coming, and the planet will heave a sigh of relief when I'm done. It will thank me, and that is all the thanks I need.' The music fractured into patterns of notes and she closed her eyes. 'I *know* you feel the same way I do, Bartholomew.' She sighed. 'And that is why I trust you.' She played the final refrains of the piece, letting the last note hang in the air.

Chapter Twenty
Mud Wallow

Darkus lay awake in his hammock listening to Uncle Max snoring. The rustling of the others twisting in their hanging beds had stopped half an hour ago. He carefully sat up and looked around. Everyone was asleep. Slowly, as quietly as possible, he untucked the mosquito net that formed a tent around his hammock and slipped down to the ground, holding still for a moment to make sure his movement hadn't woken anyone. He was fully dressed, with his boots on and Baxter's cage hanging around his neck.

His backpack was where he'd placed it, at the foot of

his hammock, packed and ready to go. He pulled open the top and peered down at the Base Camp beetles. Before going to bed, he'd emptied the bag of everything, poured a thick layer of oak mulch into the bottom of it, placed a few pots of beetle jelly on top, and then quietly transferred all of the Base Camp beetles into it. Only Virginia had asked him what he was doing, and he'd fooled her by saying he was feeding and resting the beetles. Looking into the bag, he made a few gentle clicking noises with his tongue against the roof of his mouth. The beetles all looked up at him, nodding their heads and chittering. They were ready.

He lifted the open bag, easing his arms through each of the straps and took one last look at the sleeping camp, its fire a tumble of glowing embers. It was better this way. He soundlessly crept to the path that Emma Lamb had told him led to the Biome. He walked for about ten minutes, until he was sure he was out of sight of the camp, before he stopped to pull out his plastic pooter.

'Hey, fireflies, I need a little light,' he called in a whisper.

In answer, twenty-seven fireflies zoomed up out of his bag.

Darkus unscrewed the lid of the pooter. 'Please could you fly into here? It will keep you safe and make a light for me.'

The fireflies obliged him, fluttering down into the pooter. He put the lid back on and held his firefly lantern aloft as he slowly picked his way down the path. After a while, the darkness and the isolation ate away at his certainty that he was heading in the right direction. 'What if Emma Lamb was wrong about this path, Baxter? I think I'd better check the map, make sure we *are* walking towards the Biome.'

He pulled out the map and a compass from a side pocket of the rucksack, and set the beetle lantern on the ground next to it.

'Let me do that,' a voice hissed. 'I'm better at it.'

'Gaaaaaah!' Darkus spun around, dropping his compass. Virginia was standing at his elbow. 'Flipping heck, Virginia! You frightened me!'

'Sorry,' she giggled.

'What are you doing?' Darkus was flustered, his heart racing.

'I might ask you the same thing.' Virginia tipped her head and grinned at him maddeningly. 'I wonder where you could be off to in the middle of the night?'

Darkus scowled at her.

'Well?'

'I just wanted to try something, that's all.'

'Really?' Virginia raised an eyebrow. 'What could that be?'

'I couldn't sleep, so I thought I'd try out the remote controller thing on that trapdoor,' Darkus said. 'Because, you know, if it doesn't work, then we'll need to find another way into the Biome.'

'And if it *does* work?'

'Then . . . I was going to come back and tell everyone,' Darkus lied.

'Right, of course you were.' She pointed at his backpack. 'And you brought all of the beetles because . . .'

'To be safe,' Darkus said. 'I need them for light and in case, in case . . .'

'In case what?'

'What are *you* doing up, anyway?' he challenged her.

'I'm watching you,' Virginia shrugged, as if it was obvious.

'Watching me?'

'Yeah, we've been taking in turns to watch you since Christmas.'

'What?'

'We're worried about you.'

'I'm fine.'

''Course you are. You watch your dad walk away from you and get on a helicopter with Lucretia Cutter, after you went all the way to America to help him. Why wouldn't you be fine?'

'Virginia, I said I'm fine.'

'Really?' She folded her arms across her chest. 'You're fine, are you? Is that why you've got weirder and weirder since the Film Awards? It's not just me, Bertolt's noticed it too.' She shook her head. 'You get cross really easily, Darkus, and you don't talk to us about what you're thinking any more.'

'I don't?'

'No. It's like you think we don't understand, or that this is something that's only affecting you.' She let her arms drop. 'And sure, we don't *feel* it like you do. But the whole world is under siege, Darkus, not just you.'

'Do you think I don't *know* that?' Darkus burst out. 'All the newspaper reports, food supplies running out, bombs dropping. What will it be next? Starving children? People dying? I can't stop it, Virginia. I don't know how.' He shook his head. 'I just want my dad back, and I want to go home.'

'Darkus, this affects all of us, and the people we love.' She leant towards him. 'Don't we all have a right to fight for what we believe in? I'm here for my mum, and my dad, and my brothers and sisters. We need to work together to stop Lucretia Cutter. You've got to let us help you.'

'How can you help me? I don't know what the right thing to do is. I don't want to be in a war. I just want to be with my dad.' Darkus heard his voice waver. 'If they are going to drop a bomb, then I want to be with him when it lands.'

'Is that why you're running away in the middle of the night?'

'I want to get into the Biome. I thought if I went alone, with the beetles, it would be easier to find Dad undetected.' He looked at Virginia. 'And, if I take the thingamabob, then none of you will be able to get in, and you can go home, and be safe. I don't want people to get hurt because of me. Everyone seems to think I'm some kind of hero, that's going to come up with a plan, but I don't have one. I don't even want to hurt Lucretia Cutter's beetles.'

'I guessed as much.' Virginia put her hands on her hips and sighed. 'Such muddle-headed thinking. That's why I told Marvin to wake me if you did anything weird.' Marvin uncurled from around Virginia's braid and waved a metallic red claw at Darkus. 'You should have told me you felt like this.'

'I'm sorry, I . . .' Darkus looked at the forest floor.

'Because you're gonna need someone to watch your back.'

Darkus looked at Virginia. 'What?'

'Two heads are better than one, right?' Virginia smiled.

'You're not going to tell me to go back to camp?'

'Nope.' Virginia shook her head. 'Look, I get it. Bertolt's hurt, you want to get your dad. It makes sense. I'd probably do the same thing.'

'You would?'

'But I can't let you run off into the rainforest alone. What if you get hurt? Bitten by a snake? At least if there's two of us, one of us can go for help.'

'I'm not alone,' Darkus replied. 'I've got the beetles.'

'And if you can get that Biome door open,' Virginia leant forward, eyeballing him, 'I'm going in with you.'

Darkus smiled, finding he was relieved. 'Good.'

'So, I don't want to hear any more about it . . .' Virginia pulled her head back. 'Did you say *good*?'

'Yes!' Darkus laughed. 'I didn't want to ask you to come, because it's unfair to ask someone to do something so dangerous. But now . . . I'm glad.'

Virginia grinned and picked up the firefly lantern. 'C'mon, then, what are you waiting for? You are on the right path, by the way. I checked – oh, and I brought your snake stick.' She handed it to him. 'We need to be careful of the pit vipers. Did you know there are over a hundred and thirty-five different species of snake in the Amazon? At least that's what it says in Bertolt's guide book. There's probably more.'

'Don't say things like that when we're about to do a night hike.'

'OK. Sorry.'

Darkus folded up the map, and they walked in silence, side by side, marvelling at the phosphorescent fungi growing on mossy tree trunks and glancing at each other for reassurance each time they heard a startling noise. Darkus felt braver with Virginia by his side, and they covered ground quickly, helping each other over and warning each other of obstacles. They saw snakes and were startled by monkeys, but the creatures of the Amazon showed little interest in the children.

'Darkus!' Virginia yelped.

Darkus spun around and saw Virginia frozen to the spot. She talked through tightly pursed lips.

'I've walked into a massive web.' Her eyes were wide and he could see she was frightened.

'Hold still.' Darkus lifted the lantern. He saw a golden orb-weaver on the back of her head. It was the size of a yo-yo. He recognized it by the stripes on its legs and the flash of white at the top of its body. 'It's OK. I see it. I think she's an orb-weaver. She won't hurt you. They're not aggressive.'

'Can you check on Marvin?' Virginia said.

'I see him. He's OK. Hang on.' Darkus took a deep breath and scooped the spider up with his right hand. He'd never picked up a spider this big before. He deposited it on a fallen tree trunk and watched it spindle-step away. 'It's gone.'

Virginia performed a convulsing dance as she pulled the sticky webbing from her hair, face and shoulders. 'Ewwww, man, that was gross. There was lots of dead stuff in it.' She shivered. 'Marvin are you OK?' She wiped her hands on her trousers and lifted the frog-legged leaf beetle down to the cage around her neck. I was worried you were going to end up being a spider's supper! Into the cage you go.'

They drank some water and chewed on dried mango that Darkus had pilfered from Motty's supplies.

'It's crazy that even though we're out in the middle of the night, we can't see the stars,' Virginia said, looking up. 'The canopy is too thick.'

'Good job we've got our own stars here.' Darkus

nodded at the firefly lantern. He offered Baxter a piece of mango in his bamboo cage.

'Being in here, in the rainforest, is like being in another world.'

'I know what you mean.'

'I'm not sure I understood the word "wild" before we came to this place,' Virginia said. 'There's no human systems here. It's a different kind of being alive.'

Darkus nodded. 'It's fascinating.'

'It's frightening. I'm pretty impressed that you were going to do this walk alone. I'm not sure I'd have had the guts.'

Darkus didn't reply. He wasn't sure how far down the path he would have got on his own.

'Shouldn't we be seeing the Biome soon?' Virginia asked. 'We've been walking for ages.'

'I know. We want to get to the trapdoor before the sun comes up.'

'Emma said it was half a day's walk. What's that, four, five hours, maybe six?'

'How long have we been walking for now?'

'Three?'

'It can't be much further. Come on.' Darkus marched forward.

Virginia got up and followed him, only to be stopped dead by his hand shooting up in warning.

'What is it?' she whispered, creeping up behind him.

'I don't know.' Darkus looked over his shoulder at her.

'Can you hear that?'

There were odd squelchy noises and snuffling sounds coming from their left.

'Whatever it is,' Virginia's eyes were wide with fear, 'we don't want to meet it.'

Darkus motioned that they should go around the noise. As he shuffled backwards he skidded on a fallen mossy branch and crashed sideways into a pile of stumpy tree ferns, crying out as he tried not to crush Baxter or the beetles in his backpack.

There was a blood-curdling squealing as the creature that had been squelching and snuffling thundered towards them. Terrified, Darkus scrambled on to his feet, pushing himself as far as he could into the tree ferns. Virginia leapt backwards over a large rock, ducking down behind it.

Exploding through a curtain of tree vines came a creature as big as a cow, with the face of an anteater. It blundered past them and disappeared into the forest. Darkus and Virginia were silent for a few minutes, staring at each other from their hiding places and glancing at the spot where the animal had disappeared. As its footfalls grew fainter, Darkus heard it squeal again. He crept from the ferns as Virginia came out from behind the rock.

'What was that?' she whispered.

'I think,' Darkus said, scratching his head, 'it was a tapir.'

'Whatever it was,' Virginia put her hand to her chest, 'it nearly gave me a heart attack.'

The walked to the spot where the tapir had thundered into view, and saw a sunken, trampled pit of muddy earth beside a pool of stagnant, brackish water.

'It was having a mud bath.' Virginia smiled at Darkus.

'That's what the squelching noise was.'

They laughed with relief about disturbing the tapir's mud wallow, and walked a little quicker, more aware now that there were large creatures in the forest, and some of them were dangerous.

'Wait, where's the path?' Virginia spun around.

Darkus looked at her in panic, then searched the ground. The path that they'd been following was gone. 'Let's move over there, where there's more light.' He pointed to where the trees opened up and the sky was visible.

'We must've got spun around by the tapir,' said Virginia, annoyed with herself.

'It's all right, we'll stop there and check the map with the compass. We can get ourselves back on the right track. We can't have gone far wrong.'

They knelt down in the clearing, which seemed brighter because of the light from the moon and stars in the night sky. Darkus unfolded the map and smoothed it out.

'Give me the compass.' He held out his hand.

Virginia checked her pockets and then looked at Darkus. 'You've got it.'

'I don't. You took it, when you said you were better at map-reading than me.'

Virginia's eyes widened. 'I must have dropped it, when that tapir ran at us.'

The two looked at each other in panic. Darkus looked down at the map and realized he didn't know where they were. Fear gripped his lungs and he found it hard to breathe.

'We mustn't panic,' Virginia said, anxiously glancing about. 'The path's got to be here somewhere.'

'Face it.' Darkus slumped down on to the ground and slid his rucksack off. 'We're lost.' His heart felt like lead. 'The best thing we can do is stay here until daylight.'

'Oh, Darkus,' Virginia's big brown eyes filled with tears. 'I'm so sorry. I didn't mean to drop the compass. It was an accident. I, I . . .'

'We don't know you dropped it,' Darkus said, pulling Virginia down next to him. 'It could've been me, when I slipped.'

'You're just being nice,' Virginia said, looking away from him. 'I messed up.'

'Hey, look!' Darkus pointed. A trail of dung beetles were eagerly clambering out of his backpack. He stared as the beetles crawled on to the ground and then across the clearing in a straight line.

'Where are they going?' Virginia asked.

'Ha!' Darkus sprang to his feet, grabbing Virginia's shirt and yanking her up to stand. 'They're showing us the way!' He pointed up to the star-speckled sky. 'Dung beetles can navigate using the Milky Way. *They don't need a compass!*' He shook Virginia shoulders with excitement. 'We're not lost, as long as we've got the beetles and the stars.' He grabbed his rucksack and the pooter full of fireflies. 'Come on, we can't be far away now.'

They walked beside the dung beetles, clearing the way and protecting them, like two giant bodyguards.

A space beyond the trees opened up. The dung beetles marched to the edge of the trees then lifted their elytra and flew up, looping over Darkus's head and dropping back into his rucksack.

'Holy macaroni!' Virginia exhaled, reaching out to steady herself against a tree.

Darkus's jaw dropped as he gawked at the view. Nestled amongst the trees and plants of the rainforest was a building as big as St Paul's Cathedral, made entirely of glass and metal. He couldn't see the smaller domes in the darkness, but he knew they were there.

'We made it.' Virginia looked at him and grinned.

Darkus nodded, but he couldn't stop staring at the Biome. His dad was in there somewhere, and he was going to find him. 'C'mon.' He grabbed Virginia's arm and they skirted around the edge of the helipad clearing until they were as close to the trapdoor as possible. Darkus took the black device from his pocket and held it out towards the Biome.

'Look!' Virginia pointed to a tiny triangle of light in the top right corner of the screen. It grew bigger, and then, in the centre of the dark screen, a word briefly appeared.

ONLINE.

'Eureeeekka.' Virginia breathed out a sigh of relief.

The word was replaced by the hexagon. Darkus pointed the device at the trapdoor again, touching the hexagon. The trapdoor dropped down a foot and slid open, revealing a gaping black hole in the ground, the size of a van.

There was a noise in the bushes behind them, like a man sneezing. Darkus looked at Virginia with alarm.

'Quick, run,' she hissed, already sprinting low through the darkness towards the opening.

Darkus dashed after her, and the pair of them pelted into the entrance tunnel of the Biome. A glaring ceiling of hexagonal lights flickered on and the door began to close.

'Here! Look! Quick!' Virginia called out, dropping to her knees beside a hexagonal tile in the floor with a handle hole. She lifted it and beneath was a ladder shaft. 'We have to get out of here. Emma said there are cameras.' Darkus looked up and spotted a glass globe on the ceiling. 'Come on, Darkus. Get down here.'

He shinned down the ladder fast, and Virginia followed, lowering the floor tile with her head. They dropped down into a dimly lit tunnel.

'Do you think they saw us?'

Virginia cocked her head and listened. 'There are no alarms going off. Let's hope the security guards are asleep.'

'Hang on a minute. How did you know that tile would lift?'

'It had a handle in it, for one thing, but Emma said there were maintenance tunnels running under the building. Dr Lenka told her that they're not watched, and that's how we are going to get around without being spotted.'

'When did she say that?' Darkus frowned.

'When I plugged her for info, as she was tying up the hammocks.' Virginia looked smug. 'Bet you're glad you brought me along now, eh?'

'What else did she say?'

'That the insect farm is in the basement under the giant dome, and there's only one or two cameras down there that we need to watch out for.'

'Then we're going down.' Darkus searched the floor for another hexagonal slab with a sunken handle. 'Because I want to meet the Biome beetles.'

CHAPTER TWENTY-ONE
The Queen's Consort

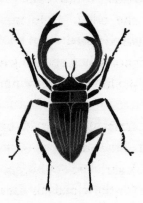

Two men in white lab coats came for Novak. Last time it had been Dr Lenka; Novak remembered him forcefully pushing her up the steps into the pupator. She hadn't known what was going to happen to her then, but this time she knew, and she struggled.

'Get off me! Let me go!'

The men lifted her on to a stretcher. They strapped down her arms, legs and then her neck. She stopped fighting and started screaming.

The men ignored her screams, raising the stretcher up on telescopic legs and wheeling her along the corridors of the Biome. She watched the hexagonal ceiling tiles zoom past, screaming and screaming as she frantically tried to work out how she was going to get away.

The trolley slowed to a stop. She could see a doorway. Darkus's dad was standing beside it, Spencer at his side, both of them dressed in white coats.

'Let me go!' she cried. 'Help me!' She looked at Spencer and he looked away.

Darkus's dad ignored her, speaking in low tones to the men who'd been pushing her. They nodded and walked away.

'Hello, Novak,' Darkus's dad said, brightly, coming to stand at the head of the stretcher.

'Traitor!' Novak shrieked at him, spitting at his face.

Bartholomew Cuttle wiped his face with his sleeve and turned his back to her. In a low, insistent voice, he said: 'Please listen carefully to *everything* I say. Even if I'm not talking directly to you.' His tone brightened, his voice growing louder as Spencer came to stand by Novak's feet. 'We are conducting an important experiment here today, and you are very lucky to be a part of it. Isn't that right, Spencer?'

Novak looked at Spencer, uncertain of what to make of Darkus's dad's behaviour. With his right eye, Spencer gave her the tiniest of winks.

'Yes, sir.' Spencer grabbed hold of the bar at the foot of her stretcher and pushed the trolley, Darkus's dad steering it down the corridor.

'Well, first things first,' Bartholomew Cuttle said, 'I'd appreciate it if you didn't scream any more. It upsets me, and will make it very difficult for you to hear what I'm saying, and, as I said, you must listen carefully to what I say at all times.'

Novak didn't reply.

Spencer nodded and smiled.

They turned down another corridor, and then another.

'Oh, drat it!' Darkus's dad turned around and made a play of looking exasperated. 'Spencer, I must have taken a wrong turn. I have to admit, I don't know exactly where we are! I'm not sure I'll ever get used to the geography of this hive. Do you know which way it is to get to the pupation lab?'

'Lost, are we?'

Novak immediately recognized Dr Lenka's snarl, and her blood ran cold.

'No,' Bartholomew Cuttle replied, turning to face him. 'We're not lost, we are, ah, just . . .'

'Where are you taking the girl?' Dr Lenka asked, stepping up to the stretcher and staring down at Novak.

'Oh, come on.' Darkus's dad laughed, lightly. 'You know where we're taking her,' – he paused – 'don't you?'

'Yes,' Dr Lenka sounded uncertain, 'of course I do. I meant, which direction do you want to go in to get to the err . . .'

'Pupation lab?'

'*What?*'

'I'm taking the girl to be prepared for the pupation chamber. We are performing the holometoboly today. But of course you already know that.' Bartholomew smiled. 'Will you be there to see it? I presume Lucy's invited you? It's very exciting. Today is the pinnacle of all her hard work.'

'I'll be there,' Dr Lenka replied. 'I'm sure Lucy will send for me.'

Bartholomew Cuttle narrowed his eyes. 'Are you?'

'*Yes!*' Dr Lenka barked. 'I was asking because I wanted to know why you are wheeling the girl into the maintenance dome.'

'The maintenance dome?' Bartholomew Cuttle looked around, surprised. 'This is not the place I want to be! It seems I may have to admit to being lost.'

'Ha!' Lenka laughed.

'But, Henrik, what on earth are *you* doing in the maintenance dome? Shouldn't you be in the lab with the other scientists, preparing the genetic material from the beetle for the pupation chamber? They'll be starting any minute now . . . Oh, no, I forgot . . .' Bartholomew Cuttle stepped right in, so that his face was close to Dr Lenka's, '. . . you've been put in charge of the toilets, because you're a traitor.'

Lenka didn't reply. He stared at Darkus's dad with a burning hatred.

'You *weren't* told about the pupation, were you?'

Bartholomew whispered.

There was silence.

'I thought not.' Bartholomew stepped back. 'You know, if the pupation works on the girl, Lucy has promised me that I can be next.'

'Next?'

Bartholomew Cuttle nodded. 'Oh, yes. Lucy and I will be Beetle Queen and consort.' He smiled. 'We are going to rule this world together.'

'Ha!' Lenka tried to laugh, but his throat was dry and his voice sounded hollow. He stepped back.

Novak stared up at Darkus's dad, unable to believe what she was hearing.

'Of course, I haven't selected the genus I would like to have introduced into my DNA yet.' He tapped his lips with his finger. 'I was thinking of the Hercules beetle. They are so strong. I think Lucy would like a strong beetle by her side, don't you think?'

Novak heard Dr Lenka march away and a door slam.

'Oh, dear,' Darkus's dad muttered, 'I appear to have upset him.' Novak thought she saw a smile peeking out from behind his blank expression. 'Now Spencer, we really should be taking Novak to the hospital, to check all of her vital signs. She shouldn't step into the pupation chamber until we have checked her blood pressure, heart rate, temperature, et cetera. I know the others are waiting for us, but they can wait a little longer. It wouldn't do to introduce any kind of a virus into the metamorphosis.'

'Yes, Dr Cuttle, sir,' Spencer replied and turned the trolley around. 'It's this way.'

Novak wasn't sure what was happening. The pupation chamber was in the Arcadia dome, in the lab, but they seemed to be wheeling her from one outer dome to another.

When they arrived at the infirmary, Darkus's dad freed Novak from her restraints, lifted her gently and sat her on a hospital bed. He made a great show of measuring her height, her weight, her pulse. He did reflex tests on her knees, taking his time and writing everything down. He made her hop across the room, and then walk in a straight line. She kept trying to look him or Spencer in the eye, to glean something from their expressions as to what was happening, but both men were too preoccupied with ensuring she was healthy to notice her glances. They pulled out her tongue and swabbed it. Spencer looked down her throat, and in her ears. Bartholomew Cuttle asked her to unfurl her antennae and then measured them.

'Has anyone made a full study of you since your first pupation?' he asked.

Novak shook her head. 'I think they were only interested in if I died or not.'

'That's a shame.' He shook his head. 'Would you mind if I took a look at your eyes?'

Novak pulled back: no one had seen her beetle eyes.

'No? OK. Not to worry.' He pointed his pen at her

wrist. 'I'm afraid you won't be able to wear jewellery in the pupator. The metal will interfere with the process. You're going to have to take it off.'

'Oh!' Novak covered her bracelet with her hand.

'Would you like me to look after it for you?' Spencer asked. 'Just until this is over, then I'll give it straight back.'

Novak thought about the way Hepburn had kissed Spencer's nose, and she nodded, slipping the bangle off her wrist.

'Right. I think that's everything.' Bartholomew Cuttle slowly read down his list of checks a second time. 'I'll just double check.'

Novak looked at Spencer, and it suddenly hit her that Darkus's dad was stalling for time.

'Um, excuse me,' she said. 'May I go to the bathroom?'

'Yes, of course!' Bartholomew Cuttle replied, sounding oddly delighted by the idea. 'We can't have you stepping into the pupator with a full bladder. In fact, do – erm, you know – take your time. Make sure your bowels are empty too. Take as long as you need.'

Novak grimaced, but she nodded, and Spencer escorted her round the corner to a toilet and positioned himself outside, a polite distance from the door.

Novak sat down on top of the toilet seat. She didn't need to go, but if this was a game to play for time, then she wanted to help. Darkus's dad had told her to listen carefully to everything he said, so she ran through the conversation he'd had with Dr Lenka. It didn't make much sense. Bartholomew Cuttle was obviously trying to make him cross, but Novak couldn't see how that would help her.

After a while, Novak flushed the chain, and then slowly washed her hands and dried them thoroughly. Finally she came out of the bathroom.

'All set?' Spencer asked, cheerily.

Novak nodded and followed him back to the room where Bartholomew Cuttle was waiting for them. 'I'm going to ask you to hop back up here, on to the trolley, please, Novak,' he said.

She dutifully did as she was told. He made no attempt to strap her back down.

'You must feel so proud to be helping your mother with her experiments today,' he said. 'There are many people who would give anything to be such an important part of her work.'

Confused, Novak looked at Spencer. His hopeful face calmed the fear leaping about inside her chest. Hepburn trusted Spencer, so she would too.

CHAPTER TWENTY-TWO
Silphidae

'*I* can't hold him for much longer!' Novak heard Mawling bellowing. 'Lock the door! LOCK IT! *NOW!*' She tried to sit up on the stretcher, but Bartholomew Cuttle gently put his hand on her chest, indicating she should stay lying down. She'd been wheeled at a leisurely pace from the infirmary dome, back along the connecting corridor and around the perimeter of the Arcadia dome until they were approaching the laboratory.

Darkus's dad stepped into the laboratory with Spencer at his heels, leaving her lying outside. Novak stared up at the ceiling, trying to make sense of the commotion and shouts she was hearing.

'*What the hell is going on?*'

Novak sat bolt upright at the sound of Mater's voice. Lucretia Cutter darted towards her, with the speed of a huntsman spider. She shook her head, to show she didn't know, and her mother skittered past her into the laboratory. Silently slipping off the stretcher, Novak crept to the doorway and peeped into the room.

'It's Lenka, he, he, got into the pupator. He . . .' Spencer was standing in front of Lucretia Cutter, staring at the floor.

'Where is everyone?' Mater's head swung in a wide arc, examining the room with her compound eyes.

'Dr Vikhrov is hurt.' Novak saw Darkus's dad crouching down beside one of Mater's scientists. 'We need to get him to the infirmary immediately.'

Novak saw a spray of red drops on the glass wall between the laboratory and the pupation chamber. She gasped. It was blood.

'What happened to the lab team?'

'I think they ran away,' he replied.

'Ran away?' Lucretia Cutter spat.

Ling Ling stepped forward and bowed. 'Mawling and I responded to a call for help from Dr Vikhrov,' she reported. 'When we arrived Lenka was in there,' she pointed through the glass wall, 'attacking Dr Vikhrov. Mawling threw Lenka off as I dragged Dr Vikrov out, and then together we fought with Lenka, driving him back into the pupation chamber. Dr Vikrov managed to lock the door before collapsing to the floor. During the fight the lab team fled.'

'Lucy, Dr Vikhrov is losing blood,' Bartholomew said, his voice urgent. 'We need to stem the bleeding.'

'Do we know which beetle genome Dr Vikhrov used for the pupation?' Lucretia Cutter stalked over to the desk, ignoring him. She tapped at the computer keyboard. 'Which beetle did Lenka have introduced into his DNA?'

Darkus's dad looked to the door of the laboratory and spotted Novak.

'Novak, bring in the stretcher.' He waved her forwards and she saw that his hands were covered in Dr Vikhrov's blood.

She nodded and quickly dragged it into the laboratory.

'Novak,' Darkus's dad said in a commanding whisper, 'I need you to pull the handle and lower the bed to the floor.'

She didn't move. She couldn't stop staring at Dr Vikhrov. There was blood everywhere, there were gashes across his neck and forehead, and his left ear was gone.

'Novak, listen to me. Dr Vikhrov needs our help. I need you to lower the bed so that I can lift him on to the stretcher.' Darkus's dad had removed his lab coat and was ripping the sleeves out of it, folding them and using them to stem the bleeding.

'Is he dead?' Novak asked.

'No.' Bartholomew looked her in the eyes. 'And he is going to be just fine, as long as we get him to the infirmary as soon as possible. You can help me do that, can't you?'

Novak nodded and sprang into action, lowering the bed and helping Darkus's dad as he carefully moved Dr Vikhrov on to the stretcher.

'Oh, no!' Spencer held up a labelled syringe. '*Silphidae*. I think the genome was from one of the *Silphidae*!'

'A carrion beetle,' Lucretia said, 'how interesting. Well, that would explain Henrik's insatiable desire to eat flesh.' She laughed. 'Unfortunate that Dr Vikhrov didn't think of that before he agreed to perform the pupation.'

Bartholomew Cuttle pulled the handle that lifted the stretcher to waist height, taking the remains of his lab coat and carefully wedging it under Dr Vikhrov's injured head. 'I'm taking him to the infirmary,' he told Lucretia Cutter.

'No.' Mater pointed at Mawling. 'He can do that.'

'But he needs immediate medical attention,' Darkus's dad protested. 'Without it, he could die.'

'I don't care if he dies,' she said. 'Dr Vikhrov is no use to me any more.'

'But . . .'

'I said *no*!' Lucretia said, drawing herself up to her full height.

There was silence as Novak watched Mawling wheel Dr Vikhrov away.

'You will help me examine what has become of Henrik.'

'He's still in there,' Ling Ling said. 'Inside the pupation chamber.'

Looking through the glass wall at the pupator, Novak stared at the white pod that she'd been shoved into all those years ago. She remembered the three steps, stumbling through the door and curling up on the floor of the pod, frightened. As it was sealed shut she heard fluid filling the outer chamber. Novak didn't remember coming out of the pupator, just waking up in a bed and feeling like a stranger inside her own body.

'What do you want me to do?' Bartholomew Cuttle asked. Novak saw that his face was grey. He looked upset.

She thought about the conversation in the hallway with Dr Lenka, when he'd said he was going to be next into the pupator, and then all their time-wasting in the hospital. *He knew this was going to happen!* He'd made it happen, in an attempt to save her from the pupation chamber, and now Dr Vikhrov was hurt and possibly dying.

'I want to see how well the metamorphosis worked.' Mater clapped her hands together like a delighted child. 'I've never tried it on a grown man before.' She flicked a switch on the console. 'Henrik, can you hear me? I'm going to open the door.'

Ling Ling drew back her left leg, moving her hands

forward into a defensive stance.

Novak found herself shuffling backwards towards the door. She didn't want to see what had happened to Henrik Lenka.

The pod wall peeled back in segments, like the petals of an opening flower, and the door of the pupation chamber slid open. Novak's blood ran cold. Lenka's face was that of a murderous beetle pirate. One beady compound eye stared at them, underlined by a stripe of chitinous scales running across his face to a decimated nose. They stopped where his top lip should have been. The left side of his face was still human, one cold blue eye staring out of pale acne-puckered skin. His mouth was a blackened pit out of which protruded huge jaws lined with razor-sharp mandibles and dripping with blood. With his one human arm, he held a strange bloody lump up to his mouth and took a bite.

Novak's stomach turned as she realized he was eating Dr Vikhrov's ear.

'Well, hello, Lucy,' His voice came over the speakers in the laboratory. 'What do you think of my new look?' He waved his left arm, which had a black and orange exoskeleton and a vicious claw where his hand should have been.

'I'm impressed,' Lucretia replied. 'I didn't think you had the courage.'

'I did this for you.' There was a scratching noise, chitinous legs against metal, as he clambered out of the pupation chamber, approaching the glass partition. Novak saw that he had two stunted misshapen beetle legs sprouting out of his torso.

'We're alike, you and I,' he said. 'You don't have to be alone any more, Lucy. We can rule the world together.'

'I'm not happy, Henrik,' Lucretia replied. 'You've chased my scientists away, and hurt Dr Vikhrov.'

Lenka rolled his human eye and laughed – a chilling, gurgling sound. 'I was hungry.'

'You monster!' Spencer cried out, surged forward. 'Dr Vikhrov's my friend!'

Bartholomew grabbed his shoulders, holding him back. 'Spencer, why don't you take Novak back to her cell?' he said, gently pushing Spencer towards Novak and the door. 'Please.'

'Oh, no, let the boy come at me.' Henrik Lenka leered at Spencer through the toughened glass. 'I'm still hungry.'

Bartholomew turned his back to the glass. 'We can't leave him in there,' he said to Lucretia, 'and we can't let him out. What do you plan on doing with him?'

She flicked a switch so that Henrik Lenka couldn't hear them. 'I'll tranquillize him. Ling Ling can put him in a cell.'

'And then what?'

'He will make a very useful live specimen for you and Master Crips to work with, don't you think?' Lucretia Cutter replied.

'He's dangerous, Lucy,' Bartholomew said. 'He's a carrion beetle, a dead flesh eater.'

'Well, then, you'd better be careful, hadn't you,' Lucretia laughed, 'because he really hates you.'

CHAPTER TWENTY-THREE

The Hatchery

*D*arkus dropped to the floor and listened, looking at Baxter for reassurance. He and Virginia had taken Baxter and Marvin out of their bamboo cages, and most of the larger Base Camp beetles were sitting on top of the rucksack, antennae alert. They'd climbed down three ladders so far, and hadn't encountered anyone, although – Darkus reminded himself – it was about four o' clock in the morning. They searched around on hands and knees, but couldn't find any tiles with sunken handles.

'This must be the bottom floor of the Biome,' he said,

looking up and down the corridor. The section of the passage they were in was lit, but both ways were dark.

'Which direction?' Virginia asked.

'The big dome is that way,' Darkus said. 'I think.'

Virginia nodded, and they set off in silence. The light sensors in the floor were unnerving: they only lit the section you were walking on, making it impossible to know if anything was waiting in the darkness beyond, and so they depended on the beetles' senses and listened, alert to the slightest noise, as they crept in the direction of the big dome.

'Look, here's a door.' Darkus placed his hands and an ear on the hexagonal door to his right. He stepped back and looked around the frame. 'How does it open?'

'Try the thingamabob,' Virginia suggested.

'Oh, yeah.' Darkus pulled it out of his pocket and pressed the white hexagon. The door slid up and a warm, earthy smell invited them into the room beyond. Red lights flickered on. The room was long, stretching out parallel to the corridor they'd been walking along. It was divided by four troughs that spanned the full length of the space.

Stepping up to the nearest trough, Darkus dipped his hand into it, scooping up what looked like earth. He rubbed it between his fingers.

'Look, Baxter, oak mulch, like we put in your terrarium.' He lifted his fingers to Baxter's face so that he could smell it with his antennae.

Virginia grabbed his arm as a distant rumbling noise

grew louder, accelerating towards them like a ten-pin bowling ball being returned to a player after a strike. Darkus leapt backwards as a giant white boulder dropped from the ceiling into the trough in front of him, sinking down into the mulch.

'What on earth is that?' Virginia whispered.

Darkus looked up at the ceiling. It was a grid of wide square holes.

'It fell through one of those holes.'

'Yeah, I get that, but what is it?' Virginia came forward, reaching out and poking it gently.

Darkus placed his hands either side of the giant ball. It had a texture that reminded him of elephant hide. 'It's an egg!' he realized.

'An egg?' Virginia frowned. 'What kind of creature lays an egg that big?'

Darkus looked at her. '*Escarabajo gigante*.'

'It's a dinobeetle egg?'

'Lucretia Cutter is breeding giant beetles in her insect farm!' He looked up. 'The adult beetles must be on the floor above us.' He thought for a moment. 'Their eggs get sifted down through those holes into these troughs of oak mulch.' He moved along the trough and pointed. 'Look, there are more.'

'This is a hatchery!' Virginia exclaimed.

There was a thunderous rumble above their heads as another giant beetle egg dropped down into a soft bed of oak mulch.

Darkus ran alongside the trough, counting the eggs. 'There must be at least thirty eggs here.' As he ran, he felt exhilarated, like he could run for miles – even though he'd been walking all night, he realized he didn't feel tired. He stopped. 'Virginia, do you feel different in any way?'

'Different?' Virginia frowned. 'How do you mean?'

'I don't know, like . . . energized,' Darkus struggled to explain. 'My body, it feels strong.'

Virginia blinked. 'I know what you mean. Like, right now, I feel like I could run up that wall and do a back flip.'

'Can you?'

'No, of course not,' Virginia snorted.

'Well, *I* don't know.' Darkus shrugged. 'You're good at gymnastics.'

'Yeah, but I can't run up a wall and do a back flip. If I could, you'd have seen me do it by now. I'd be doing it all the time. Although,' she eyed up the wall, 'now I'm thinking about it, my muscles are bursting to try.'

'Try it,' Darkus said.

Virginia looked at him for a second, spun around and burst into a sprint, running back down the room as fast as she could, speeding up as she approached the wall. Slamming her left foot down, she hurled her right leg up, landing one, then two steps up the wall, before thrusting backwards, into a back flip, and landing in a crouched position.

'Whoa!' Darkus clapped. 'That was cool!'

Virginia stood up straight, looking down at her body. She walked towards Darkus. 'You do something.'

'Do what?'

'I don't know. Anything. Run. Jump. Just do something.'

Darkus sprinted towards her, slamming both feet down hard to jump, he sprang high into the air, his arms windmilling as he travelled nearly four metres before landing.

'What's going on?' Virginia asked, her eyes wide as she looked down at her legs. 'It's like we've got superpowers.'

'But *we* haven't changed.' Darkus looked at his hands and then around. 'It's this place. It's the atmosphere,' he waved his hand in front of his face, 'it must have a high level of oxygen in it.' He narrowed his eyes as he stared at the trough. 'Yes, of course! There has to be more oxygen, otherwise the giant beetles wouldn't be able to breathe! They're too big. That's what was killing the dinobeetle in the forest.'

'Slow down.' Virginia frowned. 'Explain.'

'Beetles breathe through holes in their exoskeletons.'

'Yeah, spiracles, I know.'

'Air travels through the spiracles and the oxygen in the air is absorbed into the beetle's body by diffusion. The reason beetles don't grow bigger is because the air can only travel a certain distance into a beetle's body before the oxygen in it is absorbed and runs out. Even the tissues deep inside a beetle need oxygen to stay alive.

This makes it impossible for beetles to grow beyond a certain size. They have to stay small . . .'

'Unless . . .' Virginia's eyes lit up, 'there's more oxygen in the atmosphere!'

'Yes!' Darkus nodded. 'In the Palaeozoic era, three hundred million years ago, the atmosphere was thirty-five per cent oxygen and there were giant insects.'

'And the oxygen is working on our muscles too.' Virginia bent her knees and jumped high in the air. 'I wonder if it does anything to Marvin?'

Darkus looked to his shoulder. 'Baxter, can you feel it?'

The rhinoceros beetle nodded and rocketed off Darkus's shoulder, flying more like a falcon than a beetle.

'Nice!' Darkus laughed as all the Base Camp beetles perched around the opening of his rucksack decided to join Baxter in the air, zooming about.

'These eggs,' Darkus looked out across the vast hall of troughs, 'they're all giant beetles.'

'You think she's breeding an army of giant beetles?' Virginia's eyes grew wide.

Darkus frowned. 'But surely they wouldn't be able to survive in the earth's atmosphere.'

Virginia shrugged. 'Lucretia Cutter is a giant beetle.'

Darkus shook his head. 'No, she will *never* be a real beetle.'

Chapter Twenty-Four

Larvae Farm

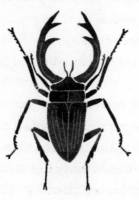

They walked beside the troughs, and Darkus saw that beneath the eggs and the oak mulch was a slow conveyor belt. The further along the belt they got, the larger and more jelly-bean-shaped the eggs became, until they reached a couple of eggs that were hatching. The translucent flat heads of larvae were breaking through or protruding out of the giant eggshell.

The largest larva Darkus had ever seen until now was the size of a cocktail sausage, but these dinobeetle larvae were the size of human babies.

'Oh, wow.' Virginia lowered her head till it was the

same height as the larva wriggling out of the egg. 'You are ugly!'

'The conveyor belt ends here. Look, there are chutes.' Darkus came alongside the closest chute. It was labelled *Hercules*. There was a diagram of the larvae.

'This one says *Tiger*.' Virginia pointed. 'And this one says *Titan*.'

There were eight chutes.

'Larvae must get sorted by someone, and put into the relevant chute.'

'I wouldn't like to have that job.' Virginia pulled her chin in. 'Those guys look bitey.' She pointed at the rearing larva opening and closing its black jaws.

Darkus poked his head down the chute marked *Tiger*. 'Urghhh!' He jerked his head back. 'It stinks down there.'

Virginia came and stood beside him, wrinkling her nose. 'Oh, man! I see what you mean.'

'It smells like rotting meat.'

'Tiger larvae eat other insects,' Virginia said. 'They're vicious.'

'I wonder what giant tiger beetles eat.'

'Let's not find out.'

'Well,' Darkus looked back up the hall, and then back at the chutes, 'we either go back the way we came in, or . . .'

Virginia saw where he was looking. 'Oh, no. I'm not going down there.'

'This one is the Hercules larva chute.'

'Are you kidding me?'

'They eat rotting wood in their larval stage,' Darkus said. 'They won't be interested in you.'

'But we don't know what's down there.'

'Exactly. I want to know what happens to the larvae once they've hatched. There are often three or four stages of larval growth, called instars, before pupation. It's the feeding phase where they do all their growing.' He gazed down the chute. 'A fully-grown larva is bigger than the adult beetle. I have to see.'

'I'm OK with not seeing,' Virginia said, pursing her lips.

Darkus sat on the edge of the chute, swung his legs in and grinned at her. 'See you down there,' he said, pushing off.

'Wait!' he heard Virginia cry as he slid down.

The chute was like a playground slide. It launched him into a dimly lit room carpeted with a woody mulch. He stood up and dusted his hands off against his trousers. His feet sank into the soft floor. Most larvae like to bury themselves, so he took extra care not to step on anyone's rear end as he picked his way to the middle of the room.

Piles of compost were liberally scattered about and the surface of the mulch undulated and cracked like the precursor to an earthquake, as the larvae beneath moved about. Darkus reached down into the soil until he found a larva and, lifting it, he saw it was the size of a sausage dog. In the middle of the room, the larvae he uncovered were the size of seals.

A squeaking noise heralded Virginia's cautious entrance, as she edged herself down the slide backwards, a foot wedged hard against each side of the chute, moving a step at a time.

'What are you scared of?' Darkus laughed.

'Er . . . sliding out into a mound of dung?' Virginia replied.

'It's just mulch and compost . . . rotting wood and vegetation.'

'It's still revolting.' Virginia wrinkled her nose as she looked around. 'Is this room full of Hercules larvae?'

'There must be a room for each species of giant beetle she's breeding.' Darkus nodded. 'You know I'd really like to go and look in the titan beetle larvae room. No one has seen a titan beetle larva in the wild, they must be massive.'

'Are you crazy? A giant titan beetle larva could bite your head off!' Virginia shook her head. 'No way.'

'It could,' Darkus nodded, 'but it probably wouldn't.' He gestured to the room. 'They're gentle giants.' He smiled at a Hercules beetle larva burrowing its flat rust-brown head into the substrate, digging with the hairy rounded ends of its stubby amber legs. 'Look, see those dark spots along the side of the larva's body?' He pointed. 'They're the spiracles.' As the larva dug down, its fat, semi-translucent rear end waggled about.

'They're not pretty, are they?' Virginia said peering at a larva munching on watermelon. 'That's a face only a mother could love.'

'Watch your ankles,' Darkus said as the sharp black jaws of a larva rose out of the soil beside her.

Virginia skipped away from it. 'How do we get out of here?'

'There's a door over there.'

'Of course, it would have to be as far away as possible,' Virginia muttered, clambering over to Darkus.

'Look!' Darkus pointed. 'The larvae get bigger and more developed as you cross the room. Check out how massive they are. That one's as big as a walrus.'

'That one is all stiff. Is it dead?'

'No, it's a pupa.' Excited, Darkus clambered over to the pupa and ran his hand over the hard-edged surface. 'Isn't it amazing?'

'Yeah, brilliant.' Virginia jumped over to the door and tried the handle, smiling with relief when it opened. 'C'mon, let's get out of here. This place is weirding me out. We need to find your dad.'

Darkus took one last look around the larvae room. It wasn't fair to breed such amazing creatures when they couldn't survive in the earth's atmosphere. And to breed them for what? An army? That was perverting their nature. Everything about this was wrong. He felt sorry for the giant beasts, and he knew that if he were confronted with these creatures, he could not fight or hurt them.

CHAPTER TWENTY-FIVE
Beetle Borg

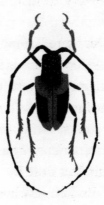

They found themselves back out in another white hexagonal corridor.

'All the corridors look the same,' Virginia complained.

'I think we're still heading in the right direction,' Darkus said, 'but we need to find stairs or a lift. At some point we're going to have to go up,' Darkus said.

'The higher we go, the more likely it is we'll be spotted,' Virginia replied.

As they walked they kept their eyes peeled for cameras. They found a warehouse-sized room with a carpet of soil on the floor, where, laid out with a metre of space between them were hundreds of giant pupae.

'Inside,' Darkus whispered, 'they're transforming into fully-grown dinobeetles.'

'Metamorphosis is a weird kind of voodoo,' Virginia replied.

They continued on down the never-ending corridor. Darkus pulled out his device, tapping the hexagon to open another door. They peeped their heads into a white room; at the far end were thirty or forty dead beetles, of normal size, lying on their backs, legs in the air. Along the right-hand wall of the room was a bank of TV monitors, all appearing to show images of the sunrise or jungle foliage. Baxter leapt off Darkus's shoulder and flew over to them, wandering between the corpses, his antennae quivering. Darkus knelt down on the floor beside the macabre scene.

'Are you OK, Baxter?' The rhinoceros beetle bowed his head, and using his horn, pushed one of the dead beetles towards him. Darkus picked it up gingerly between his thumb and forefinger. 'It's a male monkey beetle,' he said as Virginia came over. 'I recognize it from my book. Look at the long, strong, back legs and the shiny blue exoskeleton.' He looked up at her. 'These guys are only found in South Africa.'

'What's that on its head?' Virginia bent down. 'It's got a metal thing on its thorax and a tiny bobble glued between its eyes.'

'I wonder why?' Darkus looked around the room, as Baxter returned to his shoulder. Beneath the flickering screens was a long desk. There was a notebook beside a computer. Walking over to pick it up, he saw that the back wall of the room was covered with shelves of Perspex tanks. Handing the notebook to Virginia he went to look in the tanks. 'This one has giant African flower beetles in. This one is monkey beetles. More African flower beetles in this one.' He looked at Virginia. 'These are all beetles that are strong flyers.'

'She's making beetle cyborgs,' Virgina said, flicking over the pages of the notebook and looking up at the TV screens. 'They've got microchips on their thoraxes, allowing an operator to control their flight by administering electric shocks and the blob between its eyes is a pinhead camera.'

'Beetle surveillance!' Darkus looked down at the dead monkey beetle on the palm of her hand. 'Using electric shocks? That's so cruel.'

'First dinobeetles, now beetle cyborgs.' Virginia slid the notebook into one of the large pockets in her trousers. 'I dread to think what else she's doing. I'm going to give this book to Emma Lamb. She's going to need evidence, if she's ever going to win that Pulitzer prize, because no one is going to believe that beetle borgs exist.'

'This place is horrible.' Darkus wanted to get out of the room. He put the dead monkey beetle down on the desk. 'Let's go.' The plight of the beetle cyborgs upset him, but then, he thought, they are no worse off than the giant beetles who will never see the sky or breathe the earth's air. He wanted to set all the beetles free. He thought back to Lucretia Cutter's beetles at Towering Heights, angry and aggressive, head-butting the walls of their tanks. He'd thought they were evil, because Lucretia Cutter had bred them, but now he wondered whether they behaved that way because of what she'd done to them. *Maybe they just wanted to get out.* No beetle started out bad. Lucretia Cutter made them that way by using genetics and her knowledge about the insects to make them to do bad things . . . but if beetles could be used to do bad things, then by the same logic, they could do *good* things.

They continued on down corridor until they came to a junction.

'Left, right or straight ahead?' Virginia asked.

'I say we keep going,' Darkus said.

'We might end up going under the whole dome and coming out the other side.'

'Emma said there was a central lift that goes up into the main dome, to the laboratories. We haven't seen a lift yet.'

As they walked, Darkus opened doors and peeped into rooms. There was a stockroom stacked with bags of soil and mulch, a room that stank of antiseptic and was clearly for cleaning the insect farming equipment.

'There's the lift,' Virginia whispered, pointing to double doors at the end of the corridor. She looked up to see if she could spy cameras.

To the left, right before the lift, was a door. Darkus pressed the hexagon and it lifted. 'I'll just take a quick look in here,' he whispered, ducking inside.

The room was dark and warm. There was a glowing thermostat to the left of the doorway. A soft red light radiated from a tiny bulb on the far wall. Light from the corridor spilt into the room and Darkus could see it was empty but for four huge cylindrical tanks lying horizontal on white stone slabs.

He crept towards the tanks, unable to see what was inside them. He went right up to the nearest tank, pushing his face against the glass. All four tanks seemed to contain the same thing, a pale ridged object. He moved and realized that the surface of the rigid object was semi-translucent, that there was something inside. He saw two dark circles, eyes, and claw-like jaws.

Gasping with shock, he stumbled backwards, his eyes flitting from one tank to the next, then he turned and ran out of the door. Slamming his hand down on the black screen, he hammered at the hexagon until the door slid shut.

'What's the matter?' Virginia asked. 'What's in there?'

'It's her.' Darkus couldn't breathe. 'She's in all of them.'

'Who is?' Virginia stared at him, frightened. 'I don't understand.'

'There are four of her!' Darkus's heart thudded furiously. 'She's making clones of herself.'

'Who is?'

'Lucretia Cutter.'

'What?' Virginia sucked in her breath.

'Virginia, we've made a terrible mistake. We shouldn't have come here on our own. We need Bertolt, and Uncle Max.' Darkus grabbed her arm. 'We have to get out of here and get back to camp, right now.'

'Leaving so soon?'

Darkus froze, and every single hair on his body lifted in fright at the sound of that horribly familiar voice. He turned around. The lift doors were open, and standing inside was Lucretia Cutter.

Chapter Twenty-Six

Darkus Decoy

*L*ucretia Cutter had dispensed with the wig, sunglasses and gold lipstick at the Film Awards. She no longer had a chin, but in its place were beetle jaws and mandibles. The top of her head was a patchwork of black scales, tufts of wiry hair and her long antennae. Standing on her hind legs she was nearly nine feet tall. She still wore her lab coat, but underneath her dress was slashed up the front so her chitinous limbs could move freely. Darkus and Virginia walked in front of her into the lift. There was no need for restraints: she could sense they were going to move before their brains had even sent the message to their muscles. There was no escape.

Baxter had retreated, clambering inside the collar of Darkus's T-shirt and down his back. He was now nestling in between his shoulder blades, just above the rucksack. All the Base Camp beetles had scurried down into the bag.

Lucretia Cutter took them up in the lift. As it travelled up the glass shaft Darkus saw a misty sunrise casting a rosy light through the roof of the enormous greenhouse on to an impossibly beautiful rainforest, but the icy fear that was gripping his insides eclipsed all of his senses.

'How do you like my new home?' Lucretia asked.

Darkus looked at the ground, 'What you're doing here is cruel.'

'You father loves it here.'

Darkus bristled. 'You're lying.'

'I can't wait to tell him about your visit. He will be surprised.' She brought her jaws close to his ear. 'Or perhaps I won't tell him. I might save the news for when it will have the most . . . impact.'

Darkus glared so hard at the floor that he could have burnt a hole in it. A bell sounded and the lift doors opened.

'For children, you're surprisingly resourceful.' Lucretia shoved Virginia with a claw, pushing her out of the lift. 'Like rats, but what I really want to know is, how did you know where my Biome was?'

Darkus and Virginia glanced at each other, clamping

their lips shut.

'It was that hack, Emma Lamb, wasn't it? I know she's out there in the forest. Did she tell you about my Biome? I'll bet she did, didn't she? Who else has she told?'

Darkus kept his face blank. 'I'll never tell.'

'Ha!' Lucretia Cutter snapped. 'Be certain, young Cuttle, anything I want to know, you'll tell me in seconds.'

'Don't bet on it,' Virginia muttered.

'I'd be careful, girl.' Lucretia swung her head round angrily. 'You are of no use to me at all.'

'Leave her alone.' Darkus jumped between Lucretia Cutter and Virginia.

'Darkus Cuttle, you have broken into my Biome uninvited, which is a crime.' She bent down so that her saucer-sized black eyes were an inch from his face. 'I'm going to put you in my cells and have a good long think about what I'm going to do with you.' Her antennae quivered. 'It would be good to have more children to experiment on.' She grabbed hold of Darkus's shirt and Virginia, by her braids, striding up the corridor, dragging them, stumbling behind her.

They arrived at the cells and found Mawling sitting on a chair, snoring, his eyes closed and legs splayed. Lucretia Cutter kicked him. He choked on his own saliva as he woke up, stumbling to his feet when he saw who'd it was.

'Yes, boss, I mean, Madame, errr,' he saluted, 'ready for duty.'

'I have two for the cells,' she said, letting go of Darkus and Virginia.

'There are only two vacant cells left.' Mawling scratched his bald head. 'Shall I split them up?'

'No, put them in a cell together. I have a sneaking suspicion that there will be more rats out there in the jungle. Am I right?' She looked at Darkus and he kept his face blank. 'Tell Craven and Dankish to use the beetle borgs to find them, and then go out and bring them in. I don't want any more surprises.'

Darkus felt sick. Uncle Max, Bertolt, Emma and Motty would be caught as they woke up, just as they realized that he and Virginia were missing, and it would be his fault.

'And,' Lucretia placed her hand on Darkus's rucksack, 'I think I'd better have that bag, don't you?'

'*No!*' Darkus jerked away, but Dankish grabbed him and wrenched the backpack off, handing it to Lucretia Cutter.

'Leave him alone!' Virginia cried.

'Thank you for bringing my beetles back to me.' Lucretia waved the bag at him, her mouth a slash of smiling malice, all trace of gold lipstick gone. 'I'm going to enjoy analysing these.'

Darkus felt Baxter scrambling up his back. The rhinoceros beetle shot out of his T-shirt, hissing as he fired towards Lucretia Cutter. At the same time the Base Camp beetles exploded out of the bag, swarming around her head, stabbing, biting, shooting acid and scratching where they could.

'Marvin!' Virginia cried as the frog-legged leaf beetle flew to his cousins' aid.

Lucretia Cutter lurched backwards, momentarily stunned by the attack, then rallied, brushing off their offensive like it was nothing. She hammered beetles aside, grabbing Baxter between her jaws as she crushed others underfoot. The rhinoceros beetle screeched as it writhed about, trying to escape her bite.

'Aaaaaarrrrrghhhhhhhhhh!' Darkus yelled, throwing himself at Lucretia's legs, knocking her backwards. She let go of Baxter and he tumbled to the ground with a sickening clunk. Darkus curled up in a protective ball on the floor around his fallen friend.

'Baxter, are you OK? Baxter? Oh, no, *please no*. Baxter? I'm here, buddy.' The rhinoceros beetle didn't move. He gently ran his finger over Baxter's elytra. 'Can you hear me? It's OK now. I'm here.' Hot tears streamed from his eyes. He saw that one of Baxter's legs was missing. 'Please, Baxter,' he whispered. 'I need you.' Darkus gently picked up the beetle in his cupped hands, blinking furiously to clear his eyes of tears.

'You're a monster!' Virginia shouted, as Lucretia got to her feet.

There was a loud bang from the closest cell door. 'Lucy?' a man's voice shouted. 'You can't keep me locked up in here like this. Do you hear me? We can rule this planet together!'

Ignoring the children, Lucretia made a series of unwholesome clicking noises, and the beaten Base Camp beetles filed back into the bag obediently. She picked it up, cantering off down the corridor like an angry stilt-walker.

There was a second bang. '*Lucy!*' Through the small window in the door, Darkus saw a black compound eye and a scaly face; a second later it was replaced by an ice-blue eye. 'Mawling, my old friend,' the man said, 'you've got to let me speak to the old shrew. She can't keep me locked up in here. I'm on your side. Remember?'

'I'm just following orders,' Mawling replied, grabbing Darkus by the scruff of the neck, pulling him to his feet, and yanking Virginia's arm.

'Get off.' Darkus aimed a well-placed kick at Mawling's ankle.

'Ow!' Mawling grunted, let go of Darkus, and then hit him across the back of his head with the flat of his hand. Darkus cried out as he stumbled forward, his ear ringing.

'Why don't you pick on someone your own size?' Virginia tried to throw a punch at Mawling, but he held her, thrashing, at arm's length. Ignoring their protestations, the thug marched them past the cell containing the man with two different eyes, past another, and then opened the third using his thumb print on a sensor pad. He shoved them both inside and waved, as the door closed.

Darkus threw himself to the floor and opened his cupped hands.

'Is he OK?' Virginia knelt down beside him.

'He's not moving,' Darkus whispered, 'and his middle leg is gone. Is Marvin . . .?'

Virginia pointed to her braid, and Marvin was there, clinging to it. 'He's a lover not a fighter. He got thrown to the floor almost immediately and I grabbed him.' She reached into her trouser pocket and pulled out a tiny pot of banana jelly, opened it and handed it to Darkus. 'Here, try this.'

Darkus lifted Baxter and held the jelly in front of his mandibles. The rhinoceros beetle's antennae shivered. 'They moved! I saw his antennae move,' he said, hope rocketing up inside him.

'I saw it too,' Virginia agreed. 'Maybe he needs a bit of time to recover.'

Darkus rolled over on to his back, carefully putting Baxter on to his chest and holding the banana jelly where the beetle could reach it. Slowly, but steadily Baxter's strength seemed to return and soon he was nibbling away at the jelly. 'I think he's going to be OK,' Darkus said with relief.

'We need to get out of here.' Virginia looked around the cell. 'It's a triangle. Each cell must be an equilateral triangle, meeting at the point to make a hexagon, which means there are five other cells, all full except one. I wonder who is in the other cells?'

Darkus didn't reply, he was tired. He couldn't help but imagine Craven and Mawling discovering their camp, and Uncle Max realizing Darkus was gone.

'One roll-up mat and a folded blanket, not much of a bed. No windows. White walls, white floor and a white door.'

'What are you doing?' Darkus said.

Virginia was running her fingers around the edge of the door. 'Do you think your thingamabob will open this?'

'Of course it won't,' Darkus snapped. 'Dankish used his fingerprint.'

'Well, we could at least try.' Virginia gave him a pointed look. 'It's better than giving up and sulking.'

Pulling the device out of his pocket, Darkus threw it to Virginia. '*You* try.'

'Thank you. I will.' Virginia turned her back on him and started pressing the screen.

What use were two beetles and two kids against Lucretia Cutter's armies? He'd hoped to come here and rescue his dad, but he'd just made everything worse. Now, Dad would have to do everything Lucretia Cutter asked him to, because she had Darkus in her cell. This was the exact situation his father had warned him about, when they had argued before Christmas. He closed his eyes.

'Darkus?' a soft voice whispered. 'Darkus, is that you?'

'Novak?' Darkus sat up, on his elbows, wondering if

he was imagining things, but Virginia had spun around and was looking at him.

'*Oh, it is you!*'

It was definitely Novak's voice. Darkus looked up at Virginia. 'Novak, Where are you?'

'I'm over here, by the vent.'

Darkus scanned the wall and saw towards the triangular point was a small white air vent. He scrambled over to it, Virginia was right behind him.

'Novak? Are you OK? I'm in here with Virginia.'

'Hello, Virginia.'

'Hi, Novak.'

'Did she . . . put you in the pupation machine thing yet?'

'No. She tried, but your dad and Spencer, they saved me . . .'

'Spencer's here? You've met him?' Darkus looked at Virginia who gave him a double thumbs-up.

'Oh, yes, he's really nice. He's got a dung beetle called Scud.'

'Did you say that Darkus's dad saved you?' Virginia asked.

'Yes. Oh, Darkus, you were right, he *is* on our side. I'm sorry that I said he wasn't.'

Darkus felt a warm flood of relief. 'That's OK.'

'Where's Bertolt? Is he with you?' Novak asked.

'No,' Virginia replied. 'He's with Uncle Max and two other grown-ups.'

'Novak, I've messed things up,' Darkus admitted. 'I wanted to rescue you, Spencer and Dad. I thought it would be better if it was just me and the beetles, slipping in unseen to free you, so I ran off. Virginia tried to stop me, but she couldn't persuade me, and so came with me. Now, Lucretia Cutter has caught us and we're as trapped as you.'

'What about the others?' Novak asked.

'They're outside in the forest,' Darkus replied.

'Well, then, there's still hope,' Novak said.

'I don't think so. Craven and Mawling are being sent out to catch them.'

'Um . . .' Virginia started to say something and then bit down on her lip.

Darkus looked at her; her eyes were wandering all over the place and she was blinking. 'What is it? What's the matter?'

Virginia lowered her head right to the vent, and waved Darkus closer.

'I have to tell you something, but you mustn't get mad,' she mouthed.

Darkus stared at her and nodded.

'We're a decoy,' she whispered. She watched his confusion and winced.

'What do you mean, "we're a decoy?"'

'It wasn't just me that got up when you did last night.' She gave Darkus a meaningful look. 'We *all* got up.'

Darkus shook his head and frowned. He still didn't

understand what she was trying to say.

'It was Bertolt's idea.' Virginia put her finger to her lips. 'We're a decoy,' she whispered again. 'To distract attention from the others. It's good that we got caught.'

'They're *here*?' Darkus hissed.

Virginia nodded, her eyes wide. 'And Craven and Mawling have been sent out to search for them.'

'So the rescue is happening right now!' Novak squeaked.

'I'm tired,' Virginia said loudly, stretching out her arms and doing a fake yawn. 'Let's bring the bed over here and get some rest. We've been up all night and NEED SLEEP.' She looked at Darkus.

Darkus got up and helped her drag the roll mat and the blanket over to the vent. His head was reeling. That whole night trek through the forest, Uncle Max and the others had been following them the whole way? And they were here, inside the Biome? He felt shocked and hurt that they'd made a plan without talking to him – but then, he had planned to go off on his own and leave them. A spark of excitement ignited a tiny blue flame of hope at the thought that the others were here some-where, and they had a plan.

'Let's rest here, until . . .' Virginia paused, '*something wakes us up.*'

On the other side of the grate, Novak had dragged her bed over too. When the three children lay down their heads were beside the air vent, separated only by a wall.

Darkus pulled the blanket over his and Virginia's legs. He turned on his side, his back to Virginia, so he could hold Baxter in the palm of his hand, against his chest.

'Darkus? Virginia?' Novak whispered.

'Yeah,' they both replied, lifting their heads.

'There's something you need to know. There's a man in the cell on the other side of me.'

'The one who was shouting earlier?' Darkus asked.

'Yes.' Novak paused. 'Whatever happens, you must not go near him.'

'What happened to him, he looked . . . I mean, I thought I saw a compound eye.'

'He's been through the pupator. He's very dangerous.'

'Did Lucretia Cutter . . . ?'

'No, he did it to himself, but it's turned him into a monster. He eats people.'

'Eww, gross.' Virginia pulled a face.

'Just, whatever you do,' Novak said, 'stay away from Dr Lenka.'

CHAPTER TWENTY-SEVEN

Unrequited Hate

Pickering paced back and forth in his cell. Something was bothering him and he couldn't put his finger on it. The angry shouts from the man in the cell next door were irritating, yes, but it wasn't that that was bothering him.

'I mean, of course, I've been bitten by a billion nasty beetles,' he muttered to himself, scratching at his itchy thighs through his bright green cotton jumpsuit. 'That must be it.'

He'd hoped for a tuxedo, or at least a suit, to wear when he finally got to see the lovely Lucretia, but

Dankish had said the only spare clothes in the place were the overalls used for mucking out the beetles. Pickering hadn't realized beetles could be mucked out, but he didn't protest about the lurid green jumpsuit handed to him, it was clean and far better than his dirty pants. Humphrey had struggled into the largest size they had, but the poppers didn't do up over his belly, so his waxy white stomach bulged out. Pickering had been secretly delighted. Any fears that he'd had that Lucretia would be more attracted to his cousin than him were banished by the amusing sight of Humphrey bursting out of the outfit like a giant bald baby in an ill-fitting Babygro.

He shook his head. No, it wasn't the bites or the scratches and bruises from the past week in the jungle that were bothering him. It was something else. He was feeling decidedly odd. It was like there was a black hole inside him. He patted his tummy. He wasn't hungry any longer. Dankish had brought him a massive bowl of vegetable stew with a hunk of bread, and it was one of the tastiest things he'd ever eaten. He'd wolfed it down, and now his body was full, but he wasn't happy.

'What is wrong with me?' Pickering sighed and sat down on the floor, leaning his back against the white cell wall, drumming his fingers on his kneecaps.

It must be because I'm going to be seeing my true love soon. He smiled to himself at this thought. Yes! What he was feeling were the butterflies he'd read about in Harriet Harooroo's romance novels. He was nervous and excited, because he knew that once his sweetheart Lucretia heard that Dankish had mistakenly thrown him and Humphrey into the cells, she'd rush here and liberate them. He pictured the delighted expression on her face when she realized that they'd come all the way to the jungle especially to see her. She'd be outraged at their treatment, and apologetic. He imagined her bursting through the doorway, in tears, clasping his head to her breast, apologizing again and again, begging for his forgiveness.

The vision pleased him, but it didn't soothe the black hole in his chest. *It's like someone has died*, he thought. Although, he'd known people who'd died, and he'd never felt like this. Maybe he'd caught some kind of disease in the jungle? He wished that Humphrey was with him, so that he could ask him about it. He frowned, and reminded himself that he and Humphrey were only stuck together because they wanted the money that Lucretia Cutter had promised them. Once they got it, they'd go their own separate ways, and good riddance. Humphrey was a stupid greedy bully, who'd made his life a misery for years.

He looked around the empty white triangular cell. It wasn't very friendly. If he didn't know that Lucretia Cutter would be delighted to see him, he might be a little bit afraid. After all, he was in the middle of a jungle, in a foreign country, in a prison cell, and no one knew he was there. This would all be very scary if he wasn't such good friends with Lucretia Cutter. He wrapped his arms across his chest and hugged himself, wondering how long it would be before she came.

He had to admit, it was boring without Humphrey around. He had no one to talk to. No one to shout at or prod. He hadn't been separated from his cousin in months. They'd shared a prison cell, stayed in the hospital in adjacent beds, slept rough together, journeyed to LA together, squished into bins and the helicopter together, fought the jungle together, waded through the river together – and after all that, they'd been separated.

'Oh, no!' Pickering covered his face with his hands. 'I *miss* him!'

He couldn't believe it. He scrambled to his feet and punched himself hard in the face, knocking himself to the ground. He sat up, examining how he felt, but despite his throbbing nose, he felt the same. He had a giant Humphrey-sized hole inside him. He was never frightened when he was with Humphrey, because his cousin was strong and violent. They did not agree on anything and they argued all the time, but they'd been on the same side since they'd met Lucretia. Pickering didn't have any friends, but Humphrey would at least suffer his company. He was family.

When I next see Humphrey, Pickering thought, *I'm going to thump him really hard and give him a dead arm.* He felt a bit better.

There was a noise outside the cells, voices. Whoever was in the cell next door started banging on the door and shouting to be let out.

Pickering sprang up. Perhaps it was Lucretia Cutter, finally come to get him. He arranged his face into what he hoped was a winning smile and walked to the cell door, expecting it to slide open. When it didn't, he pressed his face up to the little window.

Dankish's chair was empty. There was no one there.

'I must be going mad!' Pickering muttered.

'You were already mad,' came Humphrey's gruff voice.

Pickering turned his head, trying to look to his left, but he couldn't see round as far as the cell next door. 'Humphrey, is that you?'

'Who else is it going to be, you thickie?'

Hearing Humphrey's voice cheered Pickering up. 'We won't have to stay much longer in these cells,' he said. 'I'm sure Lucretia Cutter will come and get us out as soon as she learns we're here.'

'I don't mind it in here,' Humphrey sniffed. 'It's better than being out there with the spiders and the snakes.'

'But don't you want to get our money?'

'I'm beginning to think this is way too much effort for a bunch of money,' Humphrey harrumphed. 'I've had my peanuts bitten by beetles, my front teeth knocked out by monkeys, and I haven't eaten a pie in months. I want to go home.' He sighed. 'If we'd ignored Lucretia Cutter when she'd come to our front door with a handful of dead beetles, we'd still have the Emporium.'

'No, we wouldn't,' Pickering replied. 'The council was going to throw us out, remember?'

'That was your fault for writing to them,' Humphrey grumbled.

'I think you'll find you wrote to them too,' Pickering snapped back.

Humphrey fell silent.

'Don't get downhearted, Humpty. We'll get the half a million pounds Lucretia Cutter owes us, fly home first class and buy a new place to live – we might even be able to find one above a shop.'

'I thought you were going to marry Lucretia Cutter and live with her?'

'Oh, well, err . . . um, obviously, I do love her . . .' It hadn't occurred to Pickering that if he married Lucretia Cutter he'd have to live with her. He looked at the walls of the cell. He wasn't keen on living in the jungle.

'Sorry, I thought for a minute there, you were saying you and I should live together when we get back home.'

'What?' Pickering screeched out a high peal of forced laughter. 'Why would I do that? I mean, we hate each other!' He paused. 'Don't we?'

'Yeah. I hate you,' Humphrey said, moving away from the cell door. 'I'm going to sleep. Night-night.'

'Oh, right, OK.' Pickering turned and looked at his

roll mat, then dragged it over to the wall beside Humphrey's cell. 'Sweet dreams,' he called out as he pulled the blanket over himself.

'Weirdo,' Humphrey called back.

Chapter Twenty-Eight

Team Beetle

Darkus closed his eyes, but he couldn't sleep. Images of an injured Bertolt stumbling through the forest at night, and his father's concerned face, floated into his head. All the people that he cared about were in this Biome, but he didn't know where they were.

Bertolt cried out his name, and then Virginia's. He was searching for them, but they had left him behind. 'Darkus! Virginia! Are you there?'

Darkus blinked open his eyes. He must have drifted off. He'd dreamt that he could hear Bertolt's voice.

'Darkus? Can you hear me?'

He sat bolt upright. His movement triggered a sensor, and the lights came up. Virginia stirred beside him on the floor.

'Virginia,' he shook her, 'wake up. I thought I heard Bertolt's voice.'

Virginia scrambled on to her knees, pulling the square device from her pocket. She pressed a tiny button on the top and spoke into it. 'Bertolt, is that you?'

'Yes, Virginia, I'm here.'

'We've got Novak,' Virginia said.

'I know, I can see you on the security cameras,' Bertolt's voice came out of the device.

'Where are you?' Darkus asked, grabbing it.

'We're in the security dome,' Bertolt replied.

'Is Uncle Max there?'

'We're all here.' Uncle Max's voice came through the device and Darkus felt so relieved that he thought for a second he might cry.

'We hid in a maintenance tunnel until Lucretia Cutter sent Craven and Dankish outside and then we broke in,' Uncle Max said.

Bertolt's voice came back on. 'It took me a bit longer than I thought to hack the comms device, sorry about that.'

'Darkus? Virginia? What's going on?' Novak's voice came through the air vent. 'Is everything OK?'

'Get ready, Novak,' Virginia said into the grate. 'We're about to escape.'

'Listen to me,' Bertolt said. 'I can open the cell doors,

but I don't know which one is which, so I'm going to have to open all of them at once. You need to go and stand at your cell door and get ready to run. There are six cells, one is empty, but the ones to the left of Novak have an angry beetle man, Pickering, and then Humphrey in them. You don't want to get caught by any of them.'

'Can you see Mawling?'

'Yes, he's sleeping.'

'Darkus, listen.' It was Emma Lamb's voice. 'Instead of heading towards Mawling, and the way you came in, you need to go right, the other way. Two metres from your cell, in the floor, is a maintenance tunnel entrance. Go down the ladder and turn right. The tunnel will meet a turning off for a mini dome – that's the staff quarters. Don't take that one. Keep going – the second turning is for the security dome. Your uncle will be there waiting for you.'

'OK, got it.' Darkus nodded. 'Down in to the maintenance tunnel, past the first exit, meet Uncle Max.'

'Good luck,' Bertolt said.

'Bertolt,' Darkus paused, 'thanks for coming to get me.'

'What are friends for?' Bertolt replied. 'Now, I'm going to open all the doors. Are you all ready?'

'Novak, are you by your cell door?' Virginia whispered through the air vent.

'Yes,' replied Novak.

Virginia nodded as she came to stand beside Darkus. He did a quick check to make sure Baxter was OK, on his shoulder, and nodded back.

'We're ready,' Darkus said.

'Go, go, go,' Bertolt said and there was a click as the cell door lifted up.

Darkus ran out and grabbed Novak's hand, following Virginia to the right. She fell on her knees, searching the floor for the maintenance tunnel entrance.

'Got it,' she whispered, lifting the floor tile up. Darkus grabbed it, indicating that Virginia and Novak should climb down first.

Virginia's feet were on the ladder when they all heard a blood-curdling roar.

'It's Dr Lenka!' Novak's eyes were wide. 'Run!'

Virginia bolted down the ladder and Novak raced down after her.

Darkus heard Mawling shout, and then a horrible crunch was followed by a scream of pain.

Darkus froze, hypnotized by the sounds coming round the corner.

Pickering squealed. 'You monster!'

'Aaaarrrrrrrgghhhhhhh!' Mawling cried. 'My hand!'

'Spit his hand out,' Humphrey bellowed.

'*Get down here now!*' Novak called up. Darkus jumped on to the ladder, clambering down. He heard a clatter and the sound of fists flying, and as he yanked the floor tile down over his head he heard Humphrey shout.

'Run! Pickering, run, *RUN!*'

'He will have known we were there, and where we

went,' Novak said between breaths, as they ran down the tunnel away from Dr Lenka. 'He has beetle senses. We have to hope he doesn't decide to come after us.'

They passed the turning to the first dome and slowed down to a gentle jog, so they could catch their breath.

Novak tipped her head. 'I don't think he's following us,' she said, listening.

'How did Bertolt and Uncle Max get into the Biome?' Darkus asked Virginia.

'We let them in.'

'We did?'

'Do you remember that sneeze, when we were at the edge of the forest, and I told you to run, just as the trap-door opened? That was them. They were following us the whole time. I was worried that the tapir might have separated them from us.'

'But, but . . . how?'

'Emma knew about these tunnels. She has a map of them.' Virginia smiled. 'I got you down the ladder, and blocked your view as quickly as possible, so you didn't see them run into the Biome behind us. They went down a different ladder, to a tunnel that led straight to the security dome. Then they waited for us to get caught.'

'You could have told me.' Darkus felt a spark of anger, but knew it was his pride that was hurting.

'Darkus, you weren't listening to anyone,' Virginia pointed out. 'We're a team, but you were planning on going solo. We didn't know what to do, so we decided to support you all the way, until you needed us, which now you do, because Lucretia Cutter caught you.' She grinned. 'You can't be mad that we guessed this would happen. We let you go it alone anyway, turned it to our advantage and then rescued you.'

Darkus blushed. 'I guess not,' he admitted.

'We started this as a team and we will finish it as a team.' Virginia put out her hand. 'Team Beetle.'

'Team Beetle.' Novak laid her hand on top of Virginia's.

Darkus put his hand on top of Novak's. Baxter

fluttered down from Darkus's shoulder, landing clumsily on the back of his hand, lifting his horn high, as Hepburn scrambled out of her bracelet, and Marvin dropped from Virginia's braid, tumbling down her arm, landing beside Baxter.

'Team Beetle,' Darkus said.

CHAPTER TWENTY-NINE

Out of the Jaws of Beetles

Uncle Max was waiting at the next junction. He opened his arms and Darkus ran straight into them. 'I'm sorry. I'm so sorry,' he mumbled into his uncle's shirt.

'This is not the time for apologies.' Uncle Max tipped Darkus's chin up so that he could look into his eyes. 'This is the time for a daring rescue.' He waggled his eyebrows. 'As far as we can tell, Lucretia Cutter has no idea that we're here. So we need to act quickly. C'mon, this way, Bertolt's waiting.'

Darkus followed Virginia and Novak up a ladder,

Uncle Max behind him. He blinked furiously as his eyes adjusted to the light. A quick sweep of the room told him he was in a security control centre. There was a wall of monitors, each one showing a different part of the Biome.

'Oh, Bertolt, thank you!' Novak rushed past Darkus, grabbing Bertolt, kissing him on both cheeks. Newton zipped around their heads, flashing with delight. 'Thank you for rescuing us.'

'Welcome back to the squadron, soldier.' Emma Lamb saluted Darkus, and Motty smiled at the children over her gold-rimmed spectacles.

Bertolt limped over to Darkus, punching his arm weakly and then hugging him.

'What was that for?' Darkus laughed.

'I'm cross with you for running off and trying to do this alone. Virginia would have given you a dead arm' – Virginia nodded – 'so I thought *I* should – but then I didn't want to hurt you, so I gave you a hug.'

Newton flew over and landed on Darkus's shoulder beside Baxter, and the two beetles waggled their antennae at each other in silent conversation.

'I'm sorry, Bertolt. I shouldn't have run away. We're a team and I promise I'll never forget it again.' Bertolt nodded. 'And you are amazing, walking through the forest all night with your bad leg.'

'Thanks.' Bertolt blushed, proudly.

'How did you know you could talk to us through the

thingamabob?' Darkus asked.

'I spotted that when I first looked at it.' Bertolt smiled. 'I noticed a tiny circle of mesh, which usually covers a microphone. On each side are two tiny squares – speakers. When we got in here, I set up an exclusive frequency, so that I could talk to you on the device without anyone else listening.'

'You're a genius.' Darkus shook his head. 'Was it you that came up with the idea to use me as a decoy?'

'Ah, no, that was me, I'm afraid,' Uncle Max admitted. 'I thought we should turn your headstrong attitude to our advantage.'

'It was a good idea,' Darkus said, ruefully, 'but Lucretia Cutter has taken the Base Camp beetles from me, and she hurt Baxter.'

'Is he OK?' Uncle Max leant over to look at the rhinoceros beetle.

'She bit one of his legs off,' Darkus replied, 'and he had a fall. He's weak, but he seems to be recovering.'

Baxter waved a foreleg at Uncle Max, to reassure him.

'What about the fireflies?' Bertolt asked.

'She's got them too,' Darkus said.

'Oh no!' Bertolt gasped and Newton flickered anxiously.

'We'll get them back,' Virginia said. 'Don't worry.'

Darkus stepped towards the monitors, scanning the screens. 'Have you seen Dad? Or Spencer?' he asked.

'No,' Bertolt shook his head. 'Everyone's asleep.'

'Can you see into the room by the lift? The one in the basement.' Darkus asked, his eyes flicking from screen to screen.

'This dark one?' Bertolt asked.

'Yes.' Darkus pointed up to the screen. 'Can you zoom in on the tanks that are in there?'

Bertolt frowned. 'I'll try.'

The camera picked out the dark outline of a tank, but none of the detail of what was in it.

'In this room,' Darkus turned around to talk to everyone, 'are four tanks. In each one is a giant pupa.' He took a deep breath. 'Each contains a clone of Lucretia Cutter.'

'She's cloning herself?' Emma Lamb gasped.

Darkus nodded. 'Whatever happens, we have to destroy those pupae.'

'Look, there are the prison cells.' Virginia pointed at the six empty rooms, all doors open.

'Did you see what happened to Mawling?' Darkus looked at Bertolt.

Bertolt grimaced.

'Is he . . . dead?' Novak asked.

'No, but, um, well . . .' Bertolt stammered.

'There's no nice way to say it.' Uncle Max cleared his throat. 'Mawling tried to punch that giant bug man in the face.'

'He punched Dr Lenka?' Novak said.

'That thing is Henrik Lenka?' Emma Lamb whistled.

'What happened?' Novak pressed.

'Henrik Lenka caught Mawling's fist in his mouth and chewed his hand to pieces.' He shook his head. 'I've never seen anything like it. It was brutal.'

'Did he get away?' Novak clasped her hands together.

'Humphrey and Pickering tried to run past the fighting men,' Bertolt said. 'Dr Lenka shoved Humphrey backwards, which made him angry. He roared and barrelled into the bug man's stomach like an angry bull, pushing him back into his cell.'

'Humphrey knocked Dr Lenka on to his back,' Uncle Max said. 'Lenka struggled to get back on his feet.'

'Then all three of them ran away,' Bertolt finished.

'Where are they now?' Darkus turned back to the screens.

Bertolt pointed.

'It's the infirmary,' Novak said. 'I was there yesterday.'

Darkus could see Mawling lying on a bed, trying to bandage his own arm. There was blood everywhere.

Pickering was looking in a mirror, liberally applying cream to the insect bites all over his face and neck, while Humphrey was looking at bottles of pills, reading the labels.

'Are they helping him?' Darkus asked.

Bertolt shrugged. 'After Humphrey knocked down the bug man, he slung Mawling over his shoulder, and carried him here, but I think they needed his help with directions.'

They watched Humphrey open a pot of pills and

empty them into his mouth, then carry on picking up pots and reading labels.

'If Mawling is in the infirmary, and Craven is with Dankish searching the jungle, then we only have to worry about Ling Ling and Lucretia Cutter,' Darkus said.

'Only!' Virginia rolled her eyes. 'Oh, boy, I hope you've got a plan.'

'As it happens,' Darkus stood up straight, 'I do.'

Chapter Thirty

Rhipicera femorata

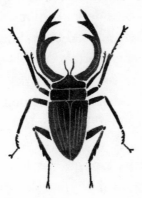

'There's Gerard!' Novak let out a little cry and leant towards the wall of monitors. Darkus saw a bedroom. The butler was rising and going about the business of getting dressed. 'Darkus, I can't leave him here,' she said. 'Can we bring him with us?'

Darkus nodded. 'Yes, although I've no idea how we're going to get out of here.'

'I think I've got that covered,' Motty said. 'There's a beautiful helicopter out there, a Sikorsky S-92. They're the best in the business, two hundred million dollars apiece.'

'Can you fly that thing?' Uncle Max asked, impressed.

Motty shrugged. 'How different can it be from a plane?'

'Don't you need a key?' Virginia asked.

'No, cars start with keys, not helicopters.' Motty chuckled. 'If the doors have a locking system I'll bet one of those will open them.' She pointed to a rack of keys on the wall.

'Motty will go outside and commandeer our escape vehicle.' Uncle Max said, and Motty nodded.

'I'm staying here,' Bertolt said, stepping up to the desk of buttons and switches. 'My leg would only slow me down, and I can help by communicating what I see on the screens – *and* I can control all the doors from here.'

'What do those buttons do?' Darkus asked.

'This is power, I think.' Bertolt waved at a grid of switches. 'These are the lights, and this is the climate control system.'

'The what?'

'Look – here are the different domes, and this counter shows the oxygen percentage in the air. This is a thermo-stat for the whole Biome, but there's also one for each dome, and I think this is a sprinkler system for watering the plants.'

Darkus's mind was racing. 'OK, this is what we are going to do. Bertolt will open all the doors between the beetle farm and freedom. Then find a way to turn the heating down in the big dome, right down, as cold as you can make it.'

Bertolt nodded. 'I'm sure I can do that.'

'And the oxygen, you need to bring it down to a normal level.'

'20.95 per cent?'

'Yes.' Darkus nodded.

'But why?' Virginia asked. 'We'll lose our superpowers, and we may need them in a fight.'

'Yes but if *we* have superpowers, then so does everyone else. If we dial the oxygen down to a normal level, it will give us a fighting chance, because beetles like it warm and oxygen-rich. Less oxygen and a colder temperature will slow down Lucretia Cutter and Lenka.'

'Speaking of the bug bloke . . .' Emma Lamb pointed. 'Look.'

On one of the monitors, they could see Dr Lenka in a room full of giant emerald-green tiger beetles. He grabbed one of the largest beetles around the head and was strapping a muzzle over its jaws. They all watched, transfixed, as he lifted a bizarre-looking clear bubble helmet with a bag attached from a row of similar devices on the wall, and fixed it to the beetle's head.

'What is that?' Darkus said.

'I believe . . .' Uncle Max paused, 'it's an oxygen mask. The only thing I've ever seen that looked vaguely like it is a First World War horses' gas mask.'

Dr Lenka leapt up on to the beetle's back and with a whip that he held in his right hand he harried the beetle out of view.

'He's riding a giant beetle, like a stallion,' Virginia said.

'There he goes.' Bertolt pointed at a different monitor. The tiger beetle was fast, speeding down a corridor, nimbly running upstairs.

'The trapdoor's opening.' Emma Lamb pointed.

They all watched, spellbound, as Dr Lenka fled the Biome on the back of a giant tiger beetle wearing an oxygen mask.

'Now I've seen everything.' Uncle Max shook his head. 'Well, at least we don't have to worry about him eating us.'

'What happened to make him . . .' Emma searched for the words, 'I mean how did he get like that? You know, half beetle.'

'He pupated himself, hoping to please Mater,' Novak explained. 'He introduced the DNA of a carrion beetle into his own body and experienced metamorphosis.'

'A carrion beetle?' Darkus gasped.

Novak nodded. 'That's why he eats flesh.'

'Wait.' Darkus looked at Novak. 'Do you know which beetle DNA Lucretia Cutter has?'

She nodded. 'Titan.'

'I knew it.' Darkus was pleased that he'd guessed correctly.

'And what about you?' Virginia asked. 'Do you know what beetle DNA you have?'

'*You* are half beetle?' Emma Lamb's eyes grew wide.

'I'm sorry, I didn't know. You look so normal.'

'*Rhipicera femorata*,' Novak replied. 'The feather-horned beetle.'

'But you don't have horns,' Virginia said.

'Actually,' Novak tipped her head, so her chin touched her chest and her silver hair fell over her face, 'I do.' She lifted her antennae, and then her head, rolling back her human eyes and opening her compound ones.

'Whoa!' Darkus stared at Novak's flagellate antennae, as silver and delicate as the finest lace hair, fanning out and twitching as they tasted the air.

'You're beautiful!' Bertolt whispered, stepping forward and taking Novak's hands.

'That is *seriously* cool!' Virginia shook her head in disbelief. 'Can you do things? Can you see things? I mean, what is it like? Does it hurt to do the eye-rolling thing? I mean, how does that even work? Can you fly? Do you have elytra?' She craned her neck to try and look at Novak's back.

'Virginia!' Bertolt's sharp bark silenced her. 'Don't be so rude.'

'Sorry.' Virginia looked shamefaced and bobbed her head apologetically. 'But you are *totally awesome*, Novak.'

'Thanks.' Novak smiled bashfully and turned to Darkus. 'I did what you said. I've been trying to build up my beetle senses. But it's still very new, because I've covered it up for so long.'

Darkus stepped forward awkwardly, 'You shouldn't

ever hide who you are. You're brilliant.'

Novak's smile grew into a wide beam. 'Oh, thank you.'

'Ahem,' Uncle Max coughed politely, 'Novak, you are lovely, but time is of the essence. Motty's going for the chopper, Bertolt will stay here and man the screens. Darkus, what do you want us to do?'

'I want to stay here with Bertolt,' Emma said. 'I can see everything that is happening from here, which will help when it comes to writing up this crazy story. Also, if Motty's going to fire up the helicopter, I can help Bertolt get outside when we're ready to go.'

Darkus nodded. 'Good. Uncle Max, you come with me and Virginia.'

'I'm coming with you. Your father will be wherever Mater is,' Novak said, her silver antennae turning towards Darkus. 'I can't let you fight Mater alone, but I need to find Gerard first.'

Darkus dipped his head. 'OK, Bertolt, keep your eyes peeled for Dad on the screens. Let me know where he is and we'll head straight for him.'

'Got it.' Bertolt nodded.

'OK, good luck, everyone.' Darkus let out a deep breath.

CHAPTER THIRTY-ONE

Beetle Run

As they ran along the corridor beside the hatchery, the thingamabob buzzed in Darkus's pocket. He pulled it out.

'There's a man getting out of the lift on your level,' Bertolt said. 'He's coming your way – *you need to hide.*'

Darkus, Virginia and Uncle Max darted through the door into the Hercules larvae room.

'Wait.' Novak stayed out in the corridor, her antennae twitching. 'I think it's Spencer.'

Darkus looked down at the giant larvae. He made a high-pitched noise with his mouth, mimicking stridulation, to get their attention. The larvae moved, their plump white bodies undulating as their heads churned in his direction. 'Baxter, you have to tell them. Explain they've been born into a world that doesn't have an atmosphere they can breathe. Tell them they are slaves. Tell them we're opening all the doors. That they have a choice to stay here or be free. Tell them to spread the word.' He crouched down and held Baxter close to the waggling head of the nearest curious larvae.

'Darkus, it *is* Spencer!' Virginia said.

Darkus waited until Baxter had finished talking to the larvae, and then came into the corridor to find a confused young man staring at Novak. He looked just like the pictures all over Iris Crips's mantelpiece.

'Did she put you in the pupator again?' Spencer asked, looking up at Novak's antennae.

'No,' Novak replied. 'This is me.'

Darkus spotted the dung beetle, Scud, poking his head out of Spencer's lab coat pocket. 'Hello, Spencer. I'm Darkus.' He smiled and held out his hand.

'Dr Cuttle's son?' Spencer blinked furiously through his rectangular glasses as he shook Darkus's hand. 'How did you get in here?

'It's a long story, but we're here to honour a promise we made your mum, to bring you home,' Darkus said. 'She misses you.'

'She knows where I am?' Spencer swallowed, and Darkus saw his eyes fill up. He nodded. 'She knows

Lucretia Cutter took you.'

'I'm Virginia.' Virginia grabbed Spencer's hand and shook it.

'Maximilian Cuttle.' Uncle Max took Spencer's hand from Virginia. 'I'm Barty's brother.'

Spencer looked past them down the corridor. 'Are there only four of you?'

'There are *seven* of us,' Darkus replied. 'With you and Dad, and Gerard, that makes ten, and then there are the beetles, but we don't need lots of people,' he smiled, 'because we're not here to fight.'

'You might not have a choice.' Spencer pushed his rectangular glasses up his nose, then gaped as a walrus-sized grub dragged its white belly forward, with six stubby amber legs, out into the corridor. It was swiftly followed by another. 'What the . . .?'

'We're setting all the beetles free,' Darkus grinned.

Spencer's eyes grew wide. 'You're doing what?'

'We're setting them free,' Virginia echoed. 'Darkus, I'm going to head up the ladder to the giant adult beetles.'

'Wait,' Spencer said, pulling off a backpack. 'Is this yours? I've been sent to take it to the dissection lab. It's full of beetles.'

Darkus whooped as he grabbed his bag from Spencer and unzipped it. Twenty-seven fireflies shot out of the top of it, fizzing and flickering. 'It's OK, my friends. It's me,' he called calmly up to them. 'Bertolt is along the corridor and up the ladder. I'm sure he'll have the trapdoor open by the time you get there.' They flew off to find their favourite human.

Darkus held the rucksack open and Virginia put her hands into it, pulling them out covered in shimmering purple and green jewel beetles. The beetles marched up her arms and parked on her shoulders.

'We're actually going to escape!' Spencer's eyes lit up.

'That's the plan.' Virginia grinned at him, stepping on to the ladder.

'I can help you.' Spencer sprang forward and Scud waggled his forelegs excitedly. 'I feed the adult beetles every day. They know me, and I know where the others are – Lucretia Cutter's Darwin beetles and her stags.'

'We'll meet you out by the helicopter once we've got Dad and Gerard,' Darkus said.

'Brilliant.' Virginia stepped off the bottom of the ladder and gestured for Spencer to go first. 'Lead the way.'

He climbed up past her. 'It will be my pleasure.'

'Gracious me!' Uncle Max exclaimed, pressing himself up against the wall as a flood of migrating larvae wormed their way towards freedom. 'These things move fast!'

Picking their way through the stampede of giant larvae, they came to the beetle borg room. Darkus ran in, followed by Uncle Max and Novak, and they opened each and every Perspex tank, making gentle clicking noises as they did it. One by one, they peeled the chips off the beetle's thoraxes, while Baxter explained to the monkey beetles and the giant African flower beetles that they were free to leave.

'Have you done them all?' Novak asked.

'Yes, but Novak . . .' Darkus replied, 'I know you're worried about Gerard. Why don't you see if you can find him? Tell him what's going on.'

'OK,' Novak smiled. 'He'll be in the kitchens, sorting out breakfast. I'll come find you straight after.' she called out as she dashed away along the corridor.

Ever since he'd seen the four cloned pupae in the next room, Darkus had tried to put them from his mind. He knew they had to be destroyed, but he didn't want Novak to see it happen.

'Are you ready?' he asked Uncle Max.

'Ready as I'll ever be.' Uncle Max nodded.

Darkus spoke into the device as he entered the darkened room. 'Bertolt, are you there?'

'I'm here,' came the immediate reply. 'All the Biome doors are open, and I can see on the monitors that the beetles are on the move.'

'Blistering bombardiers!' Uncle Max exclaimed as he peered into one of the tanks.

'Listen. I'm in the room with the Lucretia Cutter clones. Can you see if there's a lock for this door? Preferably one that can't be opened ever again.'

'Yup, I've got it,' Bertolt replied. 'Tell me when to shoot the bolt.'

Darkus walked over to the glowing thermostat and turned the dial down to freezing as Uncle Max lifted down an axe from the fire safety unit on the wall beside the furthest tank. Darkus reminded himself what Professor Appleyard had told them, that freezing insects was the humane way to kill them.

'Stand back, Darkus,' Uncle Max said, 'Glass will fly.'

'I've done the thermostat,' Darkus said, backing towards the door.

'Here we go.' Uncle Max lifted the axe high above his head and brought it down with a jarring shock, smashing the first tank. There was a hissing noise as the atmosphere inside the tank seeped out. He strode swiftly to the next tank and swung the axe in an arc, bringing it down to destroy the second tank, and then he was at the third. 'One more to go!' he called out as he strode over to the fourth, hurling the axe up and letting it fall with a crack and shatter on to the house of the final Lucretia pupa.

The momentum of the axe seemed to turn the glass into a million droplets of water which cascaded away from the giant pupa. It writhed and wriggled its rear end, rolling off the bed and on to the floor at Uncle Max's feet. He jumped back as the features of Lucretia Cutter's beetle face pressed against the hard white skin of the pupa. Her jaws opened wide, splitting it, and she began to emerge, wriggling violently and biting viciously at the air. A clawed foreleg shot out of the pupa.

Uncle Max ran towards the door. Darkus was already outside. The beetle arm grabbed Uncle Max's ankle, its sharp claws cutting through his skin.

'Arghhh!' Uncle Max roared in pain, dragged himself towards the door, the pupa clinging to his ankle.

'Bertolt, are you there?' Darkus cried.

'Here.'

Uncle Max hurled his body forward through the doorway.

'NOW!' Darkus shouted. 'LOCK IT NOW!'

The door dropped down and there was a crunch.

Uncle Max looked down. A chitinous claw was wrapped around his bloodied ankle, but it was no longer attached to a beetle leg. 'That was a close shave!' he said, bending down and prising the razor-sharp pincer off his foot.

'Are you OK?' Darkus asked.

'Oh, yes.' Uncle Max dusted off his hands and grinned. 'I've wrestled with alligators, lad. That was nothing!'

Bertolt guided them into the lift and up to the corridor outside the laboratory, where Darkus's dad was talking to Lucretia Cutter.

Darkus peeped round the corner and drew back. Ling Ling was stationed at the door. 'How are we going to get past her?' he whispered. 'Ling Ling's deadly.'

'We need to get her away from the door.' Uncle Max frowned.

'I could send Baxter to distract her,' he looked at his shoulder, 'but I'm not sure he's strong enough and I don't think she'd fall for it.'

'I'll make her chase me,' Uncle Max suggested.

'But your ankle, and what if she catches you?'

'I'll run fast, down those stairs.' Uncle Max pointed. 'I'll lead her into the jungle and lose her amongst the trees. Then I'll swing back here, meet you and we'll go and face Lucretia Cutter.'

'OK,' Darkus nodded.

'Righto.' Uncle Max crept to the edge of the wall where the corridor intersected.

'I'm ready,' Darkus whispered, retreating back round a corner to hide.

'Do not, under any circumstances, go into that room without me. Do you hear me?' Uncle Max hissed, before taking a step out into the corridor and whistling a tune loudly. He looked towards Ling Ling, said, 'Oh, crikey!' and sprinted across the corridor and down the stairs. Seconds later Ling Ling burst into view, running sound-lessly after him, her hands held up like knives.

Darkus crept back to the intersection and peered around the corner. Leaning up against the wall, where Ling Ling had been standing was a harpoon gun. *Why would Ling Ling need a gun?* he wondered, then an image of Dr Lenka chewing off Mawling's hand sprang into his head, and he knew why. *Lucretia Cutter must know her cells are empty.*

'Uncle Max said not to go into the laboratory,' Darkus whispered to Baxter, 'but he didn't say anything about sneaking up to the doorway and grabbing a very handy weapon.'

He shuffled forward, wondering if he'd be able to see his dad from the doorway. He desperately wanted to catch a glimpse of him, just to make sure he was OK. He reached the weapon and wrapped his hand around the handle of the harpoon gun, putting his other hand on the shaft, lifting it. The gun was reassuringly heavy. He brought it up to his shoulder and looked down the sight line. It sent a thrill of power through his body, and he stood a little taller. He'd never held a weapon before.

He could hear Lucretia Cutter's voice. Was she talking to his dad? He leant forward, craning his neck to hear.

'What do you say, Bartholomew? Shall I unleash my rice weevils in China? They have a lot of stored grain. If I wipe it out, it certainly would take this game up to the next level, don't you think? The political situation would become *very* interesting if we brought China into play. Did you know their rice harvest is the most valuable on the planet? I might tell them that the American president is a fan of the idea.' She laughed. 'Isn't this fun? Eeny-meeny-miny-moe, which population is next to go?'

CHAPTER THIRTY-TWO

Anthropocene

'**N**o!' Darkus shouted, standing in the doorway of the laboratory, shaking with anger. He raised the gun, pointing the harpoon at Lucretia Cutter. 'I won't let you.'

'Ha! Look, Bartholomew, it's your son, the hero.' Lucretia Cutter threw her human hands in the air, and said with mock fear: 'Oh, no, please don't shoot me.'

'Darkus, what are you doing here?' His dad looked shocked. 'Lucy, did you know he was here?'

'You are an evil, power-hungry monster!' Darkus said, suddenly aware of how heavy the harpoon gun was, and the panicked look on his dad's face.

'Darkus, put the gun down,' his dad said, taking a step towards him.

'NO!' Darkus cried, rage suddenly sweeping away every intention he'd had not to fight. 'You said you were going to try and stop her, but you're doing nothing! You're standing by her side as she sends beetles out into the world to destroy harvests and start wars. Millions of people will starve. Children will die. Don't you care?'

'Darkus, son, listen to me. It's not that simple.'

'Yes, it is. She wants the world to bow down to her.' Darkus straightened his arms, pointing the gun at Lucretia Cutter's heart, his finger on the trigger. 'She's breeding an army of giant beetles, and cloning herself.'

'Cloning?' Barty looked at Lucretia Cutter, and she shrugged, feigning ignorance.

'She kills without thinking or feeling anything. She kidnapped you. She burnt down Beetle Mountain. She's forcing millions of people to die of starvation. She's a killer.'

'Answer me this, Darkus,' Lucretia Cutter hissed his name. 'How many creatures do you think mankind has killed?'

'I don't care,' Darkus shouted, 'it doesn't change what *you* are.'

'Isn't an animal life still a life? Isn't it just as bad to kill an elephant as it is to kill a human? Let's talk about extinction. Let's say it's not as bad to kill an animal as it is to kill a man, but how about destroying every single type of elephant that ever existed? Is that as bad as killing one human? How do *you* measure life and death, Darkus?'

'Lucy, he's just a child.'

'You underestimate your own son, Bartholomew,' she snapped. 'This is the boy who befriended thousands of beetles, broke into my house, rescued you and took a bullet for you. He followed me to America and ruined my broadcast at the Film Awards, and now, he's somehow made his way to Ecuador, into the Amazon cloud forest and found my Biome, when all the governments of the world have failed.' She stared at Darkus, her antennae twitching. 'And now he's pointing a harpoon gun at me, looking as if he wants to kill me.' She snorted. 'I would not call him "just" a child.'

Lucretia Cutter took a step towards him and Darkus shuffled back, trying to move towards his father, without taking his eyes off her.

'Darkus, I'm not destroying the crops out of a desire to rule, but out of necessity. The human race is growing. The planet cannot cope.' She shook her head. 'As humanity spreads like a plague, we chop down rain-forests and flush plastic into our oceans, we release carbon dioxide into the atmosphere, causing the planet to heat up.' She opened her arms as if she were going to offer him an embrace. 'The ice caps are melting, habitats are being destroyed. We live in a new epoch, the

Anthropocene. Humanity is changing the climate, and it is a time of mass extinction.' She bent down, so that her face was at his height. 'How does that make you feel, Darkus? To be growing up in a time when the worst thing for this planet is your own species? You say that I am greedy for money and power, but you're wrong. Look at me.' She framed her face with her human hands, inching forward. 'I'm a beetle. What use do I have for money? I can't bear what we are doing to this planet. It tears at my heart and mind every day. I was ashamed to be a human, and so now,' she held up her arms, proud, '*I am a beetle.*' She stepped closer. 'I cannot stand idle, not when I have the power to do something. I will stop human population growth by cutting off the food supply. Hunger will make the humans fight for food, and they will kill each other. A cull, if you will. We justify culling deer or badgers for the greater good – well, I'm culling humans. When I rule the world, people will have to request permission to have a child. I'll re-wild the planet. Humans will live in urban habitats, powered by eco-fuels and the only jobs available will be as planet gardeners.'

Darkus stared into Lucretia Cutter's fathomless black eyes and his arms burnt from the weight of the harpoon gun.

'Doesn't that sound good, Darkus?' She moved a bit closer, nodding. 'Hmmm? Wouldn't you like to be a planet gardener? Wouldn't it be *better* with the beetles in charge?'

Darkus felt Baxter's horn against his neck, the soft

brush of wings against his skin telling him the rhinoceros beetle was frightened and ready to fly. He heard a low warning hiss.

'No!' Darkus shouted, jumping back. 'You're no beetle. You are the very worst kind of human. You think you know better than everyone else alive. You built a mountain of money and power from making people feel that they're not pretty, or wearing the wrong clothes, and now you're using it to force the whole world to agree with you. Do you think a beetle would do that? *NO!*' He stamped his foot. 'Beetles are noble, hard-working, selfless creatures.' He looked at Baxter. 'They are true heroes, and *you*, you have,' he struggled for a word, '*perverted* that. You have turned beetles into an army, into a plague. You have made them monsters in the world's eyes.' He was so angry he was shaking.

'Enough!' Lucretia Cutter turned her back on Darkus.

'No, *you will* listen to me.' Darkus was adamant. 'Do you know what the real battle is? It's teaching people how important, how beautiful, beetles are – all insects are. If people went outside and said good morning to the insects in their garden, knowing how they helped make things grow, then they wouldn't fear them or kill them with pesticides. But you,' he poked Lucretia Cutter's back with the harpoon gun, 'you've given people a reason to fear, to want to kill them.' He shook his head. 'The real battle of the beetles is not to conquer the world, but to be appreciated and understood. Turning yourself into a beetle and killing lots of humans won't win that battle or change anything. The human race will rise up and fight back. You will bring war and destruction. It's a *human* instinct to be violent first and think second, and that is exactly what *you* have done. It doesn't matter if you have six legs, two elytra and compound eyes, you are behaving like a human. YOU WILL ALWAYS BE A HUMAN!'

Bartholomew Cuttle was looking at Darkus with pride. 'He's right!'

'No, he's *not*!' Lucretia Cutter whirled around.

'Son!' his dad cried out as Lucretia knocked the harpoon gun from Darkus's hand and grabbed him with her middle legs, lifting him off the ground.

'Dad!' Darkus cried out as he felt the spikes on Lucretia Cutter's legs scratch his stomach. She held one of her sharp claws against his throat.

Baxter reared up, flying up from Darkus's shoulder, charging at Lucretia's eye. He struck a blow, but he was weak and she barely noticed, smacking him out of the air as if swatting an irritating fly.

'Baxter!'

'Lucy, put him down.'

'Now we shall see whether you're really committed to the Fabre Project,' she spat.

'Lucy, Darkus has nothing to do with this. Just let him go and I, I . . .' Darkus could see the fear in his father's eyes.

'You'll what?' Lucretia looked down at Bartholomew.

'What are you prepared to do, in exchange for the life of your son? Hmmmmm?'

'Lucy, don't.'

'How about stepping into my pupator?'

'No! Dad!' Darkus felt like his chest was going to burst open. This was what his father had been frightened of. *If she has you, son, she'll be able to make me do anything.*

'Lucy, I . . .' Bartholomew's shoulders slumped and Darkus saw him give in. Just like that. And Lucretia Cutter knew it too. She laughed, a peal of spite. Darkus punched and kicked at her abdomen, not caring how her spikes tore his skin.

'I have everything prepared,' she said, ignoring Darkus's struggling. 'I thought you'd like to be bonded with the genes of the Goliath beetle that started this whole beautiful project.'

Barty's head snapped up, his expression shocked. 'You have Prometheus?'

'Of course. Where do you think I got your DNA from?' Lucretia smiled. 'Esme gave him to me.'

'Esme?' His father's voice was strangled.

'Yes, Bartholomew. When you and that old fool Appleyard decided to abandon the Fabre Project and close it down, some of us refused to let our years of work be tossed away like garbage. Esme believed, like I do, that something needs to be done to change the path humanity is on. The path of self-destruction. She happily gave me Prometheus, and copies of the parts of your work that I needed.'

'Mum helped you?' Darkus couldn't believe what he was hearing.

Bartholomew was shaking his head. 'No. She wouldn't have done that.'

'Your mother was an eco-warrior,' Lucretia Cutter told Darkus. 'More militant than your father here. She wanted the work of the Fabre Project to continue, but oh no, Appleyard and Cuttle decreed that the work was leading us down a dangerous path, and that was it, all the funding stopped. So I took it upon myself to continue, and set up a fashion business to fund the work. Esme did what she could to help.'

'You're lying,' Barty growled.

'*Am* I?' Lucretia laughed. 'Then how do you explain this?' She opened a specimen drawer beneath the lab work bench and pulled out a dead Goliath beetle by the pin stabbed through its elytra and abdomen.

Bartholomew gasped.

'You see, and soon you'll know what it feels like to be him.' She waved her human hand towards the room that contained the pupator. 'Go on. In you get.'

'Dad, no!' Darkus shouted, struggling desperately to free himself from Lucretia Cutter's iron grasp.

His father looked at him with sad eyes. He swallowed. 'I love you, son,' he said, then he turned and walked through the metal door into the room behind the glass and up the steps into the pupator.

'NO!' Darkus screamed, as Lucretia Cutter slammed her hand down on a button on the control board and the door slid closed. He kicked at her, and she tightened her grasp on his neck, choking him, then flung him hard, into the corner. He hit the wall, and all the breath was yanked from his body. He fell, landing awkwardly on his wrist, which made a snapping sound, and he cried out in pain and anguish. 'Dad . . .'

'Pathetic,' Lucretia Cutter snarled. 'Enjoy the last minutes of your life, because after you've watched your daddy transform into a beetle, I'm going to order him to kill you.' She laughed and pressed a series of buttons, turning lights on. A strange whining noise came from the pupator.

'*You will not touch him or his father!*' came a cry, and Darkus looked up to see Novak somersault into the room. Her antennae were up and her eyes black as she hurled a barrage of kicks at her mother.

Lucretia Cutter, taken by surprise, was knocked to the ground. On her back, for a moment she seemed comical, her beetle legs flailing around in the air, but then her human arms pushed against the floor, and she was on six legs, close to the ground, scuttling towards her daughter. Novak let out a strangled cry, the kind Darkus had heard in kung-fu movies, as she delivered a jumping front kick, her foot landing under Lucretia Cutter's chin and firing her head back with force.

'Novak, where's Gerard?' Darkus asked.

'With your uncle,' she replied. 'He's hurt.'

Ling Ling ran into the room. She blinked at Darkus, her face blank.

Lucretia Cutter snarled, 'Ling Ling! Get her!'

Darkus looked at Ling Ling in alarm. There was no way Novak could fight her and Lucretia Cutter, but the bodyguard's face remained a blank. She didn't move.

Darkus threw himself across the floor, dragging his body to the console, pulling himself up with his good arm, before Ling Ling could stop him. He hit the same buttons he'd seen Lucretia Cutter press. The lights went off inside the pupator, and the whining noise died away. He sank down to the floor and saw Baxter, stuck on his back, five legs waggling, under the desk. He scooped the rhinoceros beetle up.

'I need to get Dad out of there,' he said to Baxter,

'but how?'

Lucretia's elytra flicked up, and her wings unfolded. She rose up into the air, shaking off the impact of Novak's blow.

Novak spun around, running at the wall, her claws gripping as she rose up three metres before vaulting backwards in an arch, bringing both her clawed feet down on top of Lucretia Cutter's head, making her scream.

'I'm going to rip you apart!' Lucretia cried, throwing herself after Novak, who cartwheeled and flipped away. Lucretia towered over her daughter, but although she was stronger, she was clumsy.

Darkus glanced at Ling Ling. She was just standing still watching Novak, probably waiting until the girl made a mistake and let her guard down. He had to do something to help his friend. He pulled the device from his pocket. 'Bertolt, I need you to turn the oxygen down in here. Do you hear me? I need you to turn the oxygen right down.'

'I hear you, Darkus. I'm on it. Are you OK?'

Darkus couldn't reply, his eyes were locked on the fighting mother and daughter.

'Darkus, beetles are flooding out of the Biome. There's a sea of them.'

'Beetles? Yes! That's it! Bertolt, is there an intercom? Does the Biome have an intercom?'

'Yes! Patching you through right now,' Bertolt replied.

Darkus tried to stand, but his hip burnt. He looked at his right hand hanging limply from his broken wrist. The fire of pain up his arm was so intense that he thought he might pass out. It was all he could do to keep focused on Novak, who whirled and danced around her biological mother like a sprite, landing kicks and scratches wherever she was able. He must help her. He tilted his head back and holding the device to his mouth with his good hand, he sucked his back teeth and made a pattern of clicking sounds, repeated it, again and again.

Dad was trapped inside the pupator and he didn't know how to get the door open. Uncle Max was hurt and Gerard was with him. Ling Ling was standing like a statue and Lucretia Cutter was wearing Novak down with the strength of her blows. They needed help.

He called and called, and then they came, like a rush of dark water, a multitudinous sea of invertebrates, a sparkling spectrum of colour spilling across the floor. Millions and millions of them. Darkus saw blister beetles and bombardiers, longhorns and ladybirds, fireflies and chafers, flower beetles and frog-legged leaf beetles, Goliaths and stags, Atlas and Hercules, rhinoceros and elephant beetles, titans and weevils, pleasing fungus and feather-horned, tigers and harlequins, tok-tokkies and death watch, but Lucretia saw them too and grinned. These were her beetles.

She dropped to the floor and lifted her back leg, rubbing it against her wing cases making a horrendous sound like nails down a blackboard. The beetles halted and she pointed at Darkus.

'No!' Darkus cried. 'Listen to me.' He held up Baxter. 'She bred you in captivity. I'm here to set you free. Tell them, Baxter.'

Baxter let out a series of hisses and his antennae swung wildly as he communicated with the Biome beetles.

'NO!' Lucretia Cutter shouted. 'I made you. You belong to me. You will do as I command.'

Darkus threw his head back and made a high screeching sound at the top of his throat, and the tidal wave of beetles, a fizzing sea of tippetty-tappetty legs scurried forward, washing over Lucretia Cutter, overcoming her with their sheer numbers.

Novak paused for breath and Darkus cheered as the beetles set upon Lucretia Cutter, biting and scratching, weighing her wings down. Novak smiled at him. And then, as if Lucretia Cutter had finally lost all patience, she reared up on to her back legs and spun three hundred and sixty degrees with all of her legs out, shaking the beetles off like a dog would water, and catching Novak off guard. A human fist landed a punch to Novak's ear, and a beetle claw sliced down her back, spraying blood as Novak fell to the ground.

'Novak!' Darkus screamed.

Novak's black eyes met his. 'I'm sorry,' she mouthed, as her mother stormed forward.

'You have outlived your usefulness, Handbag!' Lucretia

Cutter raged, bringing all four of her arms up to smash the life out of her daughter. But they never landed. There was a blur of movement, and Ling Ling was suddenly between mother and daughter. Her body moving in a hypnotic dance of blocks, preventing Lucretia from striking the hurt girl.

'No. I will not allow it,' Ling Ling said calmly as she danced.

'Traitor!' shrieked Lucretia Cutter.

Ling Ling parried and turned aside Lucretia's blows at a speed that was breathtaking to watch. She blocked and kept Lucretia Cutter off balance without once striking back. 'I will not stand and watch mother destroy daughter,' Ling Ling said between moves, 'nor father hurt son.'

'You work for me,' said Lucretia Cutter. 'You will do as I say.'

'I will not kill children,' Ling Ling said, a whirling windmill of arms and legs as Lucretia escalated her attack.

'Then you will die!' Lucretia Cutter shouted.

Darkus dragged himself over to Novak. His body was heavy and tired, and the pain was getting worse. He took hold of Novak under the arms and pulled her away from the fight. She was bleeding heavily.

'Novak. Novak, you've got to stay awake,' Darkus insisted as he pulled her to the opposite wall.

'I tried,' Novak whispered. Her eyes seemed to roll

back into her head as her eyelids closed.

'Novak! Novak!' Darkus shook her. Her eyes opened, and they were her blue human pupils once again.

'I'm here,' she said.

Darkus touched his good hand to her cheek. 'Please, Novak, you've got to stay with me.' He looked anxiously over at the battling scientist and chauffeur. Lucretia Cutter was slowing down, her weight was troubling her and the mass of beetles continued to harass her, but Ling Ling was tired from the barrage of blows delivered by chitinous armour. Her brow was furrowed in a concentrated look and she was sweating. The lack of oxygen was affecting both of them.

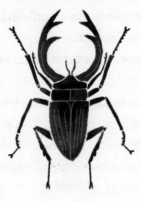

CHAPTER THIRTY-THREE

Humphrey's Recital

'Coooooeeeeeeeeeeeee! Lucretia, darling. Where are you?'

Darkus looked up. Above him, on a mezzanine floor, were Pickering and Humphrey. They were standing beside a grand piano, looking out over the forest of Arcadia and calling for Lucretia Cutter.

'DOWN HERE!' Darkus shouted. 'LUCRETIA CUTTER IS DOWN HERE!'

Humphrey turned but Pickering sprinted, almost tripping over his own feet. He leant over the railing and stared down into the laboratory. 'Lucretia, my sweet, come out, come out, wherever you are. We need to talk,' he called.

'She's there, Pickering.' Darkus pointed at the giant hovering form of Lucretia Cutter. 'That's your darling Lucretia Cutter.'

Lucretia Cutter looked up at Pickering and he started screaming, backing away from the balustrade and grabbing at Humphrey, who was stumbling up behind him, blinking and looking dopey.

'Humpty! Humpty!' Pickering squawked. 'It's a giant beetle!'

'What are you talking about?' Humphrey pushed his hysterical cousin aside and strode forward only to stagger backwards when his eyes landed on the giant form of Lucretia Cutter swiping at Ling Ling, who, tired from sustained combat, stumbled.

'Help us!' Darkus called up to Humphrey.

'That giant beetle has *eaten* my one true love!' Pickering wailed. 'The boy said she was in there! That nasty, disgusting, dirty, giant creepy-crawly has swallowed up my future wife and now we won't get our money!' He made a rasping choking noise, and Darkus realized he was crying. 'Nasty, filthy, scrabbling, rancorous, loathsome beast.' He beat on Humphrey's back with his fists. 'KILL IT, HUMPTY! That insect has eaten our money!' He grabbed at Humphrey, who was staring at Lucretia Cutter. 'Where will we live now? We have nothing.'

Humphrey turned and strode away. Darkus's heart

sank as the cousins disappeared from view. He looked at Ling Ling, who was on her knees, trying to defend herself, still not hitting back.

Lucretia Cutter was struggling too. She dropped to the ground, her heavy exoskeleton making her stumble forward. She raised her arms and Ling Ling, tired and accepting, brought her hands together in front of her chest and bowed her head, waiting for the killer blow.

'NO!' Darkus shouted.

There was a roar from above. Darkus threw himself backwards covering Novak just in time as a grand piano dropped from the balcony.

The vision of the falling piano was accompanied by a tuneless cacophony of music, hammers hitting strings, strings twanging and snapping, wood tearing.

Lucretia Cutter flew back as the weight of the piano hit her, crushing and flattening her. For a moment all that could be heard was the reverberation of the piano strings.

Lucretia Cutter's beetly body spasmed three times and then fell still.

'Ha ha ah aha ha ahahah ha ha!' Pickering's crazed laughter rang out. 'You did it, Humpty! You crushed the bug.' He flung his arms around his cousin. 'It's dead! Splat!'

Gerard ran into the room, and fell to his knees beside Darkus and Novak. 'Are you OK?'

Darkus nodded at Gerard. 'I've broken my wrist, and

my hip hurts, but Novak's bleeding.' He looked down at her. Her eyes were closed.

'Mademoiselle, it's all over now.' Gerard took Novak's hand. 'Please, for me, open your eyes.'

Novak's eyes flickered open and she smiled at Gerard.

'I'm hurt,' she whispered.

'It's OK. I'm here now.' Gerard took off his jacket and rolled her on to Darkus's lap, taking a look at the cut on her back. 'It's just the skin that is cut, *ma cherie*.' He laid his jacket under her and rolled her back into it. 'I will carry you.'

'My dad,' Darkus said. 'He's trapped in the pupator. I don't know how to open the door?'

Gerard pointed. 'The silver switch on the end.'

Darkus, pulled himself on to his knees and, with Gerard's help, stood up. He limped over to a console and flipped the switch. The door of the pupator slid open and his father lurched out of it.

'Darkus! Are you OK?'

His father half ran, half stumbled down the steps and through the metal door into the lab, groggy from the sleeping gas that had been piped into the pupator.

Darkus turned to him and smiled. 'It's over. She's gone, Dad. She's dead.'

He took two steps towards his dad when he heard Novak scream.

He spun around as Lucretia Cutter rose up screeching like a hawk, throwing off the piano and grabbing him around the waist. He didn't have time to cry out as he was dragged forward. Her jaws widened and he was engulfed by the smell of rotten bananas. He was going to die.

He heard his father shout. Lucretia Cutter's head flew backwards, away from Darkus. He fell, the sharp spikes of her legs cutting his skin. He hit the floor and cried out. He tried to roll away, but gasped in pain. He saw Gerard's face and felt the butler grab him under his armpits and drag him backwards. Darkus saw his father standing in front of him, feet astride, holding the harpoon gun. Bartholomew Cuttle reloaded it, pointed it at Lucretia Cutter's chest and fired a second shot that catapulted her backwards, against the wall. She thrashed about, screaming, pinned to the wall by the harpoon. Her legs and arms jerked twice, then dropped, and she fell still, her head rolling forward.

Darkus stared at her, not daring to believe she was gone, expecting her to rise yet again.

His dad dropped the harpoon gun and stumbled down to his knees, taking hold of Darkus and gently hugging him. Darkus could feel his dad's chest rising and falling and realized he was crying.

'It's OK, Dad. It's all going to be OK now,' he said.

CHAPTER THIRTY-FOUR

Exodus

'*D*arkus? *Darkus? Are you there?*' Bertolt's voice was calling from the device, which he'd dropped to the floor. Darkus grabbed it.

'I'm here,' he replied. 'It's over.' He looked at the giant beetle woman pinned to the wall. 'She's dead.'

'Um, we've got a problem,' Bertolt said. 'The news feed is reporting rice water weevils devouring crops in China, and the defence system is telling me there's a fleet of bombers heading this way.'

'Dad.' Darkus looked up. 'Do you know how to stop Lucretia Cutter's beetles? Can we stop the attack on the

Chinese rice harvest?'

Barty shook his head. 'I don't know how to stop them. I've looked, there doesn't seem to be any control centre, or button. I think she's pre-programmed all of it to happen whether she's alive or not. There's no way to stop it.'

'There *must* be a way,' Darkus said, leaning on his dad to get to his feet.

'I know the location of her beetle armies. She has them marked on a map, but if we tell the governments of world, they'll send soldiers, and that's what she wants. They'll trigger all her traps and make things worse. Soldiers and bombs can't stop insects.'

'We need to get to Bertolt, quickly.' Darkus tried to walk and stumbled. His hip burnt with pain. His father caught him.

'Steady now, Darkus. Where is Bertolt?'

'In the security dome. We have to get there, quickly. There are bombers in the sky and all the doors of the Biome are wide open.'

'I'll carry you.' Barty picked Darkus up in his arms.

'Anyone need a lift?' Virginia was in the doorway, sitting on the back of a giant tiger beetle wearing a muzzle.

'Virginia, can you get us to Bertolt?' Darkus asked. 'It's urgent.'

'Hop on,' she nodded. 'This bad boy is fast.'

'Hello!' Darkus heard Uncle Max's voice and turned to see Spencer sat atop the thorax of a giant Hercules beetle and Uncle Max lying on its elytra.

'Are you OK?' Darkus asked as his father carefully lifted him on to the back of the giant tiger beetle.

'Fine.' Uncle Max nodded. 'Ling Ling caught up with me and threw me in the river. Got a bit of a nasty shock from an electric eel and nibbled by a few piranha. Luckily Gerard pulled me out.'

'He's in there with Novak. She's hurt.' He looked at Spencer. 'Can you get everyone to the helicopter? There are bombers on the way.'

Spencer was already springing down from the giant Hercules beetle and running into the lab.

'Let's go,' Virginia cried, and the giant tiger beetle raced forward at breathtaking speed. The Biome became a blur of white, and they were there outside the control-room door in minutes.

Bertolt spun around in his chair. 'Hi,' he said, looking terrified.

Barty slid off the tiger beetle's wing casings and lifted Darkus into his arms, running with him to the chair beside Bertolt. 'What do we need to do?' he asked.

The pain of his broken wrist was making it hard for Darkus to think. 'Bertolt, Dad needs to put a whole series of co-ordinates – all the places in the world where Lucretia Cutter has her beetles waiting to attack – into a message.'

'But, Darkus, I told you, we can't tell the governments . . .'

'We're not *going* to tell the governments,' Darkus said, grimacing to stop the pain from overwhelming him.

'We're going to tell the *entomologists*. They're all working on the ground fighting the infestations with Dr Yuki Ishikawa using pheromone traps.'

'I can do that!' Bertolt nodded vigorously as he scrambled over to the control console, pulling a crumpled piece of paper out of his pocket. 'Mr Burton, I mean, Hank, told us how to get hold of him. He'll tell everyone.' He started typing furiously on a keyboard.

Bartholomew looked at his son, astonished. 'That is a brilliant idea. Yes! It might just work.' He leant towards Bertolt. 'Can you bring up a map? We'll mark the co-ordinates on there, and send it to Hank.'

'How close are the bombers?' Darkus asked.

Newton zipped up out of Bertolt's hair and looped around a screen with a flashing radar blip on it. Darkus could see five triangles moving towards the centre.

'Fifteen minutes away,' Bertolt said, glancing up.

'We need to get out of here,' Barty said.

'Emma sent a distress message to the bombers,' Bertolt said as his fingers flew across the keys. 'She identified herself, the location of this place and said Lucretia was dead.' He looked at Darkus. 'It's going out on repeat. We have to hope they get the message and believe it. We want them to land and see this place, not blow it to smithereens.'

A map appeared on the screen and Darkus's dad started pointing at the locations where Lucretia Cutter's plague of beetles lay in wait to do their damage.

'Darkus,' Virginia was back at the door, 'everyone is in the helicopter. We need to go.'

'Two more minutes,' Barty said, pointing at the screen.

There was a tense silence as Virginia and Darkus watched Bertolt work.

'That's it. That's all of them.'

Darkus was staggered by the number of red flags on the map. *Lucretia Cutter must have been planning this for years.*

'Sent!' Bertolt leapt up from his chair.

Barty grabbed Darkus, who took a sharp intake of breath as his father dashed across the room, putting him back on to the giant tiger beetle, who was now wearing an oxygen mask.

'Nice ride,' Bertolt said to Virginia.

'His name is Barnacle,' Virginia replied, turning the beetle around.

'*Wait!*' Darkus sat up. 'Bertolt, you have to turn the oxygen back up.'

'What?'

'In the main dome. *Quick*. Turn it back up!'

Bertolt hobbled back to the control desk and whacked a dial all the way up and hobbled back. Barty lifted him on to the tiger beetle beside Darkus and then clambered up.

Hexagonal tiles were replaced by a sapphire blue sky. Darkus heard the chugging blades of the helicopter. The sun was hot on his face and the world smelt of earth, moisture and a thousand different plants. He felt a rush of euphoria in his chest. They'd done it.

As Barnacle the beetle raced towards the helicopter, Darkus looked up at his father.

'Dad, when we get home, will you grow your beard back please?' he said.

His dad smiled, and the lines around his blue eyes were like sunbeams. 'Of course, son.'

'Baxter,' Darkus was cupping the beetle to his chest. 'Can you fly?'

Baxter nodded.

'There's one last thing we have to do,' Darkus said, holding out his hand. 'You need to tell the giant beetles that the big dome is oxygenated. They can live in there.'

Baxter jumped up into the air, his elytra up and his soft wings vibrating in bursts. He was tired, and his flight path was off kilter due to having one less leg on his right side, but he reached a giant titan beetle and gave her the message.

'Let's get out of here.' Barty slid off the tiger beetle.

Darkus heard the shouts of Emma Lamb and Spencer. Uncle Max was in the co-pilot's seat of the helicopter.

'What's that beetle doing?' Motty called over her shoulder.

'Barnacle is coming with us,' Virginia shouted above the noise of the helicopter blades.

Barnacle clambered up into the helicopter with Virginia, Darkus and Bertolt on his back. Novak was sitting on Gerard's lap, opposite Emma Lamb.

Barty jumped in and reached out to shut the door.

'Wait!' Darkus cried. 'Baxter!' He could see the brave rhinoceros beetle, struggling through the air towards the helicopter. Darkus slid off Barnacle's back, crying out as his foot hit the floor and jarred his hip. He leant out of the doorway, reaching his hand out and Baxter crash-landed, face first into his palm. A distant rumble made him look up to the skies, but it wasn't thunder. It was a fleet of bombers, growing specks on the horizon.

'Go, go, go!' Darkus cried.

As the helicopter took off, he looked down at the Biome, cuddling Baxter to his chest. The ground was awash with beetles of all sizes, burrowing, flying and gambolling in the grass. Two familiar figures in bright green jumpsuits came running out of the trapdoor in the ground. They waved their arms at the approaching aeroplanes. It was Pickering and Humphrey, and they were covered from head to toe in beetles.

CHAPTER THIRTY-FIVE

Beetle Zoo

'Are you sure you have to go? You could live with us you know. If you wanted, that is,' Darkus said to Novak's back, as she packed her case. 'I'm sure Dad wouldn't mind. I could ask him.'

'Oh, Darkus.' She turned around and smiled. 'Nothing would make me happier. It's been lovely being a part of your family for the last couple of weeks, but there's no room here, and I feel terrible with your Uncle Max sleeping on the front-room floor and your dad on the sofa, when there's a whole house I can live in.'

'You can't mean you're going back to Towering Heights?'

'When Gerard came, this morning, he told me that, as Lucretia Cutter's only living relative, I'm heir to her estate. She left no will. Everything that belonged to her, now belongs to me.'

'Whoa! What are you going to do?'

'Try and do some good with it.'

'No, I mean, what are *you* going to do?'

'Gerard – he, well,' Novak's pale cheeks flushed pink, 'he said he'd like to look after me.' She brought her hands together and her thumbs tussled nervously with each other. 'He says he wants to make up for all the times he didn't help.'

'Is he going to be your foster dad?'

'Kind of.' Novak nodded excitedly. 'And Millie, do you remember her? Our cook? She's going to come back and help him.' She beamed. 'I think she's a bit in love with Gerard. Isn't that romantic?' She drew her hands up under her chin and sighed.

'Isn't it going to be weird going back to Towering Heights? With all the memories?'

'Towering Heights is the only home I've ever had. And some good things happened there. I met you, and Heppy.' A mischievous sparkle lit up her eyes. 'And now I've got loads of money, I can change the house to be how I want it to be.'

Darkus grinned. 'What're you going to do?'

'I'm going to break down all the cells and turn the basement into a cinema. I'll give Mater's beetle collections to the Natural History Museum. I've had enough dead beetles to last me a lifetime.'

'But you must keep the books,' Darkus said.

'Oh, yes, I'm going to have a huge library,' Novak nodded, 'but I'm going to add lots of story books and picture books and books about fairies and myths and monsters, and it'll be wonderful.'

'It's a very big house for three people,' Darkus said.

'But you and Virginia and Bertolt will come over,' Novak frowned, 'won't you? I mean, now that I'm their friend too. That's what friends do, isn't it? Visit each other?'

Darkus nodded. 'If you have a cinema, you won't be able to get rid of us.'

'And I'll make a special oxygenated room for Barnacle – he's always trying to pull that oxygen mask off his face, and his spiky legs keep ripping the walls of his oxygen tent.'

'Oh, well, then, Virginia will probably move in. She loves that crazy beetle.'

'And then of course, there's Ling Ling,' Novak said, turning back to her packing.

'Ling Ling?'

'She saved my life, and with Mater gone, she no longer has a job. So, I've asked her to stay at Towering Heights and work for me, seeing as now I'm very rich and probably need protecting because my mother tried to take over the world and kill everybody.' Novak lifted her shoulders and screwed up her face into a ball of excitement. 'But the best bit is, she's going to let me train with her.'

'Train?'

'Yes. I'm going to see exactly what this body of mine can do.' She stretched out an arm and examined her fingernails, which were painted a coral pink. 'She's going to teach me the ways of the Kunoichi.' She dropped her hand. 'And I'm rather hoping that once we're friends, she'll show me how to dance. Did you know, when she was young, she was a famous ballet dancer in America?'

Darkus shook his head.

Novak sighed and sat down on the bed. 'I would love to be a ballet dancer.'

'Do you think she'd teach me some of her ninja moves?' Darkus asked. 'It would be cool to be able to deflect Robby's punches next time he decides to bully me.'

'Who's Robby?'

'Oh, just this kid at school. He never misses an opportunity to push me about. Bet he'd leave me alone if I went ninja on him.' He held his hands up, his right wrist still in a cast, and narrowed his eyes as if he was about to fight.

'Oh, and that's *another* wonderful thing . . .' Novak pursed her lips, pausing for dramatic emphasis. 'I'm going to go to school.' She clapped. 'Isn't that the best news ever? A real school.'

'School's not that great, you know.' Darkus let his hands fall to his sides.

'But I'm going to go to *your* school, with you and Virginia and Bertolt. Gerard's sorting it all out. I start at King Ethelred Hall next week.'

'That *is* cool. Although, I might not be going there.' Darkus felt a sharp pain in his chest at the idea of Novak, Bertolt and Virginia together without him. 'Dad and I will be going back home soon. Uncle Max probably wants a front room that isn't full of beetles and doesn't smell like a bonfire.'

Novak laughed. 'It's so nice being the person who knows everything, for once.' She hugged herself. 'I'm usually the one who doesn't know anything.'

Darkus frowned. 'What do you know?'

'Mater owns the Emporium, next door. She bought it from the council after the explosion.'

Darkus blinked. 'It belonged to her when she burnt it down?'

'Yes, and it's mine now,' Novak continued, 'I spoke about it with your dad and your uncle this morning. Gerard is getting a survey man to come and look at it and the buildings either side. I'm going to pay for the renovation works, and then,' she paused and her face went bright pink as she squeaked and flapped her hands, 'and then I'm getting an architect to turn it into a beetle zoo.'

'A what?'

'Well, the Base Camp beetles need somewhere proper to live, and if we're going to change people's minds about insects they'll need to be able to visit a place where they can meet beetles and see how wonderful they are. So I thought we could build a beetle zoo right here.'

'Oh, Novak, that's a *brilliant* idea.'

'Yes, and we'll make a research centre too, where we can look at the good bits of the Fabre Project and fight to make the world a better place.'

'I'll be able to visit it, when I see Uncle Max.' Darkus's voice dropped to a whisper, and he felt a lump in his throat.

Novak grabbed his arms and looked up into his eyes. 'Darkus, I want your dad to be the director of the research centre.'

Darkus blinked.

'If he agrees, and you want to, you can both live in the flat above it. I mean, it has to be built first, of course, but there will be a flat.'

'What!? Novak, that's amazing!' Darkus grabbed her arms and they both jumped up and down. 'He'll say yes, I know he will. I'll get to stay here, at the school and see you and Virginia and Bertolt and Uncle Max every day!' His heart soared. 'C'mon, lets go downstairs and ask him now.'

'Maybe you should talk to him on your own,' Novak said. 'I've got some packing to finish.'

'I'll be back in a sec.' Darkus sprinted down the stairs to the living room and burst through the door. 'Dad . . .' He stopped, seeing Gerard standing in front of the paddling pool of Base Camp beetles. 'Oh, hello.'

His dad was sitting on the sofa. 'Ah Darkus, you know Olivier.'

'Olivier?' Darkus looked at the butler, confused. 'What?'

'Olivier Gerard Laroche.' The butler bowed.

'Laroche? Laroche.' Darkus knew the name, but couldn't place it. 'Laroche! Danny Laroche. She was part of the Fabre Project . . .' He frowned.

'Danielle is my big sister.' Gerard nodded. 'A long time ago, Lucretia Cutter caused my sister great pain, a wound from which she never recovered. I trained as a butler and took a job in Lucretia Cutter's household with the intention of making her sorry for what she did to my sister, but I had no idea of the darkness I would find there.'

'Olivier made himself known to me when I was in the prison cell in Towering Heights,' Barty said, smiling at the butler. 'We've been working together ever since.'

'Monsieur Cuttle,' Gerard bowed to Darkus, 'I must offer you an apology for the first time we met.'

'It's OK.' Darkus shrugged.

'*Mais non*, it is not OK.' Gerard sighed. 'Barty, I am ashamed to say that I struck your son, a blow to the back of his head. He was resisting me and I had to get him out of Lucretia Cutter's house.'

'It didn't hurt,' Darkus lied.

'It is the only time I have ever struck a child, and it has troubled me ever since.' Gerard shook his head. 'I cannot forgive myself.'

'You were trying to help him,' Barty said, gently. 'We understand that.'

'And Uncle Max got you back by knocking you out cold.' Darkus grinned.

'Ha! This is true.' Gerard rubbed his jaw, as if remembering the blow.

'So is your name Olivier or Gerard?' Darkus asked.

'Both, but I will be using Gerard from now on, as this is how Mademoiselle Novak knows me.'

'Where is she?' Barty asked Darkus. 'Olivier's come to take her home.'

'She's upstairs packing,' Darkus replied.

'I will go and help Mademoiselle,' Gerard said, bowing his head.

Darkus watched him leave the room. 'He's going to have to stop calling her that if he's going to be her dad.'

Barty laughed.

'Dad, listen, Novak told me about the job, and what she's planning to do next door, with building a beetle zoo . . .'

'Yes,' his dad nodded, 'it's a lovely idea.'

'So you'll take the job?'

'I'll have to think about it, Darkus. Since Emma Lamb's piece on Lucretia Cutter was published, and the world has learnt the truth, I've been inundated with offers and requests. The Natural History Museum have said I can have my old job back.'

Darkus felt his stomach sink. 'But I don't want to go back to that old life,' he blurted out. 'It was lonely, and you were sad. I've got friends here, and my beetles . . .' He looked over at the paddling pool and his eyes swam with tears. He blinked them back and half shouted, 'And what about Baxter, he's only got five legs now and he'll need his friends too. I want to stay.'

'Hey, Darkus,' his dad called softly, patting the sofa next to him. 'Come over here.'

Darkus shuffled over to his father, his eyes on the floor.

'Listen to me.' His dad lifted his chin. His blue eyes were smiling and his chin covered in peppered stubble. 'You saved my life. You travelled through the jungles of the Amazon to rescue me, and you brought me hope for the future. I am the proudest, luckiest dad in the world, and I love you. If you want to build a beetle zoo, then that is exactly what we will do.'

'Really?' Darkus blinked furiously but he couldn't stop the tears from spilling down his cheeks. 'Do you mean it? We can stay here?'

'Oh, now, please don't cry. It's going to be OK.' His dad put an arm around his shoulders and pulled him close. 'I'm going to be a better dad from now on. I promise.'

'You're the best dad in the world,' Darkus sobbed, hugging his dad's chest.

They sat for a moment, until Darkus had calmed

down. 'Dad?' he sniffed. 'Did Mum really give Lucretia Prometheus, your Goliath beetle, and all your research?'

'No, Darkus, that was a lie, aimed to hurt us. Your mother was a passionate scientist, but she wanted me to stop pursuing the genetic experiments with beetles. She never would have given my research to Lucretia Cutter.'

'But she had Prometheus.'

'He was stolen from a locked vault in the National History Museum, just like Lucretia stole me.'

'Sometimes, it feels like I don't know who Mum really was, and it hurts.'

'Oh Darkus, I'm sorry. You know you can ask me anything about her and I'll tell you.'

'But I don't want to make you sad,' Darkus admitted.

'Well, I'm not going to be sad any more. I promise. I can't be. We've got too much work to do, proving Lucretia Cutter wrong and getting people to take up the environmental fight.'

Darkus nodded. 'In the new flat, next door, can we have pictures of Mum up on the wall?'

Barty ruffled Darkus's hair. 'Of course we can, Darkus. We can have anything you want.'

Darkus smiled. 'Can I have a giant tank for Baxter in my bedroom?'

Barty laughed. 'I think that brave rhinoceros beetle has more than earned it.'

There was a gentle knocking and Darkus sat up, wiping his face with his sleeve as Gerard pushed the door open. Novak was standing beside him, holding her suitcase, ready to leave.

'Are you going?' Barty got to his feet.

Gerard nodded. 'Thank you for taking such good care of Novak.'

'She's always welcome in our home,' Barty smiled, 'and Novak, Darkus and I have discussed it. I'd like to accept your offer of a job and help you build your beetle zoo.'

'You would?' Novak dropped her suitcase to the floor and jumped up and down clapping. 'That's wonderful news. We'll show everyone how wonderful beetles are and how useful they can be.' Hepburn leapt up from the corsage on Novak's Alice band and looped the loop. Novak looked at Darkus. 'Now we can see each other every day.'

'But wait,' Darkus said. 'What about Humphrey and Pickering? If we live next door, where will they live?'

'Oh, they'll be fine,' Novak replied. 'I've honoured Mater's promise. I thought it was only fair. They've each been given a quarter of a million pounds. What they do with it is up to them.'

CHAPTER THIRTY-SIX

Hamish MacTavish's Haggis and Sporran Shop

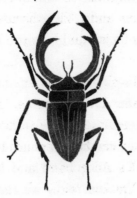

*H*umphrey and Pickering stood outside the boarded-up shop.

'That sign'll have to go,' Humphrey said, pointing above the door at a red and green tartan-checked board with *HAMISH MACTAVISH'S HAGGIS AND SPORRAN SHOP* written in gold block capitals.

'Yes.' Pickering nodded, pulling a set of keys from his pocket. 'Shall we go in and see our new home?'

The cousins tramped into the shop on the Walworth Road in Elephant and Castle, south London. It had recently gone out of business due to the decline in customers interested in buying sporrans and eating haggis.

'Look! A meat counter.' Humphrey lumbered over to the left-hand side of the shop, carrying his white bucket of cranberry sauce, which hadn't left his side since he'd got back to England. It was set up like a butcher's.

'Look! Display cabinets!' Pickering was looking at the right-hand side of the shop, his arms opened wide as if he wanted to hug the wall of glass. 'These will be perfect for my antiques.'

'This will be perfect for my pies,' Humphrey said from behind the counter. 'I wonder what haggis pie tastes like? It could be a good addition to my menu.'

'C'mon, let's look upstairs,' Pickering said, striding excitedly through the back of the shop and hurrying up a spiral staircase. He wanted to make sure he got the best bedroom.

'I hate stairs,' Humphrey grumbled. 'Bagsy the first bedroom we come to.'

Pickering silently cursed under his breath.

They came to a kitchen. Pickering opened cupboards and found a couple of old mugs and a saucepan. 'Shall we have tea?'

'Why not?' Humphrey nodded.

Pickering produced tea bags from his coat pocket and dropped them into the pan, filling it with water and placing it on the stove top. He poured the tea into the mugs and pulled out a handful of tiny pots of UHT milk that he'd stolen on the plane home, emptying a couple into each mug. The two cousins carried their mugs up another flight of stairs.

'Here's my bedroom,' Humphrey said, pushing open the first door they came to. It was a large room with a threadbare carpet over floorboards, empty apart from an old blue armchair. He went and sat down in it. 'Perfect. It has everything I need.' He slurped his tea.

'Aren't you going to come and look upstairs?' Pickering asked, annoyed that Humphrey's room was so large. 'There might be a better room up there.'

'Nope.' Humphrey shook his head.

Pickering huffed and stalked out of the room. Humphrey heard his cousin climbing the stairs.

'Oh, Humphrey, it's lovely up here. You should come and see,' Pickering's voice called.

Humphrey smiled to himself and finished his tea. He had no intention of moving. He put the empty mug on the floor and kicked it into the corner of the room. *I'll wash it up later*, he thought.

CHAPTER THIRTY-SEVEN

Beetle Girl

The children, dressed in their black and purple uniform, poured through the school gates. Darkus stood to one side, and glanced down at Baxter, who was nestled in his blazer pocket. The beetle waggled a claw at him. 'Now, remember to stay hidden,' Darkus whispered to the rhinoceros beetle, as he scanned the crowds heading to their classrooms, chattering and calling to one another. A black iridescent car pulled up, hints of violet and emerald flickering in the light. He smiled, remembering the first time he'd seen it, and how he'd thought it looked like something out of one of his comics.

Now it was his friend's car.

The rude voice of Robby sounded above the clamour of children. 'Whoa! Check out those wheels!'

Daniel Dowie pulled a comb out of his blazer pocket and dragged it through his oily quiff.

The front door opened. A woman dressed in black, with scars on her cheeks, stepped out and opened the rear door of the car. Out stepped Novak in her black and purple uniform, followed by Gerard, who held out a purple satchel.

'Your packed lunch is in your bag, and so is your pencil case. I checked with the school and they'll be providing any books you need.'

'Stop fussing, Gerard.' Novak giggled and kissed him on the cheek as she took her bag.

'We'll be here at the end of the day to pick you up,' he called as she headed towards the gate.

'Hello, princess.' Daniel Dowie called out. 'What's your name?'

Novak barely paused to give him a withering look.

Darkus heard a snort from beside him. Virginia and Bertolt had arrived to meet Novak for her first day at school. He grinned at them. Marvin was hanging from Virginia's braid, and Newton was glowing gently inside Bertolt's hair, making him appear angelic.

'They'd better not be mean to her,' Bertolt said, looking very serious.

'She'll make mincemeat of them,' Virginia chuckled.

'Yup.' Darkus nodded.

Novak saw the three of them standing inside the gate, and waved.

'What's she doing, waving at Beetle Boy?' Robby exclaimed. 'Hey, princess. You don't want to go near him. He might set his beetle on you.'

Novak ignored him and ran towards Darkus, Virginia and Bertolt.

'Welcome to your first day at school,' Darkus said. 'I see you've already met our bullies.'

Novak took him by surprise, throwing her arms around his neck and kissing his cheek. He stumbled backwards a step.

'Isn't this exciting?' she gushed.

'Not really.' Virginia shook her head. 'It's school.'

'Exactly!' Novak bounced up and down, hugging Virginia and then Bertolt.

'It's exciting to have *you* here.' Bertolt blushed as he squeezed her back.

'So where's our classroom?' Novak asked, taking Darkus's hand. 'I want to see it.'

'Oi, Beetle Boy!' Robby shouted.

The four of them turned and looked at the approaching gaggle of boys, strutting over behind Daniel Dowie and Robby.

'Aren't you going to introduce us to your girlfriend?' Robby asked, and all the clones sniggered. 'Don't go thinking she's gonna be into you for long.' He pointed at

Daniel Dowie, who pouted at Novak and waggled his eyebrows. 'Not once she's met Dowie the ladykiller.'

Darkus felt Novak's grip on his hand tighten with anger.

'Excuse me.' Novak glared at Robby. 'Would you kindly ask your friend to stop pulling those weird faces at me, he's making me feel ill.' Robby's mouth dropped open and his metal braces glinted. 'Oh, and I'll have you know that I'm *not* Darkus's girlfriend because he's never asked me out, but if he ever did ask me out, I'd say yes in a heartbeat, because he is the kindest, bravest, cleverest boy I've ever met.'

Darkus drew in a sharp breath and choked on his own saliva. His face burnt as Bertolt thumped him on the back.

'Ooooooooooooooooooo.' Robby waggled his head and made sloppy kissing noises. 'What did he do to you? Get one of his beetles to bite you?' He laughed at his own joke. 'Better watch out or you'll get turned into a Beetle Girl!'

'Beetle Girl! Beetle Girl!' the clones all echoed.

'Much as we'd love to kick your arses right now,' Virginia said, 'we have to get to class.' She turned her back on the crowing bullies, and the other three did the same.

'Beetle Girl! Beetle Girl!' The chant followed them.

Novak looked at Darkus, a wicked smile creeping across her face as her eyes went black. 'Do you want to tell them, or shall I?'

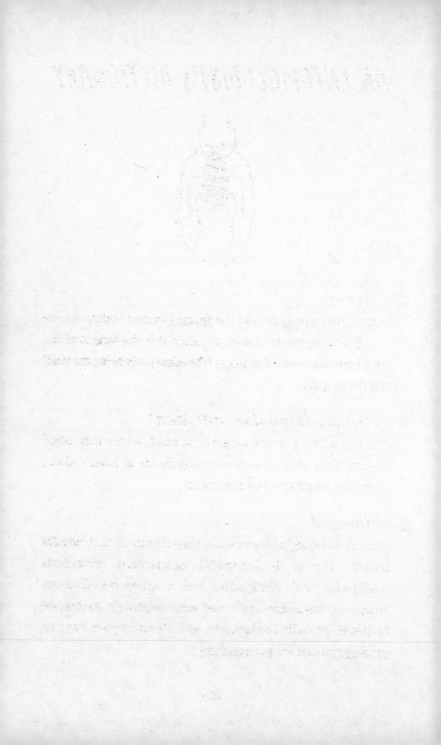

AN ENTOMOLOGIST'S DICTIONARY

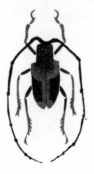

abdomen

the part of the body behind the <u>thorax</u> (human abdomens are usually referred to as tummy or belly). It is the largest of the three body segments of an <u>insect</u> (the other parts being the head and the <u>thorax</u>).

antennae (singular: antenna)

a pair of sensory appendages on the head, sometimes called 'feelers'. They are used to sense many things including odour, taste, heat, wind speed and direction.

arthropod

means 'jointed leg' and refers to a group of animals that includes insects (known as hexapods), crustaceans, myriapods (millipedes and centipedes) and chelicerates (spiders, scorpions, horseshoe crabs and their relatives). Arthropod bodies are usually in segments, and all arthropods have an <u>exoskeleton</u> and are <u>invertebrates</u>.

303

beetle

one type (or 'order') of <u>insect</u> with the front pair of wing-cases modified into hardened <u>elytra</u>. There are more different <u>species</u> of beetle than any other animal on the planet.

chitin

the material that makes up the exoskeletons of most <u>arthropods</u>, including <u>insects</u>. Chitin is one of the most important substances in nature.

coleoptera

the scientific name for <u>beetles</u>.

coleopterist

a scientist who studies <u>beetles</u>.

compound eyes

can be made up of thousands of individual visual receptors, and are common in <u>arthropods</u>. They enable many <u>arthropod</u>s to see very well, but they see the world as a pixelated image – like the pixels on a computer screen.

DNA (deoxyribonucleic acid)

the blueprint for almost every living creature. It is the molecule that carries genetic information. A length of DNA is called a gene.

double helix

the shape that <u>DNA</u> forms when the individual components of <u>DNA</u> join together. It looks like a twisted ladder.

elytra (singular: elytron)

the hardened forewings of <u>beetles</u> that serve as protective wing-cases for the delicate, membranous hind wings underneath, which are used for flying. Some <u>beetles</u> can't fly; their elytra are fused together and they don't have hind wings.

entomologist

a scientist who studies <u>insects</u>.

exoskeleton

an external skeleton – a skeleton on the outside of the body, rather than on the inside like mammals. <u>Insects</u> have exoskeletons made largely from <u>chitin</u>. The <u>exoskeleton</u> is very strong and can be jam-packed with muscles, meaning that <u>insects</u> (especially <u>beetles</u> that have extremely tough exoskeletons) can be very strong for their size.

habitat

the type of area in which an organism lives – for example, a stag <u>beetle's</u> habitat is broad-leaved woodland.

insect

in the 'class' insecta, with over 1.8 million different species known and more to discover. Insects have three main body parts: the head, <u>thorax</u> and <u>abdomen</u>. The head has <u>antennae</u> and a pair of <u>compound eyes</u>. Insects have six legs and many have wings. They have a complex life cycle called <u>metamorphosis</u>.

invertebrate

an animal that does not have a spine (backbone).

larvae (singular: larva)

immature <u>insects</u>. Beetle larvae are sometimes called grubs. Larvae look completely different to adult <u>insects</u> and often feed on different things than their parents, meaning that they don't compete with their parents for food.

mandibles

<u>beetles</u>' mouth parts. Mandibles can grasp, crush or cut food, or defend against predators and rivals.

metamorphosis

means 'change'. It involves a total transformation of the insect between the different life stages (egg, larvae, pupae and adult or egg, nymphs and adult). For example, imagine a big, fat, cream-coloured grub: it looks nothing like an adult <u>beetle</u>. Many <u>insects</u> (including <u>beetles</u>) metamorphosize inside a pupa or cocoon: they enter the pupa as a grub, are blended into beetle soup, re-form as an adult <u>beetle</u> and break their way out of the pupa. Adult <u>beetles</u> never moult and, because they are encased in a hard <u>exoskeleton</u> that doesn't stretch or grow, they can never grow bigger. Therefore, if you see an adult <u>beetle</u>, it can never grow any bigger than it is.

🪲 *palps*

a pair of sensory appendages, near the mouth of an <u>insect</u>. They are used to touch/feel and sense chemicals in the surroundings.

🪲 *setae (singular: seta)*

tiny hair-like projections covering parts of an <u>insect</u>'s body. They may be protective, can be used for defence, camouflage and adhesion (sticking to things) and can be sensitive to moisture and vibration.

🪲 *species*

the scientific name for an organism; helps define what type of organism something is, regardless of what language you speak. For example, across the world, Baxter will be known as *Chalcosoma caucasus*. However, depending on what language you speak, you will call him a different common name. The species name is always written with its 'genus' name in front of it and it is always typed in italics, with the genus starting with a capital letter and the species all in lower-case type. If you are writing by hand, it should all be underlined instead of italicized. See '<u>Taxonomy</u>'.

🪲 *stridulation*

a loud squeaking or scratching noise made by an <u>insect</u> rubbing its body parts together to attract a mate, as a territorial sound or warning sign.

taxonomy

the practice of identifying, describing and naming organisms. It uses a system called 'biological classification', with similar organisms grouped together. It starts off with a broad grouping (the 'kingdom') and gets more specific, with the species as the most specific group. No two <u>species</u> names (when combined with their genus) are the same: kingdom → phylum → class → order → family → genus → species. This system avoids the confusion caused by common names, which vary in different languages or even different households. For example, Baxter is a species of rhinoceros <u>beetle</u>: some people may call him an Atlas <u>beetle</u>, Hercules <u>beetle</u> or unicorn <u>beetle</u>, and there are lots of different species of rhinoceros <u>beetle</u>. So how do we know what Baxter really is? If you use biological classification, you can classify Baxter as: kingdom = animalia (animal) → phylum = arthropoda (arthropod) → class = insecta (insect) → order = coleoptera → family = scarabaeidae → genus = *Chalcosoma* → species = caucasus. But all you really need to say is the genus and species, so Baxter is: *Chalcosoma caucasus*.

thorax

the part of an <u>insect</u>'s body between the head and the <u>abdomen</u>.

transgenic

an animal can be described as transgenic if scientists have added <u>DNA</u> from another <u>species</u>.

Acknowledgements

This is the bit where I get to thank everyone who helped me deliver this story into the world. However, this isn't just a story, it is the completion of a trilogy and the realization of a dream.

At the end of *Beetle Boy* I thanked every friend who didn't laugh at me when I said 'I'm going to write a book about beetles', but instead helped and encouraged me.

At the end of *Beetle Queen* I thanked the entomologists I'd met on my travels who've inspired and educated me, and all the wonderful publishing companies around the world who are bringing my beetle-filled stories to new territories.

Now I'm here, at the end, I want to thank the beetles.

The last decade of my life has been characterized by my growing fascination with beetles. It began with fear and horror but has evolved into passion and respect. Welcoming these six-legged wonders into my head, my heart and my home has brought me more joy, amazement, knowledge, inspiration, delight, friendship, meaning, peace and happiness than any other single pursuit in my entire life. Beetles have changed me for the better, and I want to thank them, from the bottom of my heart. I hope they will forgive me for squealing and running away from them for thirty years. I was ignorant. I'm sorry.

The humans to whom I'll be forever grateful are almost as multitudinous as the species of beetles on this planet. Thank you to:

My husband, Sam, who has held my hand every step of the way, has read every word I've ever written, who believes in me when I do not, and loves me when I am horrible. 'We did it! We got there! Look what we made!'

Arthur and Sebastian, my bonny boys, I'm sorry I've been so busy and absent. Thank you for your patience, your pride and being the best sons a mother could ever wish for. I love you.

My family for supporting this crazy enterprise in so many ways, in particular Jane Sparling, Hannah Gabrielle and Charlie Sparling.

My invisible editors, Claire Rakich and Dr Sarah Beynon. These stories have your fingerprints all over them. I hope you feel a sense of ownership about them, because you've improved them, made them funnier (Claire) and made them entomologically accurate (Sarah).

My National Theatre family, especially those crazy cats Emma Reidy and Sam Sedgman.

My agent Kirsty McLachlan, a straight-talking kindred spirit.

The Chicken House clutch, I salute you Barry Cunningham OBE, Rachel Leyshon, Elinor Bagenal, Rachel Hickman, Jazz Bartlett, Sarah Wilson, Esther Waller, Laura Myers, Kesia Lupo and Laura Smythe.

The Riot Communications ladies, I adore you Liz Hyder, Adele Minchin, Thi Dinh and Laura Curtis.

The family of authors who've read my books, buoyed me up, given me advice, bought me a drink, talked me through this crazy business, thank you for your kindness and solidarity. In particular Holly Smale, Jess French, Maz Evans, Kiran Millwood Hargrave, James Nicol and Chris Riddell.

All the translators who painstakingly retell my stories in another language. We are all in the beetle storytelling business together, and I am grateful for your talent, care and passion.

The Branford Boase Award judges and all other beetle champions including Julia Eccleshare, Fiona Noble, Florentyna Martin, Tom Fletcher, Peter Smithers, Natasha Harding, Charlotte Eyre, Max Barclay, Simon Leather, Megan Shersby, Ashleigh Wiffin, Vanessa Harbour and Imogen Cooper.

The booksellers, the librarians, the teachers, the parents, the reviewers, the entomologists, the readers, and every Beetle Girl and Beetle Boy I've met at schools, festivals and events all over the world.

If you are hungry for more beetles then keep your eyes peeled for *The Beetle Collector's Handbook* in 2018.

Thank you, all of you, and may your life be blessed with beetles.

If you want to meet real beetles visit **Dr Sarah Beynon's Bug Farm** in Pembrokeshire. She's the scientific consultant for this trilogy and helped me get over my fear of insects by taking me into her bug zoo and giving me my first beetle to hold. It's an amazing place. Find out about it here: www.drbeynonsbugfarm.com

Here are some other brilliant organisations you should check out:

www.buglife.org.uk

www.ptes.org/stagbeetle

www.environmenttrust.co.uk

www.amentsoc.org

Standing on the Shoulders of Giants

Before I set out to write about beetles I knew very little about the creatures with which I am now so enamoured. I am incredibly grateful to be standing on the shoulders of giants, and I would like to acknowledge all of the entomologists around the world who do the hard research that is then reduced into facts for an enthusiast like me. I have absorbed information from a wealth of places, but I must acknowledge the following:

Brilliant Beetle Books

An Inordinate Fondness for Beetles by Arthur V. Evans and Charles L. Bellamy

The Book of Beetles edited by Patrice Bouchard

A Coleopterist's Handbook, edited by J. Cooter and M. V. L. Barclay

British Insects by George E. Hyde

Life on Earth by David Attenborough

The Young Beetle Collector's Handbook by E. Hofmann

The Sacred Beetle and Others, The Life of the Weevil and *The Glow-Worm and Other Beetles* by Jean-Henri Fabre

Wonderful Websites

www.nationalgeographic.com • www.buglife.org.uk • www.ptes.org.uk • www.wikipedia.org • www.thoughtco.com • www.bbc.co.uk • www.arkive.org • www.insectidentification.org • www.wildlifetrusts.org • www.amentsoc.org • www.royensoc.co.uk • www.sciencenews.org • www.livescience.com • www.featuredcreature.com • www.bugguide.net • www.drbeynonsbugfarm.com • www.nhm.ac.uk •

These are all great places to continue discovering more about the weird and wild world of invertebrates. Go beetletastic!

M. G. Leonard is an award winning, bestselling author of stories for the young of heart. She also works as a freelance Digital Media Producer for clients such as the National Theatre and Harry Potter West End, and has previously worked at the Royal Opera House and Shakespeare's Globe. Leonard spent her early career in the music industry running Setanta Records, an independent record label, and managing bands, most notably The Divine Comedy. After leaving the music industry, she trained as an actor, dabbling in directing and producing as well as performing, before deciding to write her stories down. Leonard lives in Brighton with her husband, two sons and her pet rainbow stag beetle.

🪲 www.mgleonard.com 🪲 @MGLnrd 🪲